THE DEADLIEST LEGACY

THE DEADLIEST LEGACY

Hilary Bonner

**SEVERN
HOUSE**

First world edition published in Great Britain and the USA in 2023
by Severn House, an imprint of Canongate Books Ltd,
14 High Street, Edinburgh EH1 1TE.

Trade paperback edition first published in Great Britain and the USA in 2024
by Severn House, an imprint of Canongate Books Ltd.

severnhouse.com

British Library Cataloguing-in-Publication Data
A CIP catalogue record for this title is available from the British Library.

ISBN-13: 978-1-4483-0935-1 (cased)
ISBN-13: 978-1-4483-1369-3 (trade paper)
ISBN-13: 978-1-4483-0936-8 (e-book)

Typeset by Palimpsest Book Production Ltd.,
Falkirk, Stirlingshire, Scotland.

Praise for the David Vogel mysteries

"An edge-of-the-seat crime thriller . . . This one will stay with readers for a long time"
Booklist on *The Danger Within*

"A crisply written crime novel that methodically reveals the pieces of a complex puzzle, effectively challenging armchair sleuths"
Kirkus Reviews on *Dreams of Fear*

"A cracking read, tautly suspenseful"
Booklist on *Dreams of Fear*

"This taut thriller is filled with unexpected twists and turns, leading up to a shocker of an ending"
Booklist on *Wheel of Fire*

"A gripping novel that will draw admirers of Peter James and Val McDermid"
Library Journal on *Deadly Dance*

"A formidable crime writer . . . Packed with Bonner's sharp eye for detail"
Daily Mail on *Deadly Dance*

"A suspenseful and disturbing page-turner . . . Fully fleshed characters, a masterfully constructed plot, and a shock ending make for a gripping read"
Booklist on *Deadly Dance*

"Belting cop thriller . . . Ingenious"
Sunday Times Crime Club on *Deadly Dance*

About the author

Hilary Bonner is the author of seventeen previous crime novels, including four David Vogel mysteries, and five non-fiction books. A former journalist and past Chair of the Crime Writers' Association, she divides her time between Somerset and London.

www.hilarybonner.com

For my cousin Barbara.
As ever

ONE

Detective Chief Inspector David Vogel was enjoying Sunday lunch with his wife and daughter when the call came.

He stepped away from the table to talk. As soon as he returned, Mary knew what he was going to say before he opened his mouth.

'You have to go,' she said.

'I'm afraid so,' Vogel replied.

'There's a surprise,' she murmured.

'I'm sorry,' Vogel continued. 'There's been a sudden death at the festival.'

The family were eating at the Seagate Hotel on Appledore Quay. Mary knew that the village's annual book festival was in full flow nearby. It was one of North Devon's most prestigious events, attracting big-name authors, large audiences of locals and tourists, and national media attention.

'A sudden death?' she queried. A sudden death by natural causes was hardly likely to call for the attention of her high-ranking detective husband.

'Do you mean a murder?' she continued.

'It's been called in as a murder, or a possible murder,' replied Vogel. 'Of course, we have to investigate—'

'Is it somebody important?' Mary interrupted.

'Oh, yes. It most certainly is.'

He told her then. Mary suspected she probably hadn't heard of many of those participating in the festival, but she'd heard of this one. She gasped.

'My God, if it is murder, it will be national news, David, won't it?'

'Yes. That's why I have to go straight away.'

'Good luck,' said Mary.

'Will you be able to come back, Dad?' asked his daughter, Rosamund.

'I shall try to, sweetheart, really I will,' Vogel replied.

Mary took her daughter's hand in hers. This lunch had been arranged to take Rosamund's mind off her lost cat. Storey had gone missing almost a week earlier, and Rosamund was distraught.

Mary was a good police wife. She very much loved her somewhat unusual copper husband, a naturally gentle man whose manner was more that of an academic or an old-fashioned clergyman than a senior police officer, and she did not doubt that he loved her. She had learned to accept constant disruptions to family life many years previously. On this occasion, however, she couldn't help feeling both disappointed and a little upset. Partly because it was such a rare event for the three of them to go out to lunch like this, but mostly because of Rosamund and her adored cat.

Vogel was a good husband, by and large. But something always seemed to get in the way of her little family doing what others seemed to do on a regular basis. And Vogel's days off rarely passed without some interruption, even if only minor.

At least they had all finished their main courses. But that would be of little consolation to Rosamund. And David had only just ordered his favourite dessert. Plum crumble. He was a vegetarian, had been since, as a boy, he had watched a particularly graphic documentary about abattoirs. And he had a great love for anything sweet, particularly a good crumble. Preferably with clotted cream.

'I'll get them to keep that plum crumble warm, then,' Mary said.

'Thank you, darling,' said Vogel, kissing her lightly on one cheek.

'But I won't hold my breath,' Mary added silently to herself, as she watched him stride briskly towards the door.

'You'll make sure they're still looking for Storey, won't you, Dad?' Rosamund called out.

Vogel looked back at her over his shoulder.

'I've told you, Rossy, we've got a top team on it. Docherty and Lake. You know them. They won't give up.'

'You'll make sure, though, won't you, Dad?'

'Of course I will, sweetheart,' Vogel assured her. 'I promise.'

TWO

Three days earlier, leading romantic novelist Delia Day had arrived in North Devon for the festival. She had come to believe, with dreary certainty, that she'd made a mistake even before her train chugged into the little station just across the river from Barnstaple town centre.

She'd felt ill at ease throughout the journey, for reasons she could not explain – although the now almost inevitable unreliability of Britain's rail network, coupled with a lack of what she considered to be basic creature comforts, had not helped.

That final leg had been the worst. There hadn't even been a first-class compartment. And the train really did chug. It also took for ever to complete what should have been a forty-minute leg. And because her London train had been half an hour late leaving Paddington – with a buffet of sorts, but no first-class trolley service, no hot food and, worse still, a shortage of gin – she had missed what should have been a comfortable connection at Exeter and ultimately arrived in Barnstaple an hour and a half after she should have done.

She peered despondently through her carriage window. She was in danger either of being late for the opening of the festival or of failing to have time to present herself properly. Hair and makeup both needed attention after the journey, and she had to change into one of the series of knock-'em-dead outfits that she always carried with her when making public appearances. After all, she had an image to keep up.

Insult had been added to injury by the heavy drizzle of which she had first become aware just north of Taunton, and which was still falling heavily over Barnstaple. Well, it would be, wouldn't it? Delia had recently read an article in a Sunday supplement by a clearly unimpressed travel writer seemingly commissioned to produce a series on the hidden secrets of various holiday destinations, who had suggested in no uncertain terms that the hidden secret of the West Country peninsula was that it rained ceaselessly.

She really ought to have insisted the organizers of the Appledore Book Festival send a car for her to Exeter or Tiverton Parkway – or, better still, not agreed to come to the festival at all. As it was, she was in a thoroughly bad mood, which she believed nothing in the ensuing four days was likely to succeed in improving.

Why on earth had she said yes to it? North Devon might be beautiful, but it was also godforsaken. With or without the rain. Hung on to England like Lucifer's tail, Cyril Tawney had said. Or was that Cornwall? Didn't make much difference as far as Delia was concerned. She was a diehard Londoner and failed to understand why anybody would want to live anywhere else in the UK.

She supposed it was ego that had sucked her in. She had been asked to be guest of honour at the festival before, of course, and had always said no. Finally, she had succumbed. This year's invitation from the festival director had been flattering almost to the point of embarrassment. Not that Delia was prone to be embarrassed by praise. After all, she was almost certainly the most successful romantic novelist in the world. Living one, anyway. And with that status came certain expectations.

Also, once she had learned of the proposed programme, she had made herself believe it could be used to her advantage in all sorts of ways. She was now no longer sure about that at all.

Indeed, as she pulled on the hooded waterproof cape she'd had the forethought to carry with her, largely thanks to that travel writer, she felt she must prepare for several days of misery. She disembarked without difficulty, stepping easily enough on to the shiny wet platform, but then struggled to lift down the two large bags she had brought with her. One contained the assorted paraphernalia of her work, including her laptop, a printout of her latest manuscript so far and some books she was using for reference. In the other, she carried her clothes – something, she hoped, for every eventuality, as was her wont – and her shoes. Shoes were her biggest problem.

She liked to wear designer footwear and still preferred high heels. But she also suffered from bouts of plantar fasciitis, a painful condition affecting the base of the foot, so at least a couple of pairs of lightweight trainers with insoles were a must. You would think, with all the moving around she had been obliged to undertake in her life, that she might have by this time mastered the art of travelling light. But she never quite had.

However, help was on hand.

'Allow me, Miss Day,' said a friendly male voice.

She stepped back. He moved towards her, smiling. A pleasant-faced young man, probably in his late thirties, his hairline prematurely receding, but attractive enough all the same, wearing a smart pale-grey suit.

'I'm Michael, your driver,' he said over his shoulder, as he effortlessly lifted Delia's luggage off the train. 'Very pleased to meet you, Miss Day.'

He would have had no trouble recognizing her, of course. Even in a hooded cape. The cape did, after all, bear a bold geometric design in Delia's trademark black, white, purple and silver. She had affected a distinctive personal style at the very beginning of her writing career and never wavered from it. Her hair was a geometric silver bob, with light and dark purple streaks, colour and shape both requiring weekly visits to her hairdresser. She was known to wear only her chosen colours. Be it jeans and a sweater or evening wear, or something in between, she was invariably dressed in various combinations of black, white, purple, and silver. Beneath her cape, she wore black stretch trousers, a black leather jacket – she had checked the forecast and noticed that it was cold for June in North Devon, as well as wet – a loose white linen shirt and a silk scarf in purple and silver. As ever, she had begun her journey immaculately made up, including, of course, her customary false eyelashes and a heavy application of purple lipstick, with just a hint of pink so she didn't look too ghoulish.

'And I'm very pleased to meet you, Michael,' she said, meaning every word of it.

Delia had not asked for a fee to attend the festival – she

knew it would be too low to bother with – but she had requested a car and a driver to be at her disposal throughout. A request that had been swiftly granted. The presence of Delia Day at a writing or book event was always regarded as something of a coup. And Delia knew that. She also knew that she gave good value. If she put her mind to it.

She had turned down the festival's usual offer of a room at the Seagate, very much the centre of all the action, largely because she didn't want to tempt providence. Well, no more than she had by simply being here. There could be all sorts of people lurking around with whom she wouldn't wish to be unexpectedly confronted. At the very least, she was likely to be surrounded non-stop by fans.

Instead, she had asked to be booked into the Imperial Hotel in Barnstaple. Most of her downtime was likely to be spent there indulging in room service. The deadline loomed for the book she was writing, and she was a woman of considerable discipline. Otherwise, she wouldn't have written more than a hundred novels. She had lost count of exactly how many more. At the moment, she was writing a minimum of two thousand words a day. Come what may. Festival or no festival.

Michael made sure Delia was carefully settled in the back of his excellently presented and ecologically sound electric motor car – she had no idea of the make, having little interest in cars, noticing only that this one was comfortable and almost excessively clean, and only knowing it was electric because Michael told her so. With some pride. He then loaded her bags in the boot, before asking her if it was hotel or festival first. Thanks to the tardiness of the British railway system, she only had just over an hour before she had to be in Appledore for the opening of the festival. Nonetheless, she chose to be taken first to the Imperial, only a few minutes' drive from the station, in order to freshen up and do a quick change. Delia Day had never been known to let the act drop.

She expertly renovated her makeup, ran a hot brush through her hair and chose as her outfit for the evening a glitzy silver trouser suit, with long floaty trousers, over a plain deep purple T-shirt. To the jacket lapel, she pinned a black silk rose, courtesy of one of her favourite designers, Japan's Issey Miyake.

Delia had agreed to take part in four events at the festival: including the opening ceremony, at which she would be required to make a short speech, followed by a meet-and-greet; a panel of women discussing misogyny in publishing; and an 'In Conversation' session with James Harding, the screenwriter with whom she had collaborated on the recent Netflix serialization of her first and most famous novel, *Love's Dream Eternal*. Theirs was not a happy pairing personally, but their professional collaboration was generally regarded as an outstanding success.

She arrived in time for the opening ceremony by the skin of her teeth – which she hated doing because, whenever possible, Delia was inclined to be early – largely thanks to Michael, who, having driven the eight miles from Barnstaple smoothly and swiftly, swept into the festival site, right by the sea on the Westward Ho! road, and dropped her very nearly inside the entrance to the main marquee.

The opening ceremony was presented by Janey Lucas, a local radio and TV personality who was a mainstay of the festival. Delia had never met her before but was quickly impressed by her slick professionalism. Which came as something of a relief. You rarely knew quite what you were going to get at these things.

Janey introduced Delia and two other of the more celebrated authors present, Gemma Fisher, an eminent Booker-nominated novelist, and Gerald Kauffman, a renowned literary historian. All three had been asked to speak but were required to do little more than eulogize about the festival, what it did for North Devon and its increasing prestige in the writing world. Delia knew exactly how to do this. There were two rules: you cannot ever be too short nor can you overdo the superlatives. This formal part of the evening's proceedings passed without noticeable incident, and Delia knew she had played her part well enough. As she should with all her experience.

It was during the meet-and-greet which followed that she began to really regret her presence at the festival. The unease she had experienced during her journey went into overdrive.

She told herself she was succumbing quite unnecessarily to the inexplicable sense of anxiety that was beginning to engulf her. She was Delia Day. She was rich, famous and one of the most successful novelists in the world. Of any genre. Only two authors of fiction in history, Agatha Christie and Barbara Cartland, had sold more novels worldwide than Delia Day. The critics hated her, of course, dismissing her work out of hand. It was tosh. Rubbish. Twaddle. And so on. Her readers worshipped her. She had getting on for a billion of them. And several million Twitter followers. Her bank manager loved her. As did her publishers. She was untouchable.

Nonetheless, when she became aware that she was being stared at by an elegant elderly woman with white hair and piercing blue eyes, she felt a chill run up and down her spine. Who was this? Why did she feel this way? She turned away at once. But she could still feel those eyes boring into her back.

A few minutes later, the woman approached her. Somehow or other, Delia managed to produce her usual, thoroughly professional, welcoming smile.

'Miss Day, I have little appreciation of anything you write,' began the woman bluntly. 'But I have huge admiration for everything you have achieved, most of all the work of your foundation with disadvantaged young people. You are a fine example to them, particularly to young women.'

'Well, thank you,' responded Delia as calmly as she could manage. Delia's foundation was dear to her heart, even though the woman's remark had been an extremely back-handed compliment. But it wasn't that which was disturbing Delia. Her heart was pounding in her chest. Had this woman featured in her largely forgotten past? And even if that was so, why should she be concerned? She was Delia Day, and that was that. She was concerned, though. Was there something familiar about the woman, or was she imagining it?

'May I ask your name?' Delia enquired casually.

'Of course. I'm Amelia Bowden.'

She was probably well into her eighties, Delia thought. She stood tall and straight, aided only by a narrow ebony cane. Her manner, and the look in her eye, remained disconcertingly sharp. Delia considered for a moment more. Was there something familiar about that name? She usually had an excellent memory for names and faces, but she could neither place the name nor match it to a face.

Amelia Bowden held out a thin, gnarled hand.

'How do you do,' she said.

'How do you do,' responded Delia.

She studied the other woman's face closely for any sign of recognition from her. She could see none. She decided to plunge straight in.

'Have we met before?' she asked as casually as she could manage.

Amelia Bowden looked Delia up and down with an ill-concealed lack of enthusiasm.

She shook her head.

'I believe I would remember,' she murmured.

Delia smiled more easily. She didn't mind at all the inferred superiority of Amelia Bowden's remark. It had put her mind at rest. That settled things, then, she thought. Her ever-lively imagination had run away with her again. Which, of course, was what she got paid for.

'As has always been my intention,' she said.

Amelia Bowden inclined her head slightly. It was very nearly a nod of approval.

'Is this your first visit to Appledore, Miss Day?' she asked.

'I think so,' said Delia.

She had no idea why she made such a curious reply, and Amelia Bowden had no intention of letting her get away with it.

'You think so?' responded Amelia sharply. 'That's rather a strange reply, is it not? Surely you know.'

'Uh, yes, of course.'

She was aware that she had rather backed herself into a corner. And quite unnecessarily.

'No, I haven't. But I've been close, I'm sure. I go to so many places. Can be most terribly confusing. Visiting book shops for signings usually—'

'There is no book shop in Appledore,' Amelia Bowden interrupted even more sharply.

'Oh, what a shame,' muttered Delia. 'Waterstones in Exeter, of course – pretty sure I've done a signing there . . .'

She was aware that she was waffling.

'Exeter is in East Devon, more than fifty miles away,' said Amelia rather sternly.

Delia thought the woman must surely have been a school-teacher once upon a time. Her rescue came in an unlikely form. The sound of a relatively high-pitched male voice, which she had always considered to be thoroughly disagreeable, from behind her left shoulder.

'Good evening, Delia, dear.'

She turned at once to face James Harding, his unpleasantly fleshy face stretched into what she considered to be a particularly smarmy smile. Even for him.

Out of the frying pan into the fire, she thought. This could not really be called a rescue. She loathed the man. He was, in her opinion, a toad of the lowest order. Working with him so closely on the Netflix project had been one of her very worst professional experiences.

'You look younger every time I see you, darling; you really must give me the number of your plastic surgeon,' Harding announced, loud and clear. There was a distinct lull in the buzz of conversation around them. Delia was aware of a sudden intake of breath from Amelia Bowden, who was still standing beside her. Then Harding threw back his head and emitted an extravagant peal of laughter, which presumably was supposed to indicate that he was, of course, only joking. He leaned forward and air-kissed her on both cheeks.

Delia quite desperately wanted to slap him. But that would never do. She maintained her self-control and kept the false smile firmly in place. With difficulty.

'I don't think even the greatest plastic surgeon in the world could do anything for you, darling,' she remarked pleasantly. And she had the pleasure of seeing Harding's delight at his own wit evaporate from those nasty piggy eyes, set deep in mounds of florid cheek, before she turned swiftly away to allow him no time to make any riposte.

She could, however, feel those eyes boring into the back of her head as she made her way to the far side of the marquee to greet a group of fans clutching books for her to sign. The expression 'if looks could kill' flitted into her mind. Was everyone going to stare at her tonight? Delia was also pretty sure Amelia Bowden still had those cool blue eyes of hers fixed on her. And she found that far more disconcerting than being stared at by Harding. He was now an old sparring partner. And she considered that she had always had his measure. She had to admit that he was a surprisingly excellent scriptwriter and adapter of books for stage and screen. But in every other way, she considered him to be a bit of a fool. And it was already apparent that was not the case with Amelia Bowden.

Meanwhile, it was time she got on with what she was there for. To pander to her fans. The group waiting for her, some of whom had pictures for her to sign as well as books, were all women. Her readers usually were women. Predictably so, of course. But Delia had reason to believe there were more men readers of romantic fiction than would ever admit it.

''Ave 'ee ever been to Appledore before?' asked one of the women, in an unusually broad Devonian accent.

That question again. This time, Delia was ready for it.

'No,' she replied firmly. 'But I have visited Devon before. Your county town, Exeter. A splendid city.'

'Be 'ee enjoying your stay?' persisted the woman in that inexplicably confident way exhibited by people who are smugly proud of where they live.

'Well, I've only just arrived,' replied Delia diplomatically.

She had, in fact, rarely enjoyed herself less anywhere, although she did realize that was largely due to her horrid journey coupled with her own frame of mind. The weather so far hadn't helped either. And it was also absolutely true that she had only just arrived, she reminded herself.

'I'm looking forward to having a good look around tomorrow,' she added diplomatically.

There was no doubt that this part of the world was having a strange effect on her, and she couldn't explain why. She was finding the meet-and-greet unsettling and knew she wasn't responding to those gathered with her usual aplomb. This wasn't like her.

There was a slight kerfuffle at the entrance, which heralded the arrival of two hassled-looking latecomers, each wearing a large dripping-wet pink anorak and towing a pink suitcase on wheels. As they pushed their way through the canvas flaps pulled across the entrance, they were followed by a minor squall, a flurry of wind and rain. Delia assumed it must now be raining heavily and blowing quite hard. That was all she needed. Was there anything much worse weather-wise than a raging storm by the British seaside, she pondered?

However, these were two women Delia knew well, and although, for her sins, she often found them more than a tad irritating, on this occasion she found herself inordinately pleased to see them. They did at least represent relatively safe territory. They were her very own super-fans. Tina and Tilly Tucker, identical twins from somewhere in the Home Counties. Delia wasn't quite sure exactly where. She just knew that everywhere she went, these two seemed to turn up. They always wanted to buy books and take new selfies of themselves with Delia. And more than anything, they wanted her to give them some time, to talk to them. To make them feel special. To feel as if she was their friend. She almost always obliged. How could she do otherwise? They were like a pair of devoted puppies. And they asked so little. Which had perhaps made them pretty close to the only kind of friends Delia wanted, she had reflected on more than one occasion.

She waved at them. They came hurrying over to her at once.

'We're so sorry we're late, Delia,' they said. It was a 'they' too. The twins often spoke in unison. And when not doing that, they invariably finished each other's sentences.

'Our train was over an hour late leaving . . .' began one of them.

'. . . and we missed our connection at Exeter and had to wait for ages and ages,' continued the other.

Even after such a long association, Delia had yet to learn to tell which was which, and she doubted she ever would. They were matching tiny people with identically cut coal-black hair framing round, pale faces. Delia had become very nearly fond of them over the years, and on the rare occasions she made a public appearance without their presence, she did rather miss them. They invariably dressed the same; on this occasion, the pink floral-patterned anoraks were identical and the lower part of each of them was clad in what appeared to be somewhat damp pale-blue jeans, feet thrust into pink and blue trainers which squelched as they moved.

'Then they told us there wasn't going to be another connection and we had to continue by bus and . . .'

'. . . by then it was tipping down with rain, and the link road was a nightmare . . .'

'. . . when we did get to Barnstaple, we couldn't get a taxi, and we had to wait for a bus . . .'

'. . . and we had to change at Bideford too, and we haven't been to our digs to dump our stuff, but we were still late and we've . . .'

'. . . missed your speech, Delia. It's just so annoying. You must think us so rude.'

They were quite a double act, thought Delia not for the first time.

'Not at all, ladies,' she said, when she could eventually get a word in edgeways. 'I had a horrid journey too, although it pales into insignificance against yours. But I was very nearly late myself. And that would have been baaaad, very baaaad!' She drew the vowel out long and expressively.

Tina and Tilly giggled their appreciation.

'We'll make up for it. We'll be the first in to hear you speak from now on, and the last to leave,' they said.

'Thank you, both,' said Delia. 'I don't know what I'd do without you.'

In a way, that was true, but she didn't have much more to say to them for the time being – nor ever, really, come to that. In any case, the Tucker twins were clearly not in the most responsive of states following their journey. So she wasn't displeased when the festival director arrived at her side to whisk her off to meet the local mayor. Although that too was something she could do without. In fact, she could do without all of it, the way she was feeling.

Carolyne Smedley had worked hard to persuade Delia to attend Appledore, something the writer had previously resisted. The festival in the pretty coastal village had grown considerably in stature since its inception in 2006 and now punched

way above its weight. Everyone Delia knew who had been
there always spoke well of it. But she rarely attended writing
festivals. She didn't need them to raise her profile – those days
were long over – and she didn't enjoy them. They went to the
bottom of her pile nowadays. She had not previously even
considered the Appledore festival. But there had been a change
in that regard. Not entirely facilitated by Carolyne Smedley's
persistent pressure. Something that niggled at the back of her
mind. It was probably ridiculous; nonetheless, she had become
rather curiously drawn to North Devon, and the festival
provided the ideal opportunity for her to get that out of her
system. Once and for all. Or so she hoped.

The festival director was small, dark and stick-thin. Like a
bird, she flitted everywhere. She was good at her job, invariably leaving all the writers with the impression that they were
the most important person in the programme. Delia was never
for a moment taken in by that kind of thing. Even though she
arguably *was* the most important person in the programme.
She wondered what made Carolyne Smedley tick. Carolyne
was one of those who gave little away.

'Are you from North Devon?' Delia enquired, as Smedley
led her to the far side of the marquee.

'Oh, yes, born and bred,' replied the director. 'Why do
you ask?'

Delia had little idea why she'd asked, and Carolyne Smedley
was clearly not used to her invited authors taking any interest
in her.

'Thought I'd put the boot on the other foot,' Delia murmured
vaguely.

Smedley looked puzzled for a moment, then smiled.

'Ah, I see,' she said. 'I'm from Bideford, the town just
upriver, and both my parents were also born and bred locally.
North Devon produces two types of people: those who can't
wait to get away and those who will never leave. Until
they die.'

Delia raised an approving eyebrow. An astute remark, she
thought. And probably a pretty fair assessment of how life
was in places of outstanding beauty like this, with not much
beyond their natural beauty to offer their young. Little or no

industry or culture. Virtually nothing to challenge or excite, in Delia's opinion, except the land and the sea. And if that didn't do it for you, tough.

She studied Carolyne carefully. This was not a woman to be underestimated. But it wasn't that which was attracting Delia's interest. Once again, there was something familiar about the other woman. This was getting ridiculous, she thought. Her imagination was in overdrive.

'Have we met before?' she asked abruptly. For the second time that evening.

Carolyne, who was slightly ahead of her, stopped and turned right round to face her directly.

'Goodness, no,' she said, eyes wide in surprise. 'You might not remember meeting me, but do you think I for a moment could ever forget meeting you?'

Usually, Delia would accept such a remark as only right and proper. It was more or less what Amelia Bowden had said, in abbreviated form. But that, largely because of her great age, had reassured Delia. Carolyne Smedley was a relatively young woman, in her late thirties or perhaps early forties, Delia thought. It was highly unlikely that she would have ever met her except through this festival or something similar. There could surely have been no more historic crossing of paths. So, on this occasion, Delia immediately found herself wondering exactly what Carolyne meant by her remark. Then gave herself a mental shaking. What on earth was wrong with her?

'I shall take that as a compliment,' she said mildly.

'And so you should,' countered the festival director.

By then they had reached the mayor of Bideford, Councillor Jeremy Roberts, a tall broad man with a large belly upon which his regalia of office rested as if it were a shelf.

The mayor responded most politely when Carolyne introduced Delia, but after that seemed to have no idea what to say to her. Delia thought it was likely that he didn't know who she was at all, although he would be aware that she was the festival's guest of honour, of course, and therefore would have insisted on meeting her.

She decided to go on a charm offensive.

'May I just say, Mr Mayor, how immensely fortunate I think you all are to live in such a wonderful part of the world,' she announced.

The mayor's pallid and rather unattractive face split into a wide smile, reminding Delia of two facts of life. The first was that most people, for reasons she could never quite understand, love to be complimented on the place where they live, and officers of local government more than most. The second was that the appearance of almost everyone, even a fundamentally ugly man, probably into his sixties, who has allowed what may once have been a rather decent physique to run to fat, is immensely improved by a smile.

'You have no idea how much I envy you,' she continued, lightly laying a perfectly manicured hand on his jacket sleeve. 'You must be so very, very proud to be the mayor of such a place.'

Mayor Roberts positively beamed at her, flushing with pleasure.

'I am, oh, I am,' he said. 'And we are delighted to welcome you here, I'm sure, Miss Day. Do I take it this is your first visit?'

'I really don't know how I've avoided coming here before,' replied Delia, only a touch obliquely.

'Well, I just hope you have time between your festival duties to enjoy some of what North Devon has to offer.'

'I'm sure I shall,' said Delia.

She continued with her charm offensive when introduced to the mayor's wife, Jill, his mayoress, who did turn out to be a reader, but was beginning to run out of small talk with her too when – and this time most definitely to her relief – Carolyne Smedley introduced two more people to the little group. Again, these were two people she knew quite well, probably the nearest she had to friends amongst the writers she met occasionally on the circuit. George and Felicity Smythe, who wrote crime novels together under the name of Felicity George, were mid-list authors who, through ingenuity and unfailing energy as much as talent, managed to make a surprisingly decent living out of their writing. They were also good value at festivals. They had a rather slick on-stage double act which rarely varied, except for a nod or two to their location, but was entertaining enough, and the audiences, which often moved from festival to festival, as did the contributors, seemed not to notice the repetition. Or, if they did, were too polite to mention it.

'Oh, Delia, we were so thrilled to hear you were coming, we just don't see enough of you nowadays,' enthused Felicity, a jolly woman with fluffy blonde hair. She was not much taller than Carolyne Smedley, slim and still vaguely pretty in her late fifties.

'I'm really glad to see you two,' said Delia, and she meant it. Felicity's insistent jollity could be wearing in large doses, but Delia was fond of her, and of her husband, and enjoyed their company, by and large.

George stepped forward and engulfed Delia in a big hug. He was a tall, thin man of Caribbean descent, about a foot taller than his wife, with exceptionally long arms, and much given to hugging. Rather uncomfortable bony hugs, Delia was reminded as she found herself held firmly within his angular grasp. George was affable and always seemed genuine. Sometimes it seemed to Delia that there wasn't nearly enough of either of those qualities about.

'How lovely that you're here,' he announced, in the deep growly voice which was always a bit of a surprise coming from a man of his skinny build. 'I didn't think you graced these sorts of events any more. Far too grand nowadays.'

He chuckled at his own words. There was something about him that allowed him to say almost anything without causing offence.

Delia treated him to half a smile.

'I've always been too grand for you, George Smythe,' she said.

'That's true,' interjected Felicity.

Delia smiled again. She enjoyed a bit of banter. Except with James Harding, of course.

'I think I was flattered into it, to tell the truth,' said Delia.

''Tis often the way,' commented Felicity.

'Not in our case as a rule, of course,' said George. 'We're just grateful for the fee. Such as it is . . .'

'And for selling a few books,' interrupted Felicity.

'At least they've got them here,' said George.

'We went all the way to the top of Scotland in the spring for that Highland writing festival, and they didn't even have one of our books there. Blamed the local Waterstones first. And then our publishers. Mind you, we're with them on that, aren't we, George?'

'Oh, publishers. You know what I always say about them, don't you, Delia? If publishers were in charge of selling cigarettes, you wouldn't need any anti-smoking advertising campaigns or health warnings on the packets. Nobody would be able to buy them anywhere.'

Delia laughed. Politely. She'd heard it all before.

'Still, we all know what publishers are like, don't we?' George continued.

'We certainly do,' agreed Delia.

Actually, she didn't. Or not in the way that George meant, anyway. She had led a charmed life in that regard and was still contracted to the same major publisher that had bought her first novel. Hers was an unusual story among authors. Everything had gone right from the beginning and continued to do so. Delia's first novel made a small fortune for Coldharbour, probably in the first instance saving them from liquidation, and every book since had continued to bring home the bacon. As a result, her publishers made a huge fuss of her. Mistakes were not allowed. Delia could not even imagine turning up at a book festival, or indeed any event, and finding that her books weren't in evidence. Nothing like that would be allowed to happen to her.

She noticed that the meet-and-greet gathering seemed to be drawing to an end. People were beginning to leave. George was still talking, but fond of him as she was, Delia had gone into smile-and-nod mode. One way and another, this had been the day from hell. A nightmare journey followed by an event at which she had felt inexplicably uncomfortable almost throughout. It wasn't late, only just after nine, but all she wanted now was her hotel room and her bed. She was wondering if she might be able to make her excuses and leave when Carolyne Smedley appeared at her elbow.

'Now, is there anyone else you would like to meet, Delia?'
she enquired effusively.

Was the woman mad? Delia had known only a handful of
people present and had no interest at all in any of those she
had been introduced to. She certainly didn't want any further
introductions. But she was honest enough to realize she was
being unforgivably churlish and must not let her true feelings
show. Not for a moment. After all, nobody had forced her to
accept the invitation and attend the festival. She knew the form
well enough. She made herself behave graciously.

'It's been absolutely lovely,' she lied, flashing her professional smile again. 'And I'm totally in your hands, Carolyne.
If there's anyone else you would like me to meet, of course
I would be delighted. But otherwise, well, it's been a long
day. So, if you're done with me, I really wouldn't mind heading
back to my hotel.'

'Of course,' responded Carolyne. She waved a hand vaguely
in the direction of a number of retreating backs as people
headed for the exit. 'Everyone seems to be leaving or about
to leave. That will be absolutely fine, Delia. And thank you
so very much for everything.'

'My pleasure,' said Delia, which, of course, was another
lie. A big lie.

Carolyne Smedley waved one hand around the marquee
again, encompassing both those leaving and those remaining.

'They adored you,' she enthused.

'Oh, darling, no,' murmured Delia, thinking, *So they bloody
well should have done.*

Ultimately, Delia stepped outside with George and Felicity
Smythe on one side of her. Carolyne, the mayor and his wife
were on the other, discussing the schedule for the next few
days.

The weather was terrible. Tina and Tilly had not exaggerated. The rain was being driven horizontally by powerful gusts
of wind blowing in over the Atlantic and Delia could taste
and smell the salt in the air.

Suddenly, there was a crush of people sheltering under the
canopy which covered the entrance to the marquee, unsure
whether to go back in or make a run for it to the car park or

the taxi point. Not that there were any taxis to be seen. A real storm had blown up, just as Delia had feared. But then the main festival site was right across the road from the ocean and more or less totally unprotected from the elements.

A number of the fans Delia had talked to earlier had come out. They wished her a happy stay, shouting so that their voices rose above the roar of the wind and rain. Delia tried to reply, but she doubted they could hear her. She looked up. The canopy which formed a kind of porch over the entrance was flapping disconcertingly. The entire structure was making a nasty creaking noise.

A banner bearing the name of the festival's principal sponsor, Devon Glory Apple Juice, had broken loose and was blowing all over the site, presenting quite a hazard.

Somebody pushed into Delia from one side, and she slipped precariously on the muddy grass, glad at least that she had chosen a pair of her designer trainers as her footwear rather than heels. She grabbed one of the marquee's supports for balance and was just wondering whether that was a good idea when a particularly virulent gust blew her carefully arranged geometric bob right back off her face so that it was more or less standing on end. A bit like a purple and silver bog brush, she suspected. But that wasn't her main concern. Swiftly but ineffectively, Delia attempted to smooth her hair down with her free hand. She always wore it firmly fixed in place by the liberal application of strong-hold hairspray – partially curtaining the sides of her face, right over her ears, and tucked in around her chin. A thick fringe covered her forehead. For all manner of reasons, Delia's hair was a kind of comfort blanket to her, and she hated it when that blanket was displaced. Indeed, she supposed she could be accused of being paranoid about it.

True to form, she immediately felt that everyone around her was staring at her. Mind you, she'd been feeling like that all afternoon. As usual, she told herself this was nonsense. After all, almost everybody present around the marquee entrance was probably more focused on staying upright than anything else, as she herself was. That and fighting to keep her hair in place.

George and Felicity tried to persuade her to join them for more drinks at the Seagate. Delia politely declined. She hoped her car was waiting for her and couldn't wait to get back to the comfort of her suite at the Imperial.

She just wanted to be alone. She knew it was stupid, but merely being with all these people, even the Smythes, was making her feel increasingly out of sorts. Bordering on vulnerable. And Delia Day didn't do vulnerable. Did she?

THREE

Unlike Delia, Mayor Roberts had thoroughly enjoyed the meet-and-greet. Particularly meeting the woman who was almost certainly the most celebrated romantic novelist in the world.

Delia had been right. He had known little about her before today, certainly had not read her books, and indeed had little or no interest in her or her work. However, Delia was the star of the festival, and therefore it was only right and proper that she had been brought across to him by the director. That was the way Jeremy Roberts saw it, anyway.

He was a classic example of a big fish in a small pond and had the ego, untroubled by even a passing acquaintance with reality, to go with it.

It had not occurred to him for a nanosecond that Delia had been anything less than one hundred per cent sincere when she had gushed at him earlier in the evening. Why would it? He was quite convinced that everyone he met envied him his life, as a pillar of the community in what he considered to be the most beautiful and desirable place in the world.

And so he was feeling smugly self-satisfied as he settled into the back seat of his chauffeur-driven mayoral Bentley, with his wife by his side. The borough of Bideford did not provide Jeremy Roberts with a vehicle of that class, of course. He was entitled only to far more modest means of transport when performing his mayoral duties. But Jeremy owned a luxury car-hire company, primarily in demand for weddings, one of a number of businesses he'd inherited from his father, and he'd reserved the Bentley and its regular driver for all his official appearances as mayor from the start of his term of office. He had even had a rather splendid car badge made, featuring the town crest, which clipped cleverly on to the front of the Bentley. Only right and proper, in his opinion.

He allowed himself a small smile of contentment. He was going back to the home he loved, with the woman he loved, in a quite beautiful vehicle, which he considered to be only appropriate to his status. He did realize that he was a very lucky man, but he also thought he deserved everything that he had. It wasn't the wedding car company or any of the other inherited businesses that had brought him the bulk of the considerable wealth he now enjoyed. No. At almost the beginning of the recycling era, Jeremy had spotted the potential in private waste disposal. It was possibly the only really clever thing he had done in his whole life. But he had moved fast and made a huge success of his waste management business, which was now one of the biggest in the country. And he was, of course, extremely proud of his achievement. Mayor Roberts didn't do humility.

He was undoubtedly an extremely smug man. But his smugness was about to get seriously displaced.

Just three or four minutes after he and his wife had set off, Jeremy Roberts's phone rang. The rousing tones of Elgar's 'Land of Hope and Glory' filled the back of the Bentley. Mayor Roberts only put his phone on silent when absolutely necessary. And he had been quite simply bewildered when certain of his council colleagues had expressed the opinion that his choice of ring tone might not be entirely appropriate in the modern age of diversity. The term 'woke' had yet to enter his vocabulary in any context unrelated to the act of rising from his bed in the morning.

He answered at once, even though the message 'no caller ID' appeared on his screen. After all, he prided himself on being approachable.

'Evening, Roberts here,' he began, cheerily loud as usual.

But almost as soon as the caller began to speak, he felt his heart miss a beat. Could that happen so instantly due to shock? He suspected that it just had.

'I see . . .' he began, when he was eventually allowed to speak, his voice uncertain and several decibels lower than previously.

The caller interrupted and continued to speak for another couple of minutes. Mayor Roberts had been fearing a call like this for many years. Particularly since he had been appointed mayor, his second term of office. But he was nearing the end of his mayoral year now and had begun almost to believe that his fears would never be realized. After all, times had changed, hadn't they?

'I see,' said Roberts again, when he was given another opportunity to speak. 'Of course, you can rely on me . . .'

He was quickly aware that there was no longer anyone listening to him across the airwaves. His caller had summarily ended the call, having said all that had been considered necessary, Roberts assumed.

He had hoped that he was finally free of the burden he had carried for so long. Indeed, the smooth passing of that very evening at the festival had surely indicated that. But no. It seemed he was still not entirely his own man. And he now doubted that he would ever be. Not as long as his tormenter was alive, anyway.

Automatically, he slid his phone back into his pocket. He was suddenly very aware of his wife staring at him. For a crazed minute or two, he had almost forgotten that she was with him.

'Who was that?' she asked. There was concern in her voice.

'Just one of the new councillors.'

'At this time in the evening?'

'Oh, you know, getting in a flap for no reason, as they do. Nothing for you to worry about, dear.'

'Really,' remarked Jill reflectively.

Mayor Roberts turned his face away from her and clasped his hands together in his lap. He and Jill had been married for more than thirty years and had three grown-up children and three grandchildren. His wife knew him far too well. He suspected that his normally flushed complexion had turned distinctly pale. He just hoped she couldn't see that. Nor that his hands were shaking.

Amelia Bowden was indeed watching Delia outside the marquee, from the most sheltered spot she could find, hovering in the entrance, as she waited to be picked up by one of her two great-nephews.

At one point, the famous novelist slipped and came danger-ously close to falling, Amelia reckoned. Now that would have been embarrassing, for Delia Day and the festival.

Amelia had told Delia that if she'd ever met her previously, she would definitely have remembered her. And surely that must be true. But she was now beginning to get this niggling feeling that she may, in fact, have met Delia before. It was only a 'may', and she was aware that even that could have been prompted merely by the writer's reaction to her, which she had considered to be more than a little curious. Amelia also knew that she could be intimidating, even to a woman like Delia Day, and indeed it was almost always her intention to be so. To adopt the somewhat fearsome persona she had acquired as a very young teacher – Delia had been right about Amelia's chosen profession – before and in the early days of her marriage. She had worn it like a cloak back then to conceal the fear that was inclined to engulf her when faced by entire classrooms of children, and continued to do so when it suited her. It had served her well over the years. As had her memory. Which remained better than most. If she had ever met Delia Day, it must have been a very long time ago indeed. Also insignificant, surely? Because Amelia rarely forgot anything of significance. But it was hard to imagine that meeting Delia Day could ever be insignificant.

However, the niggle remained. And became rather more than a niggle when that gust of wind blew Delia's perfectly coiffured bob out of place. This clearly disturbed the novelist who resolutely fought the wind with one arm in a not entirely successful bid to smooth her hair down again. It disturbed Amelia too.

She was transfixed by the spectacle. In fact, it was more of a pantomime than anything else. With Delia Day trying desperately to stay upright, but still seeming to be more worried about her hair being out of place than anything else. The writer was visibly distressed. However, Amelia suspected that Delia was the sort of person who couldn't bear it if things went even slightly off plan.

There was more, though. Amelia Bowden had seen something she had only seen once before. It wasn't definitive, of course. Not in any way. And it didn't make any sense at all. None. But it was certainly enough to give Amelia cause for concern.

Her musing was interrupted by the arrival of a small Italian sports car – a convertible, but with its hood up, mercifully – from which emerged her great-nephew William, unfolding a body so long and so large that it seemed barely possible that he could have fitted it into the little vehicle in the first place. He held aloft an enormous multi-coloured golf umbrella, which, under the circumstances, vaguely resembled a weapon of mass destruction. Amelia had no children of her own, therefore no grandchildren, but she had her two great-nephews, whom she had always managed to keep at her beck and call to some degree or another.

William was the stupid one. Most of the family thought he was loveable. Amelia never found stupidity loveable, although she would tolerate it in those she found useful. And William was useful – she had to give him that. He never asked questions and always did as she asked. Both highly commendable characteristics as far as Amelia Bowden was concerned.

Unfortunately, the stupidity rarely failed to manifest itself. And there he was, in a raging gale, clutching an enormous umbrella. Not to mention having arrived in that low-slung sports car – not his only vehicle, either. William was a complete petrolhead – he also owned a Land Rover and a van – oblivious to the disapproval of so many in a world desperate to clean itself up. Amelia regarded the little car with a distinct lack of enthusiasm. She knew that she could still just about get into it, but she didn't have a hope in a bucket of ever getting out of it. William would have to lift her out. Mind you, he'd done that before. Or very nearly.

He certainly wasn't her first choice of driver, but even Amelia Bowden could not always call all the shots. Her second great-nephew, her favourite, had been otherwise engaged. She was going to have to have a word with him about that. She watched as William attempted to approach her. A gust took the umbrella almost out of his hands. It wheeled and bucked in the air, ultimately turning completely inside out.

He was almost alongside her, bearing the inverted and out-of-control umbrella before him rather as if he were a human unicorn and it was his horn. Amelia dodged it with considerably more agility than might be expected of a woman of her years who used a walking stick. Mind you, her gleaming ebony cane had always been a bit of a prop for Amelia Bowden. Only not a lot of people knew that. Rather like the large translucent-pink-framed spectacles she had adopted many years previously because they masked the bags she developed beneath her eyes as a relatively young woman. Cheaper and less painful than a facelift, she had concluded. Only not a lot of people knew that, either.

'Sorry, Aunt Amelia,' said the young man as he continued to struggle unsuccessfully to control the broken umbrella.

'Why don't you put that thing back in the car before you kill someone,' she instructed.

'Yes, Aunt Amelia.'

'Not a very good idea on a day like this,' she called after him.

'No, Aunt Amelia, sorry, Aunt Amelia,' the young man called back.

'I do have a raincoat, you know – had you forgotten?'

'I don't know, Aunt Amelia. Sorry.'

He had quite a struggle getting the large umbrella into the small car. Eventually, he returned and provided a helpful arm and shoulder as he led his great-aunt across the now very muddy piece of field stretching between the marquee and the little sports car.

With further help from her great-nephew, Amelia managed to insert herself into the small low-slung vehicle without doing herself any permanent damage. As far as she knew.

'Is it straight home, then, Aunt Amelia?' William asked.

'Yes, of course, William,' said Amelia, who was yet again marvelling at the boy's stupidity.

'Where on earth am I likely to be going at this time of night, at my age?' she asked him curtly.

'Of course, Aunt Amelia, sorry, Aunt Amelia,' said William.

She settled back into the passenger seat, which was really quite comfortable once you'd jacked yourself into it, and stretched her legs. There was also plenty of legroom, something she greatly appreciated. Amelia Bowden had extremely long legs. She was five feet eleven, unusually tall for a woman of her generation.

Amelia lived in Bideford, in the area known as top-of-the-town. Her house was a big Edwardian terrace, far too big for a woman living alone, and in a rather poor state of repair because she couldn't afford the upkeep. But it was home. The only home she had known since her marriage, when she was twenty-two, to the young man who had been literally the boy next door when she was growing up, and had remained the only love of her life. His early death still plagued her. Barely a day went by without her seeing or hearing something that reminded her of her Gordon, and the family life they had dreamed of together. She had never got over the loss and never would. Nor everything else she had lost along with it. There had never been another man. There had been no substitute family life. No children with anyone else.

The usual darkness descended upon her when she started to dwell on the great tragedy of her life.

She knew she was always considered tough and steely. Maybe heartless. And soulless too. But only by those who knew nothing of her history. Her family knew. And understood. She was grateful for that. Immensely grateful.

William turned right out of the festival site and drove through Appledore, along the quay and then up the hill above the docks, once the centre of one of the biggest shipbuilding enterprises in the country, heading towards Northam.

That evening at the festival, Amelia had been reminded rather shockingly of her terrible loss. She realized that the thoughts that had come into her head could not possibly have any grounding in fact. That she was surely behaving crazily. But suddenly she no longer wanted to go home. To be all alone in that big house. There was something she wanted to do. Needed to do.

'William, can I change my mind?' she asked.

'Of course, Aunt Amelia,' replied William.

He might be stupid, but he was always amenable, thought Amelia, not for the first time. Indeed, William always seemed to have a truly lovely nature.

'I'd like to visit your grandfather,' she said. 'Do you mind?'

'No, of course I don't mind,' replied William predictably. 'But I'm not sure about Grandpa. Don't you think it's a bit late? He'll quite likely be in bed.'

'Then I shall have to get him out of bed,' said Delia. 'I am his sister, William. And I'll thank you to remember that. Sisters don't have to make appointments.'

'No, of course not, Aunt Amelia,' said William.

As he'd been heading for Bideford, he was driving in the wrong direction for his grandfather's house. The opposite direction, in fact. Grandpa Harry lived in Westward Ho! But William could easily turn right when they reached Northam and take the road above the Burrows towards Westward Ho!

William didn't grumble. But then he very rarely did.

'And will you wait for me and drive me home later, please?' asked Amelia.

'Of course I will, Aunt Amelia,' said William.

Carolyne Smedley headed straight for the Seagate. She too would have liked to go home, even though a recent divorce, after which she had swiftly reverted to her maiden name, had made home not quite as attractive as it had once been, but it was expected of her to mix and mingle. Endlessly. There would be no early nights for her for the duration of the festival.

She was a little anxious about the Delia Day/James Harding situation. She had overheard their caustic exchange at the meet-and-greet and had previously learned on the grapevine that their relationship might be more than a tad strained. It wasn't common knowledge, not yet anyway, but Carolyne's former husband – with whom she had remained 'friends' even though privately she would rather like to disembowel him – was now living with the PA to the chief executive of Delia's publishers. And had, it now seemed, been conducting an affair with her through most of his marriage to Carolyne. All the same, Carolyne was not averse to picking up and inwardly digesting the odd crumb of pillow talk when it came her way. And her ex, an unjustifiably self-important chap, she had come to realize only as their relationship had deteriorated, still seemed to get huge satisfaction from demonstrating that he knew something she didn't. Which suited Carolyne rather well.

Carolyne had felt that Delia had seemed edgy all evening. This was the third Appledore Book Festival she had organized as director. She had also helped out at several previously, and at other festivals in Devon and Cornwall. Carolyne Smedley knew her onions. She understood how even the most experienced of authors and the biggest names could suffer from nerves on these occasions, and she considered that one of her most important duties was to keep them happy. Delia Day had not been happy; she was quite sure of that. Carolyne Smedley wasn't a stupid woman. People, particularly authors, were inclined to underestimate her. But she had not failed to notice the flicker of something she couldn't quite identify flit across Delia's face when she had asked if there was anyone else the writer wanted to meet. Weariness perhaps, at the end of a long day. Or had it been something more? Frustration? Dislike? Dislike of Carolyne? Of the whole process?

Sometimes Carolyne wondered why certain people bothered to come at all. They were so susceptible to flattery, too. Didn't they realize that Carolyne would say and do anything to get the best possible line-up for her festival? Wasn't that patently bloody obvious?

James Harding hadn't seemed very happy, either. He was another one. Thought a good deal too much of himself, in Carolyne's opinion, and had a tendency to make clever remarks. Or remarks he thought were clever. Not exclusively directed at Delia Day. He had also given Carolyne the impression that he would rather be almost anywhere else than at the meet-and-greet.

This all made Carolyne uneasy. She liked things to run smoothly – although they never did, of course, not entirely. And she had to accept that. Nonetheless, she had already gained a reputation for running a tight ship, appropriately enough in Appledore with its nautical history, and she wanted to keep it that way.

She reminded herself that nothing concerning the relationship between Delia Day and James Harding was her problem, as long as it did not spill over into the festival as a whole. She just hoped that she hadn't made a mistake in inviting the pair of them. But she knew she hadn't. She couldn't have done. Apart from Delia's extraordinary record as a romantic novelist, she and James Harding had between them produced one of the biggest Netflix hits ever. Of course Carolyne hadn't made a mistake. Everybody wanted Harding and Day. They were box office. They were hot. Really hot!

What could go wrong, she asked herself as she smiled, gushed and air-kissed her way through the melee at the Seagate, intent only upon acquiring a large gin and tonic as swiftly as possible.

James Harding had also spurned the usual festival accommodation at the Seagate. He was staying in a rented cottage set in lush countryside between Bideford and Torrington, and he drove straight back to it as soon as the meet-and-greet ended.

The cottage was pretty but isolated. James wasn't normally a man who sought isolation. And certainly not solitude. But he had his reasons for choosing this location.

He was not in a particularly good mood as he began the drive back to the cottage. He loathed Delia Day every bit as much as she loathed him. And what annoyed him most about her was the way she invariably seemed to get the last word.

He had thoroughly rehearsed his comment about wanting the phone number of Delia's plastic surgeon, which he thought he had delivered rather well and in a suitably cutting fashion. But she had come back at him, lethal as ever, without missing a beat.

It was infuriating. But he reminded himself that it didn't matter. He was the one with the power. He was making a great deal of money out of adapting Delia's work. And she was stuck with him, whether she liked it or not. Netflix wouldn't trust her to adapt her books herself – they were quite right, too, she wouldn't have a clue – and she didn't dare suggest another scriptwriter. Certainly not after the little word he'd had with her a while back. She had no say in the matter, for all manner of reasons. The truth was that he had Delia Day in his pocket. And that at least was a highly satisfying thought, and one which raised his spirits slightly even before he reached his destination.

Of course, she was making a small fortune out of him, too. It was his scriptwriting that had transformed the first of what he privately regarded as her thoroughly dreadful books into an international hit on screen. But the big difference between them was that she didn't need the money. The bitch was filthy rich already. She wanted it, though. She'd always been a greedy cow. Common as muck, too, and little or no education. Not that you needed any to churn out her stuff. At least he had an English degree from a rather good university. Whenever he needed to boost his confidence, he would always remind himself, and everybody else, of that.

His spirits raised even more as he turned into the short drive leading to Honeysuckle Cottage. Carolyne Smedley had been quite right in concluding that the last place James Harding had wanted to be that evening was at the meet-and-greet. But he'd had a number of reasons for being extremely keen on attending the Appledore Book Festival. So here he was, in Devon for the best part of a week, staying in an idyllic picture-book thatched cottage. And he was not alone.

It was still raining, though not as heavily inland as earlier by the sea, and with a much lighter wind. He could see her through the window as he pulled his car to a halt by the porch. Which really did have honeysuckle growing around it. She was sitting in a tall, winged armchair watching out for him. A glass of white wine, which he knew would be a well-chilled Sancerre, stood on the little table by her side. There was just enough light inside the room for him to see that she was smiling. She wasn't a great beauty, that was for sure, but he didn't care. By God, she was eager.

He climbed quickly out of the car. She waved at him. He waved back, as he hurried towards the door. She stood up as he walked in, opening her arms to him. He stepped into her embrace. She wrapped himself around him. His soul soared. And James Harding wasn't a man often accused of having a soul.

'I've been waiting for this all night,' he murmured.

Meanwhile, William had delivered Amelia Bowden to the home of her brother, his grandfather, as requested.

And Grandpa Harry had indeed been in bed as William had predicted he would be. The house, set back from the main road just where it swings down the hill towards the centre of the seaside village and the beach, was quiet when they arrived. The curtains were already pulled upstairs, even though it was not quite dark, and both the front and back door were locked.

None of this deterred Amelia. But then, William reflected, nothing ever did deter Aunt Amelia when she was on a mission. And she definitely had that look about her. William was quite sure that Amelia had not asked him to drive her here in order to make a friendly, sisterly visit to her brother. Indeed, William couldn't quite remember when his aunt had last called on his grandfather. And he would probably know. After all, he visited his grandfather almost every day, delivering groceries and generally checking up on him.

Harry was the younger sibling, almost exactly a year younger than Amelia, but you'd never think it. He'd seemed like an old man for as long as William could remember. He was frail and had mobility problems, having suffered a stroke some years previously, which had left him partially paralyzed down his left side. Initially, the condition had gradually improved, and Harry had managed pretty well, but in recent years he had greatly deteriorated. And there were also question marks nowadays over his mental capacity. Indeed, if it weren't for his favourite grandson – and William was quite sure he was that, as he should be, he thought, considering all he did for the old man – Harry would almost certainly have found himself unable to remain alone in his own home and would be in some sort of residential care by now.

Aunt Amelia rang the doorbell persistently and called through the letterbox. All to no avail. But William had a key, of course. And Amelia knew it.

'Come on, time to use that key of yours,' she ordered.

William did as he was told, as usual, albeit reluctantly.

As they stepped into the hall, he heard his grandfather call down the stairs. His voice was loud enough but shaky.

'Who is it, who is it? Is that you, William? At this time of night. You never come this late. I'm not coming down. Is that you, William?'

'Yes, it's me, Grandpa,' William called back. 'But I didn't—'

'It's Amelia,' his great-aunt interrupted him, her voice as she called up the stairs so much stronger than her brother's. 'And you don't need to come down. I'm coming up.'

William could hear muttered dissent from above, but it was already too late. His great-aunt had attacked the staircase with confidence, and a perhaps unexpected turn of speed. She was already halfway up. With William following behind her. Not for the first time, he wondered exactly what his aunt's ebony cane was for.

As she reached the top, she turned towards him.

'William, what on earth do you think you're doing?' Amelia snapped. 'You know I hate you following me about. Go downstairs and wait for me there. I need to speak to your grandfather alone.'

As usual, William did not demur. He turned and obediently began to make his way downstairs. He paused halfway down and listened as she opened the door to his grandfather's bedroom and closed it behind her.

Maybe she would call after him, thank him for driving her, for looking after her, for agreeing to wait for her. But she didn't of course. She never did.

He adored his great-aunt. She was his heroine. She was everything William wasn't. He wanted to be like her. But he never could be. So all he could do was try to please her. Which he did, again and again. Yet he rarely seemed to succeed.

FOUR

Michael had appeared as if by magic at Delia's side just as she had begun to wonder how she was ever going to escape from the festival site without getting wet through and blown to bits. Unlike Amelia's great-nephew William, much more sensibly in view of the weather conditions, he wasn't carrying an umbrella. Instead, he handed Delia the hooded purple cape she had left in the car earlier, when she had chosen to brave a few seconds in the light drizzle that had been falling then in order to make an entrance in her glitzy silver suit.

'You'd better slip this on, Miss Day,' he instructed, helping her do so before escorting her to the car, which he had somehow managed to park closer to the entrance of the marquee than anyone else.

He settled Delia into the back seat and did whatever it was you did with electric cars to get them to move forward, proceeding to glide slowly and silently over what she suspected was becoming a thoroughly muddy field. Just as they reached the exit, Michael had to swerve to avoid two scurrying figures, presumably half blinded by the weather and the hoods of their anoraks, pulled down low over their faces. In spite of that, Delia knew at once who they were. They were each dragging a suitcase. One of them, finally becoming aware of the presence of Delia's vehicle, attempted to half throw herself out of danger, and would have fallen to the ground had she not been held more or less upright by the other.

The two sorry creatures failing so dismally in their battle with the elements were, of course, Tina and Tilly Tucker. And they really were in a mess. Totally against her better judgement, Delia decided that she should offer assistance.

'You'd better stop, Michael,' she said.

He did so.

Delia wound her window down.

'Tilly, Tina, what on earth are you doing?' she asked. 'Where are you trying to get to?'

'We're trying to get to our Airbnb. It's on the other side of Appledore, but . . .' said one of them.

'. . . there aren't any taxis, so we thought we'd just have to brave it and walk. There wasn't anything else we could do,' continued the other.

'. . . we tried to get an Uber, but that didn't work . . .'

'. . . it's the weather, you see . . .'

'It certainly is,' agreed Delia. 'And I suspect North Devon isn't big on Uber somehow. C'mon. You'd better get in. Is that all right, Michael?'

'Of course, Miss Day,' replied Michael promptly. Although possibly not with the greatest enthusiasm.

Delia didn't blame him. He was wearing a lightweight raincoat over his grey suit, but Delia didn't think it would give him much protection against the near hurricane sweeping along the coast. All the same, he climbed out of the car with apparent good grace, then loaded the twins' baggage into the boot and them into the car – one in the front and one in the back next to Delia.

Tilly and Tina appeared somewhat overwhelmed to be given a lift by the woman they had followed over most of the UK for so long. Delia just hoped she wasn't making a big mistake. The twins and their devoted attention had never previously given her a moment's concern, but everything seemed to be making her anxious that day.

The drive to the Airbnb, in one of the new builds on the outskirts of the village, only took three or four minutes. Which came as something of a relief to Delia, because the twins gabbled non-stop throughout the brief journey.

'This is just wonderful . . .' began one.

'. . . and so kind. We would never have presumed . . .' continued the other.

'. . . that you would bother with us . . .'

'. . . we are just nobody really, and we are so grateful . . .'

'. . . particularly with the weather being so awful . . .'

The only good thing about this monologue crossed with a duet was that Delia didn't have to even attempt to make conversation. Michael decanted the twins right outside their accommodation and even lifted their baggage out of the car boot for them. The rain had yet to appease and a gale was still blowing, and he looked more than a tad bedraggled when he climbed back into the car. But he didn't grumble.

'I'm really sorry about that,' said Delia. 'I didn't feel I had any choice. I couldn't just leave them there, annoying though they can be. You got another soaking too . . .'

'No problem, Miss Day,' Michael replied. 'Always pleased to help damsels in distress.'

Delia was beginning to think that, so far, this young man was undoubtedly the best thing that had happened to her in North Devon. She liked to have her drivers on her side. She decided to make small talk, asking him where he came from and how long he'd been doing this job.

'I'm a local boy,' he told her. 'And I've been doing this job for five years now, ever since I left the army.'

So he'd been a soldier. That made sense to Delia. Michael was of average height or thereabouts, but she'd noticed that he was a well-made young man. And he looked fit.

'More peaceful, I hope,' she remarked.

'Usually, ma'am,' he replied. 'But not always. I'm still getting over the time I was hired to drive half a stag party around back in the winter. I had the big people carrier I get on loan sometimes. Six of them in the back. Intent on getting as drunk as possible. Got worse as the night progressed. Three of them launched themselves into some sort of a punch-up in the back. I had to hose the whole motor out the next day. At least a couple of them had thrown up. Never again.'

Delia chuckled.

'I shall try to behave myself,' she said.

Michael turned briefly and flashed her a big smile over one shoulder.

'I don't mind a bit if you don't, Miss Day,' he said.

She didn't reply. He couldn't possibly be flirting with her, could he? Apart from any other consideration, she was certainly more than twenty years his senior. Her head was not turned, though. It came with the territory, after all. And she suspected that if she appeared at all receptive to Michael's mild flirtation, he would run for his life. She responded only with a small modest smile back. Or at least she hoped that was what it looked like.

Michael drove her swiftly and smoothly to the Imperial and rushed to open her car door for her.

'Is there anything else I can do for you, Miss Day?' he asked.

Delia wondered fleetingly if he might not run as swiftly as she had thought. In any case, she decided enough was enough. She certainly wasn't going to venture into the dangerous territory of double entendre. She would take her driver's remark entirely at face value.

'No, thank you, Michael,' she said, her voice level and without expression. 'I'll see you tomorrow. Not sure what time yet, so I'll call you in the morning.'

'Of course, Miss Day,' replied Michael smartly.

She was halfway to the hotel front door when she turned, just as he was about to get back into his car.

'Do you have a family to get back to, Michael,' she asked.

'Oh, yes, ma'am,' he replied. 'I have a wife and two little boys, the second one just three months old.'

Michael's face lit up with pride as he spoke. He was positively beaming.

Delia feared she had misunderstood the young man. She sent herself a warning. *In danger of behaving as if you are still attractive, dear*, she muttered under her breath as she hurried into the hotel.

But Michael did not go home to the little terraced house in Bideford's East-the-Water which his wife had made so comfortable. It was a pretty house too. He had been responsible, soon after they moved in, for painting its rendered walls white and the front door and window frames a carefully chosen pale blue. But his wife had done everything else. She looked after the two gardens, a tiny patch in the front and one just a little bit bigger at the back. Indeed, his wife looked after almost everything. And Michael could only marvel at how she found the time to do it all whilst looking after a baby and a toddler.

But that was Rosie for you. She was so capable. So cool. He adored her, and had done, it seemed, for most of his life.

They had been childhood sweethearts, parting only due to logistics when he joined the army. The Parachute Regiment. He would have married her then, but she was only seventeen and her parents wouldn't hear of it. Which the nineteen-year-old Michael had actually understood.

And once he began his military training and embarked on a soldier's life, he had decided that marriage was no longer for him. Certainly not for as long as he remained in the military.

He had fitted in well, which for all manner of reasons he had not expected. He'd always been a rather awkward boy. Or that's what he thought anyway. He'd had few friends and even fewer girlfriends. Only ever the one really. Rosie. But Michael had been an extremely physical, athletic lad, strong and muscular. And he possessed possibly the most valuable asset of all for a professional soldier. He rarely experienced physical fear. It wasn't that he was brave exactly. Just confident that he could overcome any level of physical threat.

Ultimately, Michael's soldierly skills reached a level where he was invited to apply for the SAS. He then had to complete what is generally regarded as the most arduous and rigorous selection processes in the British army over a period of several months. Only a very few, considered the cream, are ultimately selected every year. Michael was one of them. The day he became a Blade and was presented with his beige beret remained the proudest of his life. And his time with the SAS completely overwhelmed any prospect he might have had of sharing his life with anyone. He certainly completely dismissed any thoughts of marrying Rosie. Not with that job. It was, of course, highly dangerous and challenging. It involved very nearly leading a double life, certainly not revealing to anyone, except perhaps very closest family, what you did for a living, and travelling all over the world, sometimes for quite long periods of time, on top-secret assignments in the world's most hazardous trouble spots. But Michael loved it. He joined the SAS as a corporal, and as such there was no statutory limit on his term of service, whilst officers were limited to two tours of three years each, although most SAS men and women served only a few years at most. But Michael had intended to remain in the unit for the rest of his military service, if possible. It gave him everything he needed. Excitement, discipline and an extraordinary level of comradeship. Also, a perhaps unlikely tolerance of an individual's idiosyncrasies. Of men and women who were different. Michael was different and had always known that he was. In the SAS, nobody cared as long as you could do the job. And boy, could Michael do the job.

Then suddenly his world caved in. During a routine medical, it was revealed that he had a heart murmur. Further investigation showed that one of Michael's four heart valves was no longer working at its full potential. This had yet to cause any problems that he knew about but would need careful monitoring and, more than likely, surgery at some point in the future.

In the present, however, that was the end of the SAS for Michael. And indeed the end of active service of any kind.

In view of the respect with which he was held within his unit, and the service he had already given, he did not face discharge from the army. And he could return to his regiment. But only in a desk job.

He told himself that it was better than nothing. That he was still a military man. That he still had the comradeship and the lifestyle. But he was devastated. He could barely see the point in continuing. But he did, for a bit. As much out of habit as anything else.

Then, whilst at home on leave, he met Rosie again. She had married some years after Michael went out of her life, but disastrously. A cheating husband and – thankfully, under the circumstances, she always said – no children, even though she had wanted them desperately. She was by then divorced.

Michael quickly came to remember how much she had meant to him. Before the army, before all the other realizations about himself. He had always imagined a family life one day. A wife and children. And there was nobody he could imagine wanting to share that life with more than Rosie.

He supposed he loved her. No, he knew he loved her. He supposed that he had always loved her.

The SAS would always be at the core of his soul. He could never forget what he had seen and what he had done. And that was just one of the many facets of his character that he realized did not necessarily make him good husband material.

Nonetheless, he had suddenly wanted desperately to marry her, was determined to do his best and was overjoyed when she accepted his proposal. He promised her and himself that he would make her happy.

He quit the army at once. He was thirty-six and she was thirty-four. They didn't want to waste a moment.

The two children came in quick succession, even though they had both wondered whether that would happen, in view of Rosie's childless first marriage and her age.

Michael continued to try his absolute best to make Rosie happy, in every possible way, and he intended to devote himself to the happiness and well-being of his children for the rest of his life.

Nonetheless, instead of taking the town bridge over the Taw to take him back to East-the-Water, he turned the other way as he left the Imperial, heading for a Barnstaple town centre car park.

On the way, he called Rosie.

'I'm sorry, darling, I think it's going to be a late one,' he told her. 'I've just driven Miss Day out to a late dinner with friends in Ilfracombe. And I have to pick her up. Not worth me trying to come home in between. I'll be back as soon as I can. But don't wait up. Love you.'

Rosie took the news cheerily enough. Michael knew she had feared that she'd agreed to marry a long-serving soldier and had been unsure if he would keep his promise to quit the army. But he did. And under the circumstances, he knew that she found his intermittent late nights, when she believed him to be driving a taxi around North Devon, imminently preferable to the life of an army wife.

'I shall watch TV in bed,' she said. 'But I'd rather you were here.'

Michael made kissing noises down the phone and told Rosie how very much he would prefer to be there with her. It wasn't true, though. Not that night.

Michael had places to be and things to do. He couldn't go home.

It was nearly midnight by the time William got home, having dropped Aunt Amelia in Bideford after she and his grandfather had eventually finished talking.

Their voices had been raised. Their conversation had not been friendly. His great-aunt had sounded furious.

He had rather hoped she might choose to confide in him. But no. She had maintained a stony silence all the time she had been in his car. William had asked her if she was feeling all right.

'When I want you to know how I'm feeling, young man, I'll tell you,' Aunt Amelia had snapped. Which was unusually tetchy, even for her, William had thought.

And when he'd walked her to her front door after dropping her off, he'd seen by the light of the hall that her pale-blue eyes had turned to ice. Just as they always did if anything threatened her or her family. Or, sometimes, even if something just displeased her.

He so wished she'd confide in him. Let him help her. But there was little chance of that, was there? After all, she thought he was stupid, didn't she? William really wished he could change her mind.

Aunt Amelia always seemed so strong. She never looked as if she would be shocked or upset by anything, although he was quite aware that she had been. Aunt Amelia had known tragedy in her life. But she had come through it, of course.

Most people he knew, certainly of around his own age, had encountered Aunt Amelia as a schoolteacher. Including him and his brother. And she treated all of them in adulthood, again including him and his brother, almost the same as she had then. As if they were big, overgrown children.

But William knew how kind she could be too. When she wasn't in a fury, as she was that night. On a really bad day, Aunt Amelia treated almost everyone as if they were stupid.

But she had always looked after William. Indeed, it was Aunt Amelia who had stepped in when his parents had moved away from North Devon. He knew that his father had always wanted to leave. He was one of those for whom the sea and the beautiful countryside had never been quite enough. But when circumstances had required that he stay at home, where he was needed, he had done so. He'd turned down the chance to go to university, married a local girl and stayed close. Only when his boys were grown had William's father, Arthur, asked his wife if she'd like to move somewhere else. Indeed, to make a new home overseas. Mavis had agreed with alacrity. The tragedy that haunted the family she had married into had come to haunt her too, and she'd had quite enough of it. Their two sons had been in their early twenties by then; they could make their own choices, and stand on their own two feet.

And so Arthur and Mavis had emigrated to New Zealand.

It had been fine for William's brother, of course, just a year older, but already out there in the world building his own life. William was a very different sort of chap. He had no idea how to stand on his own feet. He'd always lived with his mum and dad, and had more or less assumed that he always would. Which was an example of him being stupid, he supposed. They had said he could go with them to New Zealand if he liked, although, in his blackest moments, William had allowed himself to believe that part of the reason for their departure was to leave their bothersome second son behind. A part of him still believed that, too.

In any case, he couldn't imagine living anywhere except North Devon. It was home. He had a job he loved, certain aspects of which he found fascinating. So much so that he had turned them into a kind of hobby. And a boss who seemed to be one of the few people in the world who rated him and treated him as if he had at least some worth.

And so he had transferred all his affections to his grandfather and Aunt Amelia. They were his substitute parents. Aunt Amelia did treat him a bit like a servant and could be hard on him, but he knew she would always look out for him. And William liked that. He liked that a lot.

His grandfather had looked out for him, too, and had given him a home when William's parents first took off to New Zealand. Grandpa Harry had nurtured and supported William. Eventually, he had found for him the isolated and somewhat dilapidated cottage out towards Buckland Brewer, which was still his home, rented for a pittance from a farmer who was just glad to have someone living there to stop it from totally disintegrating. William had always wanted to live in the country, without people all around him, and to be independent. Which was paradoxical considering his distress at being forced to part company with his parents. But he couldn't have imagined he'd ever have the strength to do it. However, Grandpa Harry had encouraged William and helped him settle into some sort of life of his own. In the early days, he even stayed with William overnight to make sure he was all right.

And it had all turned out well in the end. William was quite happy with his life.

After Harry suffered his stroke, William had felt it was his turn to look after Grandpa. He was also on standby to look after Aunt Amelia, should she ever need it. And perhaps she needed it now. Although she would never ask.

FIVE

Tina and Tilly Tucker had rented a studio on the first floor of the small apartment block.

It was comfortable enough, with a large double bed which folded up against one wall. The twins didn't mind sharing a bed. They always did at home, though they rarely discussed this in public.

There were quite a lot of things they did not discuss in public. Because in many ways Tina and Tilly were not quite what they seemed. Somewhat to their surprise, they had inherited a house, near the coast in Sussex, and quite a lot of money from a childless distant cousin. They weren't rich, exactly, but they had enough invested so that they didn't need to work and could indulge in their favourite interests in life. Actually, 'interest', in the singular – which was following Delia Day around the country. They never stayed in hotels. It wasn't the cost. They could have afforded hotels of a moderate standard, at least some of the time. But they liked to be independent. Hotels involved walking past reception, talking to staff and being found out if you broke even the most inconsequential of rules. Like no smoking. Of any kind.

They took off their pink floral anoraks and hung them over the shower to drip dry. The rain had run down their necks inside the anoraks. Their pink floral blouses were also wet. So they removed those too. Then they dressed in their pyjamas – which were, of course, pink, fluffy and very comforting at the end of such a horrid day. After all, they had no intention of going anywhere now until morning. They had everything they needed in their two big suitcases, which had seemed, even by Delia's standards, to be quite oversized for a stay of only a week or so at most. They then continued to unpack.

Out came their wardrobe for the duration, everything in matching sets of two, including two spare pairs of trainers each, one pink, of course, like the now sodden ones they had worn that day. The other black, silver and purple, as a tribute to Delia. They were the same designer brand that Delia wore. And slippers, pink and fluffy like their pyjamas, only fluffier, which they donned at once. Tina and Tilly liked to be comfortable. And they were greatly looking forward to the rest of their evening.

As well as clothes and footwear, one case also included two large bottles of Famous Grouse whisky, wrapped in a matching pair of pink sweaters for protection, and two big plastic bottles of Coca-Cola original, all of which they carefully removed and set out on the low table in front of the sofa. The twins didn't see the point of worrying about the sugar content of their mixers. They were in any case as thin as meat skewers. Not that they ever ate meat, of course. Tina poured the whisky, a hefty measure, into two half-pint tumblers. Tilly poured the Coke, just the amount they liked to make what they considered to be a perfectly balanced drink. It was their habit to do things together.

They each took a long, much-appreciated swallow, before turning their attention again to the second case, from which they removed two packs of Marlboro Red, a packet of Rizlas and a decent-sized chunk of Colombian Black.

They felt the same way about the Marlboro Red ciggies as they did the classic Coca-Cola. And the Famous Grouse and the Colombian Black, come to that. If you were going to smoke tobacco, add a sprinkling of dope and drink whisky and Coke, you may as well do the whole thing properly.

'Your turn to roll the joint,' said Tina.

'Your turn to get out the munchies,' said Tilly.

They set to work at once. Tina removed a food parcel from the second suitcase. It contained several bread rolls, some rather good vegan cheese, a small jar of Branston Pickle, and two large bars of excellent dark chocolate. Also vegan. She turned the first three ingredients into very acceptable butties, which she piled on a tray along with the chocolate.

'Dinner,' she said.

'Aperitif,' said Tilly, lighting the long, fat and extremely well-rolled joint that she had just finished making.

'Such a lovely way to work up an appetite,' said Tina.

A couple of hours or so later, well stoned and fully replete, the twins, lying in bed, propped themselves up on their pillows and poured yet another whisky and Coke.

'So, whaddya think, Tilly?' asked Tina, her diction not at all clear.

'Whadda I think about what?' responded Tilly, similarly slurred of speech.

'You know, should we tell her, d'ya think?'

'I can't think right now.'

'Well, I reckon she should know what we know.'

'I expect she does already . . .'

'That'sh not what I mean . . .'

'Well, what do you mean?'

'You know what I mean . . .'

'For goodness' sake. Let'sh talk about it in the morning.'

In their room at the Seagate, George and Felicity Smythe were having a surprisingly similar conversation.

They'd had quite a jolly time in the bar, meeting old friends and acquaintances. The Smythes were known to be both friendly and engaging, so they were rarely short of company on such occasions.

Like most people with these qualities, they looked forward to social gatherings and invariably excelled themselves, both in entertaining others and in themselves being such a receptive audience.

They had stayed up late, going to bed well after midnight, and both had had rather a lot to drink. Considerably more than usual.

Felicity invited her husband to use the bathroom first, whilst she sat on one of the two Victorian nursing chairs by the window looking out across the river to Instow. The storm had finally blown over. It was high tide on a clear moonlit night. The reflection both of the lights of Instow and the very nearly full moon shimmered on the water. The Smythes had a prime room at the front of the little hotel, overlooking the quay and the river beyond. They had set their latest detective series in North Devon, and Appledore was probably Felicity's favourite festival of all. But she did not feel her usual contentment at being there. Not this year. Not at all. Indeed, she felt distinctly uneasy. Felicity considered herself to be a decent sort, and by nature honest and straightforward. She did not like duplicity of any kind. She sighed and lowered her head into her hands, just as George emerged from the bathroom.

'Are you all right?' he asked.

'No I'm not,' Felicity replied, sitting up straight again and turning around to face her husband.

He walked across the room and laid a long bony hand on her shoulder.

'What's wrong, dear?' he asked solicitously.

'As if you don't know,' she snapped, jerking her shoulder away from his touch.

'Look, it's not our problem . . .' he began.

'How can you say that?' she replied, snapping at him again. 'She is our friend. We aren't behaving like friends.'

'Well, what can we do?'

'We can tell her. We must tell her.'

'Don't you think she knows already?'

'That's not the point.'

'I know. But I don't think we should get involved.'

'We are involved.'

'Are we? Look. We've both been drinking. Let's talk about it in the morning.'

'That's what you always say.'

'Well, not necessarily.'

'You know exactly what I mean.'

SIX

Delia could not wait to get to the peace and comfort of her mini-suite. Nonetheless, she did do her best to run up the stairs to the second-floor accommodation, ignoring the lift, as was her habit. It wasn't just that she wanted to leave that vaguely embarrassing moment with Michael behind her as quickly as possible. This was, after all, just about the only exercise she got. As soon as she entered the room, she sank gratefully on to the big double bed, closed her eyes for just a few minutes and tried to clear her head after what had been such a tiring, muddling and quite disturbing day.

She hadn't eaten anything worth mentioning at the reception – she never did – so after a few minutes, she ordered some soup and sandwiches on room service. Then she tuned in to a Poirot repeat on TV. She'd seen it before, of course, but that never seemed to matter.

She turned in well before midnight. She didn't set an alarm as she was free of any obligation the following day until her next event in the late afternoon.

She slept soundly and did not wake until the arrival of the waiter bringing her breakfast at nine a.m. Rising hurriedly then, she threw a wrap around her shoulders over her pyjamas and hurried across the room to let him in. As she did so, she noticed an envelope on the floor just inside the door, which she automatically assumed had been pushed beneath it. She bent to pick it up. There was no name written on the front. Probably some sort of hotel round-robin delivered to all the guests, she thought.

She followed the waiter to the sitting area, where he had already set the tray down on the table by the window over-looking the River Taw. It was as if she'd landed in a different world from the one she had endured the previous evening. A truly glorious day had dawned. There wasn't a cloud in the bright blue sky. The morning sun glinted on the elegant tray setting, silver coffee pot and cutlery, white china, napkin and tray cloth, and the lavish Imperial breakfast she had ordered – juice, cereal, fruit, an omelette, hash browns on the side, and a range of pastries.

Delia loved hotel breakfasts delivered to her room, and it seemed the Imperial offerings were particularly fine. She put the envelope down on the table and tucked in. Then she sat drinking coffee and simply enjoying the open outlook and the sunshine. Her anxieties of the previous day seemed a long way off. Only when she had finished the coffee did she idly pick up the envelope, more out of habit than anything else, and slit it open.

Inside was a single sheet of A4 paper which she pulled out and unfolded. It bore two lines of large print, six words of centred upper-case Times Roman, in bold – 72-point or there-abouts. Delia's writing career had been spawned in the days of print and paper. She was inclined to recognize and study fonts before she absorbed content. So the shock she was about to experience when she ultimately grasped the meaning of the short message that had been sent to her was slightly delayed. Automatically, she read it twice to make sure she hadn't misunderstood it. But she could not have misunderstood it, of course.

It was short, sharp and to the point:

I KNOW
WHAT YOU HAVE DONE

Delia dropped the piece of paper on to her lap, shaking it from her fingers, almost as if it had burned her hand. It landed with the printed words facing upwards. She glanced down and read it yet again. Not that she needed to.

Perhaps she had been right, then, to feel so uneasy the previous day. Indeed, it seemed that the sense of disquiet she had experienced ever since her arrival in North Devon could have been well founded.

She began at once to speculate on who might have written the note. She couldn't help herself. She'd met quite a lot of people the previous day. But who on earth among them might have felt moved to write such a thing? Or had any reason, real or imagined, to do so? Was there perhaps someone out there who thought they knew things about her she maybe didn't even know herself? Was that a possibility? Or was it nonsense, and yet another instance of her letting her imagination run away with her? In any case, what did any of this matter?

She was the biggest-selling living novelist in the country, if not the world. Hers was indeed a story of triumph over adversity and a rise from depths far lower than she had ever fully admitted in public. She had recently been wondering whether or not the time had come to tell her own story. Her autobiography was surely a book she should write one day. But she never seemed to quite get around to it. After all, why should she unnecessarily rock her rather splendid boat? She did not need to reveal to the world anything more about herself than she already had. Her readers wanted her to tell them stories. To entertain them. To allow them to become immersed in the fantasies she created. They did not require her to bare her soul to them. And so far, she had never done so.

Nonetheless, she still wanted to know who had written that note and pushed it under her door. The most likely candidate was probably James Harding. It would not be the first time he had threatened her. It would, however, she had to admit, be the first time he had done so anonymously. In fact, it always seemed as if he enjoyed the process of facing up to her, of looking her straight in the eye – or very nearly, because he definitely had a bit of a squint – as he unleashed his latest vitriolic rant. So maybe it wasn't him.

But who else could it possibly be? In her head, she went through all the people she had met the previous day. Those she already knew as well as those she had encountered for the first time. She could not imagine why any of them would be moved to do such a thing. Certainly not the Smythes or the Tucker twins. The festival director? The mayor? The mayoress? Amelia whatever her name was? Delia had found that woman particularly disconcerting, but at her great age, and in need of a walking stick, it was hard to believe that Amelia whatshername could even make it to Barnstaple and the second floor of the Imperial Hotel, quite probably in the middle of the night. Lift or no lift. Unless, of course, she had hired, or merely persuaded, somebody to deliver the note for her.

Delia gave herself another sharp mental shaking. That imagination again. She really should ensure it remained focused on the lucrative fiction she produced so prolifically and keep it well away from real life.

She screwed the piece of paper up into a ball and tossed it into a bin. This, of course, was not the first disturbing anonymous message she had ever received. Indeed, like all well-known writers, and almost anybody in the public eye nowadays, she had suffered her share of unpleasantness from anonymous sources all over the internet. As a romantic novelist who knew she was a damned good storyteller but hadn't the tiniest pretension of being literary, she attracted more than her fair share, she often felt, of some quite vicious reviews of her work; she accepted this as par for the course, and for decades now had been laughing all the way to the bank, but she still resented the ones that were anonymous, as so many were, on various alleged reader websites and, of course, Amazon. On Twitter and Facebook, there were usually names attached but it still seemed that, unlike in the mainstream written press, people got to write what the hell they liked without fear of retribution, in some instances contriving to successfully conceal their true identity.

She reminded herself that she had always regarded people who hid behind anonymity, and used only forms of communication that allowed them to do so, as cowards. Pure and simple. She had never previously let their pathetic outpourings affect her, and she wasn't going to start now. She had put that note where it belonged, in the bin with the rest of the small amount of rubbish she had also disposed of during her brief stay. Now she would move on from it and forward with her life.

She glanced at her phone. Her breakfast had been leisurely. Yet it was still not quite ten a.m. She would work on her book now, but she would hope to finish her two thousand words by one o'clock or even before, so she would still have most of the afternoon to kill before that five p.m. event – the all-female panel on misogyny in publishing. The third event she was committed to, the one she was least looking forward to, her interview session with the dreaded James Harding, was not until the following day.

She thought she might have a wander around Barnstaple first, maybe risk finding a quiet corner in a café or a pleasant pub where she might be able to enjoy a little light lunch unrecognized and unbothered. Although she knew that was unlikely, unless she took the time and trouble to disguise herself, something she did very occasionally, which in this instance really didn't seem worth it.

It was all her own fault for so resolutely maintaining such a distinctive image, of course. Still, she could give it a go as full-blown Delia. Sometimes people seemed to be too taken aback to approach her. Then she might perhaps call Michael to take her to Bideford. She had so far only looked down at the little riverside town from the heights of the towering Torridge Bridge, en route to Appledore the previous day, but, in spite of the rain, she had thought how attractive the little waterside market town seemed to be. After that, she supposed she should make the effort to visit the Seagate, the heart of the festival. She should really mix a little with the other contributors and perhaps meet more fans, although she wasn't in the mood. But then she rarely was in the mood. She vowed, not for the first time, that this really would be the last festival she would ever attend. Anywhere!

When she had finished her writing, she showered, applied her makeup and styled her hair with her inevitable meticulous care, and pondered what she would wear. Eventually, she chose tight black jeans – her legs were still good – ankle boots and, again, her black leather jacket over a silver shirt, this time with broad purple stripes. A chunky purple, silver and black glass bracelet, made specially for her by Andrew Logan, the celebrated artist jeweller, adorned her right wrist, and she slid the matching ring on to the second finger of the same hand. She wore no other jewellery. You didn't need anything more if you had a couple of lumps of Logan to wave about.

Once she looked right – and whilst never having been a pretty girl or a beautiful woman, she knew she had always been rather good at putting herself together – she usually felt right. It was chicken and egg for Delia Day.

She glanced at herself in a mirror one last time as she headed for the door. Job done. And she would put all those other nonsensical thoughts of the previous day, which that silly note had brought right to the surface again, firmly out of her mind and just get on with it. As she always did.

She opened the door to her room with a flourish and took a step into the corridor. Then she hesitated. It was no good. However hard she tried, she couldn't completely ignore the events and feelings of the last twenty-four hours. She took a step back in. And although it remained against her better judgement, she plucked that nasty little note from the bin, smoothed it out, folded it and popped it into her shoulder bag.

She would keep it with her just in case and perhaps make a casual enquiry or two, she told herself. Starting at the Imperial itself. As she dropped her key off at reception, she took the opportunity to have a word with one of the young women on duty there, quickly taking note of the name on the badge pinned to her jacket lapel. People liked to be addressed by name. Delia was good at that sort of thing. If only because ultimately it was inclined to make her life easier.

'Good morning, Jenny,' Delia began. 'I wondered if you might be able to help me with something.'

'Good morning, Miss Day,' responded Jenny with a big smile. 'I will certainly try.'

'Well, do you by any chance know if anyone from the hotel popped an envelope under my door sometime during the night or early this morning?' Delia continued as casually as she could manage.

'I don't think so, Miss Day; we haven't had any mail for you,' replied Jenny.

'And nobody stopped by and asked for something to be delivered to me?'

'No, not as far as I know.'

'Can you be sure?'

Jenny looked as if she was concentrating.

'Well, I've been on duty since six a.m., and certainly nobody has come to reception with anything for you since then,' said Jenny. 'I do hope nothing is wrong, Miss Day? We would never give your room number out, but I'm sure you know that, don't you?'

'Yes, of course, and no, nothing is wrong – just a little misunderstanding, I think. That's all.'

'You could check with the concierge if you like. Ian has also been on duty all morning.'

Jenny gestured towards a tall, good-looking man in a dark suit standing at the far side of the lobby, apparently giving directions to an elderly couple who were on their way out.

'I'll do that,' said Delia. 'Many thanks.'

As she turned, she could feel the receptionist staring after her. Or was it just that ever since she had arrived in North Devon, she had for some reason felt that everyone was staring at her?

Then Jenny spoke again.

'I just wanted to tell you, Miss Day, I really enjoyed your speech last night,' she said.

Delia turned back to face her.

'Oh, thank you. You were there, then?'

'I never miss the festival, go to all the events I can, and I usually get invited to the meet-and-greet. I went to school with Carolyne Smedley, and my uncle and aunty are the current mayor and mayoress.'

'Goodness, is everybody around here interconnected?'

'No, but it sometimes feels like it,' said Jenny, again with that big smile.

'So I will be seeing you again at the festival, will I?'

'Oh, yes, I have tickets for all your events.'

'I'm flattered,' said Delia.

'Thank you for taking the time to talk to me,' said Jenny.
'My very great pleasure,' said Delia, lying through her teeth
as usual. She didn't mind, though. A reader is a reader is a
reader, and Jenny must clearly be one.

As if on cue, concierge Ian approached the desk.

'Miss Day would like to ask you something,' said Jenny.

Delia did so. Had Ian delivered anything to her room?

'No, should I have done?' responded the tall young man,
just a tad uncertainly.

'No, no, I'm just trying to solve a little mystery, that's all,'
said Delia. 'Have you by any chance seen any strangers come
into the hotel and go upstairs?'

As she spoke, she knew she'd said something pretty silly,
although Ian gave no impression that he'd thought that too.

'This is a hotel, Miss Day,' he responded pleasantly. 'It's
unlikely that I would recognize everyone who was staying
here at any given time, particularly when we are busy, as we
are at the moment. It's pretty much high season, after all.
We do try not to let any non-residents go upstairs without one
of us on duty in the lobby being aware of them and finding
out what their business is, but it wouldn't be impossible for
an unknown visitor to slip in and go straight to a room without
our knowledge. Not impossible at all.'

'No, I don't suppose it would be,' murmured Delia.

She thanked both members of staff and left the hotel.
Involuntarily, she found her hand slipping into her bag. Her
fingers closed around the folded sheet of paper, which had
already caused her more concern than she felt it should have
done.

She seemed to have left herself with little choice as to what
to do next. She decided she would head for the Seagate, and
then the festival site, much earlier than she had intended. In
spite of her original intention of ignoring the unsettling note,
it had become quite clear that she was not going to be able to
do so. She needed to know who had sent her the note and why.
She couldn't help herself. Maybe there had been somebody at
the opening ceremony and the meet-and-greet who knew who
she was and had wanted to frighten her. She paused. What a silly
train of thought that was. She was Delia Day. It was virtually

certain that everybody at the opening had known who she was. That was why she had been invited to attend the festival – indeed, virtually stalked so that her presence could be achieved. And she'd got up on her hind legs and made a speech.

Delia turned the whole thing around in her head. Maybe the note itself was a red herring, designed merely to unsettle her. Perhaps in reality the person who had sent her the note was afraid that she had recognized them. There had been that odd familiarity about Amelia Bowden after all. But nothing about that made any sense. The note could have been sent merely to confuse her. And it had succeeded.

Any plans, however vague, to walk around either Barnstaple or Bideford now lay in shreds. Instead, Delia called Michael and asked him to pick her up straight away and drive her to Appledore.

SEVEN

A melia Bowden had risen early to try to make sense of the information she had gathered the night before. She doubted that her brother would have told her what he had, even then, if he were not a sick man.

She had bullied him mercilessly, mostly mentally, but at one point she had slapped him good and hard across the face. She wasn't proud of herself, but it had to be done. He had cowered in his bed, whilst she did her best to frighten the truth out of him, until he had given in and revealed the secret he'd kept for over fifty years. A secret known to nobody else alive. Except, now, Amelia.

She had been shocked to the core. He was a broken old man. A quivering wreck, as he lay before her in his bed. But Amelia had no sympathy for him.

Her last words to him as she'd left his bedroom had been absolute.

'You are no longer my brother,' she told him. And she meant it.

But now she had to decide what to do about Harry's revelation.

She had to be sure. She must have no doubts. She didn't want to ruin anybody's life for no reason. Nor did she want to look a fool. When you were into your mid-eighties, people were inclined to just assume you were a fool. Amelia Bowden was anything but. She remained a highly intelligent and highly rational woman, and she wasn't given to rash behaviour.

She had witnessed the unexpected last night, seen something that had brought long-buried memories shooting to the surface. However, Amelia was aware that very little in anyone's life is unique. You think it is. But it isn't. So she had learned nothing, here, today, in the present, that was conclusive. Not from Harry. And not at the festival earlier.

She needed to find out more. To dig deeper. She had friends who would help if she asked them. She had friends in all sorts of useful fields, including the police and the media.

But first, like most people nowadays, she turned to the internet. Amelia had a laptop and an iPhone. She wasn't the best at surfing the net, but she had typically determined not to be left behind in the modern world. She had attended classes and picked the brains of younger relatives and friends. She was certainly no mug online.

She failed, however, to find the information she sought. On social media, on various appropriate websites and on media outlets, every path led to a dead end. To a brick wall blocking the way. Until she had that information, there was nothing she could do. Or nothing she was prepared to do, anyway.

So she gave in to the reality – which was that she needed help from someone more adept than her. And someone with a wider range of life experience. She would call her great-nephew. Not William, of course; he'd be no use to her. The other one. He also might have unique access to what she was seeking. She didn't think she would confide totally in him; in fact, if she could get away with it, she would barely confide at all at this stage. She would tell him just enough to get him on board. And then see if he could help her solve the mystery she had suddenly been confronted with.

Delia made it to the Seagate around two thirty, just in time for a late lunch. Only crab sandwiches, but she couldn't believe she was able to eat anything after her huge breakfast. There was more than an element of comfort eating about it, she thought. Almost everyone she encountered was terribly nice to her. All the same, she could not stop herself from studying them carefully and sizing up the likelihood of any of them having sent her that disturbing note.

She met the mayor again, surprisingly briefly, and had a longer conversation with his wife the mayoress. The Robertses, she had now learned, of course, were receptionist Jenny's aunt and uncle, so Delia mentioned to the mayor that she had met Jenny, and how charming the young woman was. He did not seem at all interested.

Jill Roberts was a reader, which helped, because at least Delia could talk about her books.

Jeremy Roberts was not chatty. Delia had already ascertained that he most certainly was not a reader and had little interest in her. But this time he gave the impression that he really could not wait to get away from her, saying only, and most unconvincingly, how lovely it was to see her again, whilst backing off at speed and heading towards the far end of the bar.

Delia watched his swift retreat with interest. He was behaving awkwardly today. Not at all as he had the previous evening. Was he embarrassed by something? Or even afraid of something? Could it be remotely possible that the mayor was responsible for the note she had received? Surely not! She gave herself yet another telling-off. What possible motive could the mayor of Bideford have for sending her a poison pen letter?

Carolyne Smedley arrived at the pub soon after Delia and sought her out at the first opportunity.

'I was just going to call you,' she began. 'We've had a bit of a disaster, I'm afraid. Jennifer Sedgemoor tested positive for Covid this morning.'

'Ah,' said Delia.

Jennifer Sedgemoor was the respected Random House editor due to take part in the misogyny panel that afternoon. Delia didn't know her personally but was aware of her excellent reputation. The Smythes were also due to sit on the panel, along with literary historian Gerald Kauffman, who had written the book tracking the history of women writers from the days when the prejudice against them was so absolute that the only way they could get published was to adopt a male persona, which had prompted Appledore to schedule such a panel. Both panel and book were called *Women: The Right to Write.*

'I was only told a couple of hours ago that she had to drop out, and ever since I've been desperately trying to find a replacement,' Carolyne continued somewhat breathlessly. 'Without a publishing representative, the panel would be completely unbalanced. Don't you agree?'

Delia nodded in cautious agreement. Warning bells were starting to peel inside her head, although she didn't quite know why. Yet.

Carolyne was still speaking.

'Anyway, we've been just so lucky. Ridiculously short notice I know. But I've managed to find a replacement!'

She paused triumphantly, almost as if waiting for applause.

Delia obliged. Eventually.

'Oh, well done,' she murmured.

'Yes, I know,' Carolyne gabbled on. 'It's a miracle. I managed to get hold of Penelope Peabody-Jones. She lives on Exmoor now, with her sister. Only about an hour's drive away. I don't know if your paths have ever crossed, Delia? She's a very experienced editor who's moved around quite a lot in publishing; says she's more or less retired now, but she's wanted to be involved with our festival ever since she relocated down this way.'

Penelope Peabody-Jones certainly had moved around in publishing, thought Delia, stifling a desire to groan out loud. Of course she says she's retired; nobody would employ the cow anymore. Doubtless, she had been desperate to get involved with Appledore or anything else that might allow her to get her foot in the publishing door again. Delia just couldn't believe it. Not Peabody-Jones. Of all the panels in all the world, that creature had to walk into Delia's.

If Delia had known in advance that Peabody-Jones was

going to be on the panel she would never have agreed to do it. But now the dreadful woman had been slotted in at the last moment by the festival director, who was convinced she had saved the day, Delia was presented with a dilemma. She could still say no, but then a situation would be created. The director would be upset. The other panellists would be upset. The panel would then have to go ahead without Delia, or more likely without Penelope, or possibly even be cancelled. The latter was the most unlikely, because the audience which had pre-booked would have to be refunded. And, however brief, and hopefully tactful, Delia might be in explaining why she wanted to withdraw, the noise from the beating jungle drums would be deafening. Under the circumstances, Delia decided she had little choice but to accept this most unwelcome of replacements and not make a fuss.

She was vaguely aware that Carolyne was still rabbiting on. The director was so sure of herself and her achievement in finding a last-minute replacement that she hadn't even asked Delia, who, after all, was surely supposed to be the star of the show, if she was happy with the unexpected substitution. Delia decided she would not comment on that either.

'So Penelope is on her way already. She should be with us very soon. Have you ever met her, Delia?'

Had she met her? Would that she never had, thought Delia.

'Yes, I've met her,' she remarked levelly.

Many years previously, when her usual editor had been on maternity leave, Penelope had been the temporary replacement provided by her publishers. Penelope had only recently joined Coldharbour but had come highly recommended by her previous employers. In order to get rid of her, Delia had swiftly concluded. It didn't take her long to realize that the woman was very nearly incompetent, and she could not possibly work with her. Delia delivered a new book and had the manuscript returned to her by Penelope full of unacceptable amendments, particularly in relation to punctuation, most notably commas introduced both copiously and inappropriately. Delia was quite puzzled for a while before suddenly realizing what must have happened. Clearly, Penelope had put a grammar check on the book and accepted all suggestions carte blanche. It was a writer's nightmare. All Delia could do was insist that the edit be completely discarded. And Delia had requested – most discreetly, because she'd always had a first-class relationship with her publishers and had aimed to keep it so – that Penelope be moved on. Which she was. To a less high-profile role within the company, which she was fortunate to have been offered, in Delia's opinion.

However, Peabody-Jones was as slippery as a bobsleigh run. And proved to be almost as dangerous. She was arrogant, with a far too high opinion of herself, and it became apparent that if she was crossed, or imagined that she was, or slighted in any way, she could be quite malicious. Her demotion, which she no doubt regarded as totally unjustified, was soon followed by a virulent campaign against Delia, primarily on social media, but also by word of mouth. For a time, Delia would turn up at events and be aware of conversation stopping when she walked into a room and of people muttering in whispers around her. Amongst other scurrilous allegations, it became bandied about that Delia was a cheat and a bully, that she had bribed the judges of a prestigious fiction award that she'd won and ensured that anyone at her publishers who offended her in any way would be sacked.

It was all a long time ago, more than ten years. And Delia could never be one hundred per cent certain that Penelope was responsible for what had been a highly organized and quite vicious campaign against her. She knew, though. In her heart, she knew. And so did her agent and her publishers.

One result of this was that Peabody-Jones was promptly sacked by Coldharbour on some spurious excuse, because neither Delia nor her agent nor Coldharbour wanted to add flame to the coals of Penelope's fire. Plus there remained the little matter of being unable to prove, certainly to the satisfaction of any court of law, that Penelope was responsible – although all concerned were convinced that she was.

Delia had little doubt that Penelope would not have believed the spurious excuse for her sacking for one moment. She would have known exactly why she had been shown the door.

All of which did not bode well for their event together that afternoon. Delia just wanted to get through it as smoothly as possible, without incident. To keep out of trouble. She decided that her best plan was to avoid engaging directly with Penelope. And as there were five panellists, two of them people she regarded as friends, she told herself that this really should not be too difficult.

William decided he would pay Aunt Amelia a visit. He was worried about her. He really wanted to help her, and he wanted her to know that.

She might talk to him properly then, confide in him what she and his grandfather had been talking about the previous night. Maybe she would even stop treating him as if he was a complete idiot. It was true that William hadn't been good at school, and he always felt that his schoolteacher great-aunt based her opinion of him entirely on that. But in William's opinion, that was unfair.

It was mid-afternoon when he approached Amelia Bowden's home. He'd been working all morning, even though it was a Saturday. William never minded working at weekends. He got paid very generous overtime for a start. He was driving his little Italian sports job again, a classic Alfa Romeo, in the vain hope that Amelia might one day realize what a good car it was and be impressed that William was doing well enough to be able to afford a car like that.

She never seemed to think that way, though. And neither did that girl who worked behind the bar at the Seagate whom William had once offered a lift. When he'd pulled up alongside her in his newly washed and polished Alfa, she'd looked at him in horror and fled. William had rarely had much success with girls. Not the ones he took a shine to, anyway.

He didn't mind too much. He didn't really want a girlfriend telling him what to do.

He was about to park, as close to Amelia's house as he could get, when he noticed the vehicle parked just across the road. It was his brother's car.

William drove past. There was no way he was going to visit his great-aunt if his brother was already there. William was under no illusion as to which of the brothers was his aunt's favourite.

He would be her favourite one day, though, he told himself as he turned the Alfa towards home. One day, she would realize his worth.

Delia gave Carolyne Smedley a lift back to the festival site, so that Carolyne didn't have to move her car from a coveted spot in the Seagate car park.

When Michael dropped them off, there was already a queue of people, mostly women, at the entrance to the main marquee where the *Right to Write* panel was to be staged. This was only what Delia had grown to expect when making a public appearance.

Carolyne escorted her around the perimeter of the marquee, avoiding the queues, to the backstage area which had its own entrance.

The Smythes were already there, preparing to give their take as a husband-and-wife team on the misogyny issue. They were modern crime writers, a genre which surely boasted almost as many women writers as romance, and they had chosen to assume as the amalgamated author name for their co-produced books an undoubtedly female compilation in Felicity George. Delia would expect a valid and entertaining contribution from them.

Penelope Peabody-Jones was also already there. She was in the process of having her microphone fitted by the soundman. She inclined her head slightly as Delia entered but did not speak. Delia did the same. After all, her only desire was for there to be an absence of all but the most unavoidable interaction between them. She quickly appraised the appearance of the other woman before looking away. Peabody-Jones had not changed a lot. Her double chin remained. She still carried far too much weight. Her hair was the same reddish blonde colour, but frizzier than it used to be and not in good condition at all. But then, Delia suspected, Penelope would no longer be able to afford anything like the standard of colourist she employed!

She knew she was being bitchy. But who could blame her? Peabody-Jones was a bigger bitch than Delia could ever be. She was also an all-round phoney. She tried to give the impression of being far grander than she actually was. Delia was sure of it. She would guess that even the double-barrelled name was not genuine. Of course, Penelope was probably far from alone in that. Double barrels were par for the course in publishing, particularly among the women. And Delia suspected that many of those who didn't have them when they embarked on a publishing career frequently acquired them.

She could feel Penelope's murky brown eyes on her back and risked another quick glance at the creature. Penelope had an extremely large nose and, as ever, gave the impression that she was looking down it at Delia. Indeed, she invariably looked as if she was looking down her nose at almost anyone. Delia shouldn't take it personally. After all, how on earth could a failed editor look down her nose at the country's best-selling living novelist? Possibly the world's! With ease, Delia suspected. This was Penelope Peabody-Jones. And she was delusional to a degree Delia had never otherwise experienced.

Gerald Kauffman was the final panellist to arrive, just in time for the off, allowing no time for small talk before the five of them were ushered on to the stage.

Delia had met Gerald Kauffman before this festival. He was a dry old stick, and his work, whilst ineffably worthy, was even drier. His delivery on the panel proved also to be dry. Which was no surprise to Delia. It was bordering on plain old-fashioned boring. The Smythes were at the other extreme, invariably as far away from boring as it was possible to be, even bringing an air of jollity to their few serious points, taking the lightest possible attitude throughout, always trying to be funny and usually succeeding. They were inclined to laugh a little too loudly at each other's jokes – every bit as much on the panel as they did off. Delia suspected they were invited to book events not so much for the content of what they could contribute as for their entertainment value, on and off stage. The organizers liked them and enjoyed their company. As Delia did. In spite of the bad jokes.

The panel began well enough and proceeded without incident until almost halfway through its allotted hour, with Delia being careful not to respond directly to Penelope about anything, and to keep her contributions, whilst hopefully not as dull or as boring as Gerald Kauffman's, both unprovocative and uncontroversial. Then, unheralded, and in Delia's opinion quite unwarranted, her best intentions were destroyed with one sudden unexpected lash of Penelope Peabody-Jones's venomous tongue.

It started as a relatively innocuous exchange between all the panellists concerning what women writers could do to prevent being ghettoized. Kauffman remarked that although, at first sight, it would seem that women writers were treated on an equal basis in the modern publishing world, this was not always quite as it seemed, a theme he had explored at length in his book.

Delia had agreed.

'But as a romantic novelist, I have never suffered in this way,' she continued. 'It could be argued, though, that I am writing in a genre in which authors are expected to be women, by and large, writing almost exclusively for women. So in a way, I am automatically ghettoized. Of course, I don't really see it like that. I've made my own choices, and I consider myself to have been extremely lucky—'

'You certainly have been,' interrupted Penelope Peabody-Jones forcibly. 'Indeed, you've made millions out of promoting exploitation. The stories you tell and the characters you create are of the sort that could set back the emancipation of women decades. If your example was followed, we'd all be living in harems.'

There was a buzz of unease around the room, a strangled gasp from Felicity and a nervous cough from George. An expression of blind panic flitted across Gerald Kauffman's pale face. Janey, experienced moderator that she was, contrived, as did Delia, to show nothing of what she was feeling. And she jumped in pretty much straight away.

'I don't think any of us would blame Delia for single-handedly causing that, would we?' she enquired pleasantly, and not entirely rhetorically.

Felicity and George both gave one of their rather-too-loud laughs. There were cries of 'No! No!' and a few only slightly strangled giggles from the audience. Kauffman still looked like a rabbit caught in headlights.

Delia most certainly had not been happy to find herself

sharing a panel with Penelope, but she hadn't expected an aggressively offensive personal outburst. She was, however, famously good at thinking on her feet. And her first thought was that she must not be seen to retaliate. That would be the worst thing she could possibly do. She must be cool and clever. And remain calm at all costs. She needed to deflect Penelope's broadside, not return it.

'Oh, you know, on one level, Penelope is quite right,' she began, with a small smile, her voice steady. 'The women in my fictional world are not terribly emancipated in the conventional way. That's absolutely true. But without exception, they have made their own choices. Also, there are three writers on this platform who are writing fiction. And fiction means we are making it up. Which is something that should be remembered. It is also true that if real-life women behaved en masse the way my heroines do, the world would, at the very least, be a totally different place. And, of course, if there were as many murders in North Devon as Felicity and George create on a regular basis, I should think its reputation as one of the country's favourite holiday destinations would suffer substantially. Certainly, nobody would dream of attempting to organize a book festival around here. Far too dangerous . . .'

The audience laughed, a proper, more confident laugh this time. Delia could see that her calm and reasoned response had annoyed Penelope, which was exactly what she had intended. She was also aware that Penelope was preparing to speak again. Delia would soon put a stop to that.

'Indeed, Penelope has opened a quite fascinating debate,' Delia continued swiftly. 'And focused attention on one of the more serious aspects of all fiction. Its effect on real life. Does life mimic art? Or is it only the other way around? And so on. We should all be most grateful to Penelope for introducing this topic. I know I am. And, yes, debate sparks interest and is invariably good for business. Which, in my case, is selling books! Indeed, I am so grateful that, should I make any extra millions, I'll be sending you a hefty commission, Penelope dear.'

The audience laughed again. They showed their approval with an outbreak of applause, and some even cheered. They were comfortable again, reassured that all was well. Delia knew that you should never do or say anything to unnerve your audience. It always backfired. Penelope Peabody-Jones had no idea how to handle an audience, it seemed, or how to put over a contentious point of view. Let alone how to effectively attack a fellow panellist, without it harming you far more than your target. Penelope had plunged in without any kind of subtlety at all.

The woman's mouth was still open, but she appeared to have no more words. Eventually, she closed her mouth without saying another thing. She looked absolutely furious.

Delia on the other hand, for the first time at the festival, was in danger of thoroughly enjoying herself.

Janey had not enjoyed the panel. Not for a second.

She could handle it. As Delia had realized at once, Janey was an experienced moderator and a consummate broadcasting professional.

That was not the problem.

It was Janey who had suggested to a desperate Carolyne Smedley that morning that she might contact Penelope. Janey had known Penelope since their schooldays together and was aware that she could be a loose cannon. But before returning to the West Country, following her divorce, Penelope had built a successful career for herself in London as an editor working for a succession of major publishers. Or so she had told Janey, who was now beginning to doubt the accuracy of the version of her life story that Penelope had given her. She certainly couldn't believe that Penelope was now living with her sister in a remote part of Exmoor out of choice. It seemed far more likely that it was out of necessity. And that her glittering career had collapsed around her, leaving her virtually homeless. Unable to continue living in London certainly.

Janey, who had stayed in North Devon, where her Ghanaian parents, both doctors, had settled just before she was born, had at first been impressed by Penelope's stories from the metropolis, more often than not centring around how she had rewritten the work of some of our greatest authors. Gradually,

Janey came to realize that there was barely a contemporary book she ever mentioned that Penelope did not claim at least some credit for.

'Wasn't even printable when I first got my hands on it,' was a remark she made not infrequently.

It seemed likely that, at the very least, Penelope was given to considerable exaggeration.

However, they had remained friends, after a fashion. Penelope was, after all, the most wonderful and captivating gossip, and had proved to be an engaging distraction on numerous occasions over the years.

Certainly, it seemed both obvious and natural that Janey should recommend Penelope when she had learned that morning of the festival's desperate need for a last-minute substitute panellist.

Penelope lived within striking distance of Appledore and was the genuine article. Albeit given to a little fantasy now and then. And when she got into her stride, she could be extremely entertaining.

Indeed, she had thoroughly entertained Janey when they had met for a coffee that afternoon, just before the panel, with a couple of quite outrageous stories. Which, of course, Janey had taken with a pinch of salt.

'Between you and me,' Penelope had murmured, as the two women left the coffee shop, raising her forefinger to her lips.

'Of course,' said Janey, who, by and large, never repeated a word Penelope told her, as almost all of it was slanderous, and Janey was big on self-preservation.

She had, however, been looking forward to the panel, confident that Penelope, with her apparently endless store of anecdotes, would perform excellently, and hopeful that she would keep her most scurrilous tales for more private consumption.

But Janey had been shocked rigid by Penelope's outburst, by her quite violent attack on Delia Day. She had found it all the more disturbing because of their pre-panel conversation.

Janey was a big fish in a little pond. She had her regular daily local radio show and a column in the local paper, and she was a frequent contributor to regional television. The thing about small ponds, Janey had grasped early on, is that you encounter the same marine life repeatedly. Close up. And the only way to succeed and to stay successful is to make sure you don't wee in the water.

And so whilst Janey seriously considered what she should do, whether or not she should talk to Carolyne Smedley about the matters that were causing her concern, or even go directly to the police, ultimately she came to her usual conclusion.

She would do nothing at all.

Penelope Peabody-Jones left the festival site straight after the panel. She had intended to socialize at the Seagate, cosy up further to Janey, try to get to know Carolyne Smedley and attempt to ingratiate herself generally with the great and the good of the festival in order to find a niche for herself in future years. Her track record, if you didn't study it too closely, would surely qualify her for all manner of roles.

But now it was already too late for any of that. She drove at speed through Appledore and Bideford, swinging her Lexus hybrid around corners at a speed far greater than was wise. The sleek motor was just about all Penelope had left from what she regarded as her glory days. She had lost everything else.

And misfortune seemed to be continuing to follow her like a hungry old dog. She really was in a cold fury. Partly with herself, it was true. She had made a fool of herself on that panel. Not for the first time either.

She had lost her temper. Thrown a tantrum. Given in to what her mother had always called 'one of Penelope's paddies'.

She should have known better than to agree to sit on a panel with that bloody woman. Delia Day got right up the nostrils of Penelope's not-insignificant nose. Always had done. The ignominy of her brush with Delia all those years ago still stung. Actually, it was worse than that. It bit into the core of her. How dare Delia have queried Penelope's ability as an editor? Did Delia have a first in English Literature? No, she bloody well didn't. And nobody at Penelope's university had questioned her use of commas. That, of course, had been before grammar checks existed at their present level of sophistication and were readily available as a shortcut. But it wasn't as if Penelope had exclusively relied on an electronic grammar check when editing Delia's latest pile of rubbish. Of course she hadn't. Or at least she didn't think she had. It just hadn't occurred to her at the time that Delia would make such a fuss about her blessed words. Penelope had assumed she just churned out her books and took the money. It was trash romantic fiction, for goodness' sake. She hadn't thought Delia, or indeed anyone else at Coldharbour, would go through her edited copy with a toothcomb.

She had been quite wrong. And now she had been wrong about Delia again. She had lashed out like an out-of-control child and underestimated, yet again, the woman who always seemed to be at the root of her troubles.

Even the failure of her marriage was partly down to Delia.

Her husband had accused Penelope of rank stupidity after the debacle at Coldharbour, which had left her at first sidelined and then, when she attempted to regain her position in the hierarchy by launching a hapless campaign to discredit Delia, without a job. Ultimately, without a job anywhere.

She had then launched herself as a freelance editor, with some initial success because of the positions she had previously held, but gradually the work became less and less and eventually fizzled out altogether. Again her husband blamed her totally: her recklessness, her lack of common sense, her exaggerated opinion of her own ability.

He did not see any of it, not for a moment, the way it really was. He did not see the obvious at all. He did not seem to realize how well everything had been going for Penelope until Delia Day took against her. Quite unjustifiably, in Penelope's opinion.

Eventually, she and her husband grew apart. Or that was his way of putting it. Penelope had another view. He was a feckless bastard who had more or less lived off her until her career fell apart. Then he had found himself another meal ticket. He'd embarked on an affair with the editor who had replaced her at Coldharbour. A young woman who, to add insult to injury, was rumoured to be a great favourite of Delia Day.

And there it was again. Delia Day at the crux of all her misfortunes.

Penelope slammed her foot down on the accelerator and hit the narrow and winding road out of Bideford at speed, a far greater speed than was remotely safe. But she didn't much care. If she became another roadkill statistic, at least she'd be putting herself out of her misery.

There was, however, one small light glimmering on the horizon of her desolation. Penelope had met someone who, unlike her prat of a husband, had at least some respect for her and appreciated her value in all manner of spheres. Someone with surprisingly similar aims to so many of her own. And someone with information that she had been able to build on, to the benefit of them both. Because Penelope had always been a bit of an Autolycus. A gatherer up of ill-considered trifles. In this case, trifles of information concerning certain people, one of them being Delia Day, of course, collected and squirrelled away over the years. This meant that she continued to have a certain worth to certain other people.

Penelope was not dead and buried yet. But she couldn't afford any more mistakes. She knew her greatest failing was her inability to be disingenuous, to any degree at all. Of course, that could be considered a good quality, couldn't it? Honesty was a virtue after all. But Penelope had to learn to keep her feelings to herself, or she might blow her very last chance of resurrecting not only the wreckage of her career but her whole broken life.

She would slow down, try to stay alive and make a call from the car on her hands-free. She had to confess her unfortunate outburst. To ask forgiveness. But she was confident that it would be given. After all, for once in her life, she felt that she was needed. In every possible way.

Best of all, she was needed by someone who detested Delia Day almost as much as she did. And together they were going to get their own back on the woman. It was Delia who was finally going to get her comeuppance. Delia who was going to end up dead and buried in the publishing world, not Penelope.

EIGHT

Delia and the Smythes adjourned to the Seagate immediately after the panel for drinks followed by dinner. Delia was mellow, if not a little more, by the time she returned to the Imperial, driven by Michael. This time in companionable silence. Unlike so many drivers, he seemed to have an instinct for knowing when to talk and when not to. Delia had done enough talking for one day. And although she knew that she had handled the Penelope Peabody-Jones incident pretty well, it had, all the same, been disconcerting. She just wanted to switch off now and recharge her batteries for what would almost certainly prove to be another tricky day tomorrow. The main purpose of her visit to the festival was the 'In Conversation' event with James Harding, scheduled for tomorrow afternoon, which she most certainly wasn't looking forward to. And hadn't been since the moment she had, to her considerable regret now, agreed to it.

She went straight to bed and watched just half an hour or so of news on TV before falling into a thankfully heavy and uninterrupted sleep. She woke early, feeling surprisingly refreshed. Under the circumstances. She planned to complete a good two hours or so on her new book before turning her attention to other matters. She also needed to take another look at one or two possible future commitments that she really should discuss with her agent before the day was over. But, most importantly, she needed to make sure she was fully prepared for that blessed two p.m. session with her bête noire, Harding. She shouldn't let it bother her, though. After all, she almost always managed to get the better of the dreadful man. And she already had her approach worked out. He didn't stand a chance. The thought made her smile.

By and large, she was in pretty good humour – until she happened to glance towards the door. There, lying on the carpet in front of it, was an envelope. It was the same size, shape and colour as the one that had arrived the previous day. This time she picked it up off the floor and tore it open at once. Again the envelope contained one sheet of A4 paper bearing a printed message in the same Times New Roman 72-point. On this occasion, there were two sentences spread over four centred lines.

BE WARNED!
YOU WILL
NOT GET AWAY WITH IT,
NOT ANY MORE

Delia sat down with a bump on the edge of the bed. What exactly was it she would not be allowed to get away with? She was sixty-two years old. There were a number of people she had offended in her lifetime, she was sure. Some, no doubt, considered themselves grievously offended. There were aspects of her past she preferred not to dwell on. But why would anyone set out to pursue and threaten her at the Appledore Book Festival? She couldn't even remember when she had last done anything which might have caused real offence to anyone. Unless her books were really that bad, of course. And if the person writing her these notes was referring to past misdemeanours, well, there might be things she would rather forget forever, but surely that was true of almost anyone, wasn't it? Certainly, anyone who had achieved anything in their life. In any case, it was all so long ago. It was all history.

There was, of course, Penelope Peabody-Jones and her ridiculous outburst. The woman clearly remained as bitter and twisted as ever. Her career was over now, it seemed, but Delia knew that she had worked for at least two other publishers after leaving Coldharbour. The fact that neither of these appointments lasted long – almost certainly because she was such a poor editor, and quite possibly somewhat unhinged, in Delia's opinion – surely even Penelope could not have blamed on Delia. Or could she? Was she that deluded? Judging from her extraordinary behaviour on that afternoon's panel, it certainly seemed that she might be.

Again she thought about James Harding. But maybe there were others who wanted to threaten her. She also didn't think Harding was likely to risk wandering around the Imperial Hotel, most probably in the early hours.

Delia looked again at the single sheet of A4 paper. The message it contained was clearly a threat. But the manner of its delivery was also a threat. Once again, the note had been pushed under her door, and again, unless a different modus operandi had been used, most probably by the person who had written it. Someone who had found his or her way to her hotel bedroom, thus making it clear that they had acquired direct access to her. Which, as doubtless would have been the intention, raised the question of what that person might do next.

Delia made herself a cup of tea, and on autopilot opened her laptop and attempted to start work on her book. She supposed she would have to do something about these notes, but she hadn't decided quite what yet, so she might as well get on with her writing. It was what she did. But not that morning, it seemed. She just couldn't concentrate. Her mind was in a whirl. She had barely written a word when her breakfast arrived, over an hour later. She ate, but not with the relish of the previous day. The offending note lay on the table alongside her coffee cup. It was, she felt, a tad more serious than a bad review or the odd swipe on Twitter. She was resilient, she was tough, but this was definitely getting to her. She couldn't remember anything that had happened to her before which had made her look over her shoulder as she walked down the street. And she was certainly going to be doing that today. Perhaps that disconcerting feeling she had experienced ever since her arrival in North Devon, that she was being watched, and not just in the way she would expect as a celebrity author, and that feeling of meeting people who were curiously familiar even though it seemed she had never met them, notably Amelia Bowden, had not been so irrational after all.

This was a direct threat. She supposed that it might be potentially a police matter. Should she call the police? Or should she at least report what had happened to the festival director?

There was something about being a romantic novelist which made Delia reluctant to display any signs of weakness. Not that there was anything weak about Delia Day. She just always wanted to make sure nobody thought there might be.

In any case, she thought she would start with Carolyne Smedley. This could still just be some sort of practical joke, she told herself sharply. And perhaps there was a history of such a thing happening at Appledore? A local nutcase perhaps, causing trouble for the hell of it. Although, even if there was, it seemed unlikely that the festival director would admit it.

Nonetheless, Delia decided she would make that her first course of action. She would set off early for her two p.m. event with Harding, so that she would hopefully get a chance for a private word with Carolyne beforehand.

She was not looking forward to the panel. She found Harding increasingly obnoxious, but it had to be done. They were obliged to present a united front if their lucrative association with Netflix was to continue. Discussions were already going on with the giant production company and streaming service regarding several more mini-series based on her books, and they still wanted Harding to collaborate with her on the screenplays. It was more or less a condition. Netflix really rated him. It was such a shame that Delia found Harding so bloody difficult. Actually, very nearly impossible. She considered him bossy and arrogant. Not to mention rude. How was it that she so frequently found herself amongst arrogant people? Surely, with her track record, she was the one who might be forgiven for displaying a little arrogance now and then. But she sincerely believed, and certainly hoped, that she did not. And the truth was that she didn't much like what he'd done with *Love's Dream Eternal*, which they had allegedly collaborated on. He had continually taken liberties with her plot and paid scant attention to her characterizations and dialogue.

However, Netflix and their producer had been thrilled. And Delia had to admit that she had very much liked the cheque.

In spite of that, she had at one point very nearly decided that she would walk away from the whole thing. Refuse to sign a new contract. Which would have left Harding high and dry. Without her agreement, there could be no more television adaptations. But Harding was not a man who gave up easily. Delia remained under considerable pressure from all involved, particularly Harding himself. He had even taken to more or less threatening her. With all sorts of nonsense. Eventually, she had concluded that it was not worth fighting the man, that it was best to take the path of least resistance and the intelligent thing to do was to hand the whole thing over. To step back and allow Netflix and Harding to do whatever they liked with her books. To take the money, to sign the new deal which offered by far the biggest single payment she had ever received for anything, then wash her hands of it all. Better writers than her had done so. However, she still hadn't signed the new contract. And she knew how that was annoying Harding.

All the same, appearances had to be kept up. And she and Harding must continue to present themselves as a team, whilst there was even a chance of moving forward with more Delia Days on Netflix, whatever arrangement was agreed.

NINE

D elia arrived at the festival site an hour early, Michael having collected her from the Imperial promptly at twelve thirty, as she had requested. But Carolyne Smedley was nowhere to be found. Nor, enquiries had already revealed, was she at the Seagate. It seemed that, most unusually, Carolyne had allowed herself to be taken to lunch in Bideford by a publisher keen to have her authors more firmly established on the Appledore list, which continued to grow in prestige.

Carolyne arrived back just fifteen minutes or so before the Harding/Day panel, and Delia was unable to snatch even a couple of minutes alone with her. Every time she approached, there were others about, or somebody joined them, in front of whom Delia had no wish to discuss what had happened. The revelation of her unsettling correspondence would just have to wait.

She told herself that this was of no consequence. She was undoubtedly troubling herself about nothing.

Instead, she must concentrate on the matter at hand. In spite of their underlying dislike for each other, she and Harding had developed a kind of public double act which worked well enough; so far, neither any of their audiences nor the media appeared to have detected the fact that they endured a total personality clash.

Carolyne herself led Delia into the backstage area.

Janey Lucas was again to be the moderator – on this occasion, actually their interviewer: according to the programme, she was to be 'in conversation' with them.

This kind of format suited Delia well, as it indeed did most authors, as it pretty much removed the need for any detailed preparation. The interviewer had to do the bulk of the work.

Harding was already there, chatting with Janey. He and Delia repeated their air-kissing routine of the previous evening. This time without any barbed remarks.

Shortly afterwards, Janey made her way on stage and began to introduce the two writers, who were to follow her on at the appropriate moment.

As she walked forward, Delia could see posters advertising her books and the Netflix mini-series surrounding the stage. There were three chairs positioned before a long low table bearing three bottles of Devon Glory Apple Juice and three glasses, and what were presumably name cards facing towards the audience. As if anyone was likely to get any of them confused, thought Delia.

'Please welcome Delia Day, the queen of romance, and James Harding, Britain's leading writer of television blockbusters,' Janey announced with a flourish.

She gestured for them both to sit. Delia headed for the chair Janey seemed to be waving a hand at. As the two contributors settled into their seats, Delia was vaguely aware of Carolyne discreetly pouring juice for each of them, which Delia assumed was probably contractual in view of Devon Glory's sponsorship, and adjusting the piles of books and name cards on the table.

'And so,' Janey continued, 'I think what everyone here today wants to know is just how you two work together to turn Delia's wonderful books into such high-quality and captivating international television. Because, of course, we all hope there will be many more series to follow *Love's Dream Eternal*. Can each of you please tell us how you do it?'

'The most important thing is the incredible respect we have for each other,' began Harding, smooth as an oil slick as usual, thought Delia. 'There is no doubt that Delia is the foremost in her field, and it is a huge privilege for me to work with her to transform her work on to the screen.'

'And it is a huge privilege for me to work with James,' responded Delia, with a smile so broad and warm that not even her closest friends, if she had any, would detect just how false it was. 'He is probably also the foremost in his field, certainly in this country.'

Janey asked both of them about their early lives and how they had become writers. As if none of this had been recorded many times. Delia trotted out the usual story about being the daughter of a long-dead door-to-door vacuum-cleaner salesman, and how she had worked in a factory until, in her early twenties, she had entered a magazine short-story competition for romantic fiction and, totally to her surprise, had won it. The prize was for her story to be published in the magazine. She promptly wrote another, which was also accepted for publication. Then she attempted a book. Her very first book, *Love's Dream Eternal*, now the Netflix mini-series, was also accepted for publication, by the second publisher she sent it to. It remained her best-selling and most famous, which Delia always attributed to it being ground-breaking in the field of romantic fiction, particularly in the way it represented sex and sexual attraction.

'Not all hearts and flowers, but quite a chunk of pure honest lust along the way – I always say it like it is,' Delia told the Appledore audience. Just as she told every audience. 'But I was extraordinarily lucky. For your first novel to be published by a major publisher almost straight away has always been unusual. And remains so. It's not just about writing a good book, although I hope I did that. Ability, talent, originality – all are necessary to some extent. But when you start, you do need a little bit of luck. You need your manuscript to land on the desk of an editor who gets what you are about, appreciates what you do and falls in love with your book. Oh, and has a vacancy on their list. I had that little bit of luck.'

She smiled and opened her arms to the audience. As she always did. A picture of humility. The audience roared their approval, clapping her effusively when she stood up to humbly acknowledge their response, arms still outstretched, head bowed.

'The rest is history,' she continued, as she also always did, whilst wondering if there was likely to be anyone in the audience who hadn't heard this story before. After all, most of those present were likely to be fans of some sort.

The panel was to last an hour and a half. Both contributors were considered worthy of an extra-long session. After forty-five minutes or so, the event was opened up to the audience for questions. Or they were 'invited to join in the conversation', as Janey put it. Talking so intensely was thirsty work. By then, both writers had begun drinking their apple juice. Delia wondered if Harding had requested his to be laced with vodka. Or even whisky. His complexion was invariably more than a tad rosy. She considered that he was becoming more and more flushed as the event progressed. It was no secret that James Harding liked a drink, which is what often led to his belligerence and intransigence, Delia thought, and quite probably to the snide manner he had displayed the night before. She had begun to wonder some time ago if he perhaps had quite a serious drink problem.

Also, she thought he'd put on even more weight since she'd seen him last. He was several years her junior. She reckoned she looked the younger of the two. She hoped so anyway.

She also hoped she was a more interesting speaker. Harding was pontificating about his work in that annoying way of his. She thought it was annoying, anyway.

'Oh, no, I never went to film school, if you have talent and ability, it will always rise to the surface,' he announced. 'Although, of course, I do have a degree in English . . .'

He was like a cracked record, thought Delia. She was aware that she could be accused of allowing her self-awareness to desert her for a moment or two. But surely Harding was in a different league to her when it came to repeating the same old story over and over again. And his stories were persistently self-congratulatory. She didn't think she had ever heard him speak without mentioning that wretched degree. Then he began what she considered to be the even more deeply tedious, oft-repeated tale of how he had begun his film and TV career as a runner at Pinewood Studios. Which, in the modern world, surely verged on being mildly offensive.

'I learned everything I know on the job,' he said. 'As it were, if you see what I mean . . .'

There were a few titters. Unbelievable in this day and age, thought Delia.

Harding droned on, every story in some way or another boastful, and most of them probably invented, Delia thought. There was an anecdote about beating Roger Moore at backgammon during the filming of a James Bond movie, on which he had worked as a script assistant.

'Uncredited at that stage in my career, but not unheralded,' he pronounced. 'Roger made sure of that.'

Another chronicled a list of well-known actors, almost all dead, of course, who had proclaimed that they would refuse any future screenwork unless Harding was on the writing team.

Delia knew for a fact that he'd never been employed in any capacity on any Bond film. And she couldn't imagine anybody who had worked with Harding once ever fighting to do so again.

He just kept talking, too. Even though this was supposed to be a Q and A session. She studied the audience. Some did seem to be looking a tad askance, but most seemed to be lapping up Harding's nonsense. And she didn't want to butt in as she feared it might look as if she was descending to his level.

Eventually, he paused for breath. Or for a gasp, actually. He stopped talking quite abruptly. His complexion had grown even redder. He was panting and looked very hot and uncomfortable. Served him right for so resolutely hogging the limelight, thought Delia.

She stepped into the breach, concentrating her attention on a woman in the front row who she thought might have been trying to ask her a question for some time. It turned out to be the almost obligatory one from reader to author.

'Would you tell us where you get your ideas from, Miss Day?'

'Well, ideas for novels are all around us in real life, you know,' Delia began. 'In newspapers, magazines, on TV and radio news, and, of course, in our own lives. I draw on all these sources . . .'

She didn't mention something she had realized early on in her career: that there was only really one acceptable love story in the world of romantic fiction. Boy meets girl, one or both of them have to conquer adversity or become reformed characters, or both, and then they live happily ever after. She had once suggested to her publishers that it was time for a bit of a twist, perhaps for an unhappy ending. They had been appalled. More recently, she had put it to them that she should become a little more modern and introduce boy meets boy. Or maybe girl meets girl. They had not been impressed. She was Delia Day, they told her; her readers liked boys to be boys and girls to be girls, and there could be no gender bending or variation in sexuality for her.

'*Love's Dream Eternal*, the book adapted by James for Netflix, was inspired by living through the experiences of a dear friend who, as a very young woman, had to endure an enforced separation from the man she was sure was the love of her life,' Delia continued. 'She never lost faith in his love for her in spite of almost overwhelming evidence to the contrary. That became the entire basis of the book. I'll stop there, though – I don't want to give away the ending for those of you who have yet to read it or see the television series.'

This led to the question she always disliked most, the one she never actually answered. She had learned to dodge it quite adroitly, but still invariably felt uncomfortable.

'Miss Day, you have never married, and you always say in interviews that you live alone. Does that mean that you, probably our greatest romantic novelist, have never found the love of your life?'

This was unusually direct. Delia made herself beam a broad smile at the questioner, a bookish-looking young woman wearing wire-framed spectacles.

'Look, not all of us are destined to have the privilege of sharing our entire lives with a soulmate, but I have, of course, known love, great love.'

She was abruptly interrupted by a crash to her left and the tinkling sound of breaking glass. She turned around to see that James Harding had risen to his feet and had apparently knocked his chair over and caused his apple juice bottle to tumble to the ground and break. His face was purple. He looked as if he was unable to breathe properly. He suddenly clutched at his chest with both hands. Then he emitted a single gurgling noise before falling backwards, landing face up and arms akimbo. His mouth and eyes were wide open. He no longer appeared to be breathing.

A woman in the audience rushed forward proclaiming herself a nurse, dropped to the ground beside Harding and began urgently applying CPR. Delia also became aware of Felicity Smythe, who had suddenly emerged from the backstage area, holding her phone aloft and, having presumably already dialled 999, asking for the ambulance service, in a clear but rather stricken sort of voice.

She didn't hear the rest of Felicity's call, as she had moved closer to the figure spread-eagled on the ground and was concentrating all her attention on him. Delia studied James Harding carefully. He wasn't even blinking.

The woman from the audience was still pumping his chest ferociously. Delia suspected that was not going to do much good.

James Harding, the man Delia Day loved to hate more than anyone she had ever known, was dead. There was no doubt about it. He was dead, all right.

TEN

The body lay sprawled across the platform. Face up. Eyes still open. Arms and legs akimbo. Mouth frozen in what appeared to be a grimace of pure agony.

David Vogel stood to one side, quietly taking everything in. At least there was no blood. Vogel didn't like blood. He didn't like violence either. And he'd been known to be physically sick when confronted by its results, which could be regarded as rather unfortunate for a senior police officer whose principal task was investigating murder.

Apparently, there had been several crime writers, due to form a panel for the next event, in attendance when James Harding had risen rather dramatically to his feet, emitted a single strangled cry and fallen backwards. One of them, a woman called Felicity Smythe, had taken it upon herself to proclaim that Harding was dead and had declared the marquee in which they had all been gathered a crime scene.

All a bit premature, Vogel thought, in regard both to the proclamation of death – as resuscitation had been taking place at the time, albeit ultimately to no avail – and the manner of it. Vogel could, at a glance, see no reason to suspect anything but natural causes.

It was also Felicity Smythe who had called in the incident and told the emergency operator that she believed Harding may have been murdered. Based, as far as Vogel could work out, on no evidence whatsoever.

His own years of experience indicated that Harding had died of a heart attack. The man, probably around sixty years old, Vogel guessed, was overweight and of florid complexion. He was perfect heart attack material.

It would not be usual, of course, for a detective chief inspector to be called to such an occurrence, which would much more probably be dealt with by local uniform. If, indeed, a police presence was required at all. But in this case, circumstances had conspired to demand his presence. First, the somewhat over-enthusiastic Felicity Smythe had clearly over-dramatized the demise of James Harding when she had mentioned the possibility of murder to the emergency operator. Control had therefore not only dispatched a uniformed patrol, as well as contacting the ambulance service, but had also alerted Devon and Cornwall Police's Major Crimes Team and called Vogel – obeying the DCI's own instructions in the event of an incident so potentially serious. This was, after all, the Appledore Book Festival, and everybody, even the civilians manning control at Barnstaple police station, had heard of James Harding, certainly since he had adapted, or co-adapted, Delia Day's bestseller for Netflix, if not before.

It was still only a little after three o'clock. Vogel was thinking about his lunch. This was not like him. He was more of a man who ate to live, rather than one who lived to eat. But he had been enjoying the company of his wife and daughter on what was a rare occasion of its kind. And then there was the plum crumble he feared he may never get to devour.

He was also feeling guilty about abandoning his daughter at a time when he knew she needed him. Rosamund, an exceptional swimmer who suffered from cerebral palsy, was struggling to cope with the loss of her cat, Storey, named after the champion Paralympic swimmer and cyclist Sarah Storey.

And it was only with some difficulty that he turned his attention back to the matter at hand.

James Harding had died in the middle of his appearance at a venue comprising primarily a complex of marquees, just outside the village. He was particularly well known in North Devon because he had previously lived there for some years. But it was his collaboration with the world-famous Delia Day, the world's most successful romantic novelist, that had brought him much wider acclaim.

The Appledore Book Festival was one of North Devon's premier events, now pulling in high-end participants from all over the world, and had become a significant tourist attraction. The sudden death of one of its more celebrated contributors, certainly with the yet-to-be-confirmed suggestion of foul play, meant that Vogel had not hesitated to abandon both his lunch and his family and take off for the festival, not much more than a couple of minutes' drive away, thus becoming an unlikely first responder, way ahead of the uniformed patrol on its way from Barnstaple or any medical professionals.

He now rather wished not only that they would all hurry up but also that he'd held back a little before rushing to the scene. He was already pretty sure there was no real call for his presence, and he would so like to get back to his family. Mary was the most understanding of police wives, but their lunch together had been an important one in more ways than one. In a couple of weeks, Rosamund was due to depart for the residential special school at which she had recently acquired a much sought-after place. It was a big thing in all their lives. He and Mary would miss Rosamund greatly, but it was what she wanted, not least because she would have access to an exceptional level of coaching in competitive swimming and the best possible facilities. But both Vogel and his wife now feared that if Storey remained missing, Rosamund might be reluctant to leave home. Certainly, it would be likely to make the move more traumatic for her. He just hoped the cat would be found soon. Unfortunately, he was not optimistic. Rosamund didn't know this, but an above-average number of cats had gone inexplicably missing in the area over the years, never to be found. And recently there had been quite a spate. The police had come to suspect some kind of cat-napper was at work. Or worse. It was all extremely unpleasant. Vogel just wanted to get back to his little family as soon as possible. But now that he was at the scene, he could not leave it unattended.

He looked around him. The death had occurred in the large marquee which served as the festival's main auditorium. There had been three upright chairs, placed along the length of a long low table, on the small raised platform at one end of the marquee. Where Vogel now stood. One of the chairs, presumably the one occupied by James Harding, lay on its side next to the dead man, doubtless knocked over by him when he collapsed. The other two, Vogel knew, had been occupied by Delia Day and Janey Lucas, the moderator of the event, which, he had been told, was a sell-out. But the rows of chairs facing the platform were now almost empty.

Vogel had cleared the marquee of everyone except those who might be regarded as having been directly involved to some extent or other in the incident and its aftermath. He had a quick word with the nurse who had attempted CPR, but she had little to offer except to say that, in her opinion, Harding had almost certainly died of a heart attack and she had known from the start that CPR was unlikely to help. Which, of course, was also Vogel's opinion.

Most of the audience seemed relieved to have been released and hurried to leave the scene. One woman, in tears, seemed particularly distracted and kept bumping into people as she hurried out of the marquee. For a fleeting moment, Vogel considered going after her, but he decided that for the time being he would concentrate on those who seemed likely to be the most relevant witnesses. Delia Day, Janey Lucas, Felicity Smythe and Carolyne Smedley, the festival director, were sitting in the front row watching Vogel. He had asked them to remain and supposed he had better speak to them and get their version of exactly what had happened. But he was pretty sure he would be wasting his time.

Two of the four women, Carolyne Smedley and Janey Lucas, still looked shocked and upset. Understandable when someone had literally dropped dead in front of you, thought Vogel, even if there was nothing sinister lurking.

Felicity Smythe, on the other hand, appeared to be buzzing. She looked highly animated and rather as if she might even be enjoying the whole episode, Vogel suspected.

Delia Day's face was impassive. It was impossible to even guess what she might be thinking. But some people give that appearance even when they are actually in deep shock, the DCI reminded himself.

She was an extraordinary-looking woman thought Vogel. Her clothes matched her hair. They were both predominately silver and purple. As were her shoes. Only her trousers were another colour, and they were white. She had a certain aura about her, Vogel thought. But she would, wouldn't she? She was so successful and famous that even Vogel had heard of her.

He climbed down off the platform and approached the three women, speaking first to Felicity. He cut straight to the chase.

'Mrs Smythe, I'd like to know exactly why, when you telephoned emergency services, you said that you thought Mr Harding had been murdered?'

'I said I thought he *could* have been murdered,' corrected Felicity.

Vogel sighed inwardly.

'And why exactly did you think that?' he continued patiently.

'Well, he died so suddenly and so dramatically. And . . .' Felicity paused and waved one hand in the general direction of the dead man. 'Just look at the expression on his face,' she commanded.

Vogel obeyed, although he didn't mean to, as did the other three women.

'It's contorted in agony,' Felicity continued. 'As if some terrible shock had just overwhelmed his body. He stood up like a rocket . . .'

She paused. *Stood up like a rocket*, Vogel repeated to himself silently. He hoped Felicity's writing was better than that.

'He screamed and grasped his chest with his hands, before dropping to the ground. And if you ask me, he was dead before he hit the floor. I mean, I immediately thought he'd been poisoned—'

'You thought what?' Vogel interrupted.

'That he'd been poisoned.'

'Why?' asked Vogel.

'Well, you see, George – that's my husband – and I, we write crime novels under the name of Felicity Ge—'

Vogel interrupted again. 'Mrs Smythe, what have your crime novels got to do with James Harding's death?'

'Well, in our latest one, the victim dies of poisoning, having ingested a serum which has been extracted from killer spiders, and he screams, clutches his chest, leaps to his feet and instantly drops dead – just the way poor James did.'

Vogel stared at Felicity in disbelief. Out of the corner of one eye, he could see that Delia Day no longer looked impassive. Indeed, she appeared to be struggling not to laugh. He knew how she felt. But a man had died. Vogel kept his features suitably composed and his tone of voice level.

'So, your belief that Mr Harding had probably been

murdered was based on the way in which a character in one of your own books died,' Vogel recited carefully. 'Is that so?'

'Uh, yes,' replied Felicity.

'Entirely so? You are not aware of any other evidence?'

'Uh, no.'

'Did you not consider a less exotic cause of death at all?' Vogel persisted. 'Something more common, perhaps? Heart failure, for example?'

'Oh, but of course, as I'm sure you know, Chief Inspector, the cause of death is always heart failure. It's what causes the heart to fail that is so often of interest to a detective, isn't it?'

Vogel did then allow himself the luxury of a small smile.

'Indeed, and thank you for sharing your extensive knowledge with me, Mrs Smythe,' he responded.

The woman had the grace to look as if she might have embarrassed herself a little.

'Oh, I'm so sorry, Chief Inspector,' she said, erupting into a flow of verbal diarrhoea. 'I know I do get carried away sometimes . . . all the same, we do have to keep an open mind in these matters, don't we? I mean, who knows what—'

Vogel stepped in smartly to stop the flow.

'Rest assured, Mrs Smythe, I will consider all possibilities,' he said. 'And an appropriate investigation will be conducted.'

He turned to Delia.

'Miss Day, I understand that you and Mr Harding were writing partners, working closely together,' he began. 'Therefore, could I just say how sorry I am for your loss.'

Vogel thought that for a fleeting second Delia Day's expression changed. Hardened, perhaps? He wasn't sure. Then the moment passed.

But did her bottom lip tremble slightly as she replied? He wasn't sure of that either.

'Thank you, Detective Chief Inspector,' she replied. 'Such a shock. We were just about to start work together again. A clever, very talented man, and a dear friend.'

'Yes. I'm sure. You were sharing the platform with Mr Harding, were you not? Perhaps you could tell me exactly what you saw?'

'Of course. Well, only minutes earlier, James had been

talking about his life and his work, quite clearly and articulately, about how he came to be a screenwriter, about the intricacies and challenges of dramatizing a novel, and so on. And then . . . then it happened. I believe he may have coughed a couple of times. I'm not sure. A bit earlier, he'd stopped talking quite suddenly, so I did think he might be struggling, but that can happen for all sorts of reasons. I stepped in, obviously. I was answering questions from the audience when I became aware that James had suddenly stood up. He cried out only once, I think, clutched his chest and fell to the ground. Just as Felicity described it. And just as you see him.'

Delia gestured with one manicured hand towards the spread-eagled body.

'I see,' responded Vogel. 'And might I ask, did you, Miss Day, notice anything that might have indicated foul play, anything that might have suggested that Mr Harding did not die of natural causes?'

Both corners of Delia Day's mouth twitched distinctly. This time, Vogel was quite sure of it.

'Nothing at all, Detective Inspector, I can assure you of that.'

Vogel was also pretty sure there was a twinkle in her eye. Which was probably quite understandable following Felicity Smythe's rather extraordinary pronouncements, but it also might indicate, he thought, that Delia Day was not exactly overcome with grief following the death of her writing partner. He could, in any case, think of little else to say. Delia Day relieved the need.

'Look, I wondered if it might be possible for me to leave now?' she enquired. 'I have quite a lot of work of one sort and another to get through today, and if you need me again, I am booked into the Imperial for another two days, assuming the festival continues, of course . . .'

Her voice trailed off.

'I see nothing so far to prevent it, Miss Day,' said Vogel. 'Although, as I told Mrs Smythe, our enquiries will proceed for the time being. And yes, of course you can leave if you're absolutely certain you have nothing more to say that might add to what we know already about Mr Harding's death.'

'Nothing at all, Mr Vogel.'

'My card, in case you think of anything,' said Vogel, handing one over. He was aware that most police officers offered their contact details electronically nowadays. But although he was actually extremely computer literate, and indeed in one of his previous policing incarnations had been known as The Geek, there was an old-fashioned side to Vogel. And a practical one. He felt that people were less likely to ignore the relatively rare presence of a calling card – which was inclined to come to hand in wallet or pocket, as long as they didn't immediately throw it away, of course – than just another entry on their contact list.

'Perhaps, Miss Day, you would drop me a text so I have your contact details too?' he requested nonetheless.

Delia Day agreed that she would do so at once.

Vogel turned his attention to Carolyne Smedley, wanting to know exactly what she had seen.

'I was sitting at the back and haven't anything to add to either Delia's or Felicity's account, I'm afraid,' Carolyne said quickly. 'It was a dreadful shock for everyone, I can certainly tell you that. But I'm afraid I have to ask you straight away, Mr Vogel, when will we be able to continue? This is our principal venue, and I have three more major events scheduled here today, with some very important authors, and a full programme tomorrow, too.'

'I'm sure you have, Miss Smedley, but you can hardly continue whilst we have a dead body on the podium, can you?' Vogel replied, a little more tetchily than he had intended. 'Look, we have to wait for the paramedics before we can give you any such information, or indeed do anything at all, because only then can we organize for Mr Harding's body to be taken to the mortuary.'

He glanced back at the dead man.

'There will be next of kin to inform too, of course. Nobody's mentioned a wife or any other companion. Do I take it that Mr Harding came here on his own?'

'Yes. I believe he is married, but his wife did not accompany him, nor anyone else, as far as I know. Certainly, he has not brought anyone along to the festival site or any of our events, nor asked for accreditation for anyone.'

'I see. I did wonder, though . . . I saw a woman leaving the marquee in floods of tears. Did you happen to notice, Miss Smedley, and did you know who the woman was?'

'Oh, yes, I noticed, but I didn't make anything of it. That was Penelope Peabody-Jones. She has a reputation for being a drama queen, apparently, which I wish I'd known before inviting her on to a panel yesterday.'

'Ah, so you didn't think she had any particular reason for appearing to be so upset?'

'What do you mean?'

'Well, I just wondered, were she and Mr Harding close?'

'Close? You mean, were they, um, in some sort of relationship?'

'Yes, that is exactly what I mean?'

'Goodness,' said Carolyne, all wide-eyed astonishment. 'It hadn't even occurred to me. Not those two, surely . . .'

'You're probably right, and, in any case, most likely it is of no importance. But I would like Penelope's contact details if you don't mind.'

'Oh, yes, certainly. I'll text them to you. But I just can't believe . . . Oh dear. And somebody must inform James's wife, obviously. I suppose it will have to be me. My only contact is his agent. Do you think I should call her, DCI Vogel? Oh dear . . .'

'Well Miss Smedley, Mr Harding was rather a well-known man, was he not? I should think it's quite possible somebody has already posted about his death on social media, and if they haven't, they will soon. And as festival director, I'm afraid it probably does fall upon you to make the call. Albeit via his agent. Particularly, as I have no reason to believe, so far anyway, that his death is a police matter . . .'

Vogel's attention was then attracted by a bit of a commotion at the main entrance to the marquee. It was a paramedic team arriving with a stretcher and all their other equipment.

Thank God for that, he thought.

One of the paramedics, a young woman, recognized Vogel and approached him immediately.

'Afternoon, Mr Vogel, I'm Aniya Amin. Have you got any instructions for us? Nobody seemed clear on whether we were entering a crime scene or not. Do we have to wait for pathology and CSI?'

Vogel shook his head very slightly. The earlier information, as gleaned from the over-enthusiastic Mrs Smythe, had surely been quite wrong. He really could see nothing to indicate foul play.

All the same, he excused himself from Carolyne Smedley and Janey Lucas, who was still presumably waiting for him to interview her, and from Felicity Smythe, who remained sitting in the front row and clearly had no intention of going anywhere unless she was told to, and took the paramedic to one side.

'No, no need to bother either of those departments,' he told her quietly. 'Death from natural causes almost certainly.'

'Right, well, I can see he's dead all right from here,' said Aniya. 'What do you need us to do?'

'Just have a good look at him to make sure I haven't missed anything, and we need an official declaration of death, then call in the body snatchers to take him to the morgue,' Vogel instructed.

He had just received a text from uniform saying they were only five minutes away. As soon as they arrived, he intended to hurry back to the Seagate, hopefully before Mary and Rosamund tired of waiting and made their own way home. He really couldn't see that there was likely to be anything here that would continue to require the attention of the Devon and Cornwall Police MCT.

But whilst he was trapped at the scene by police protocol, he might as well continue to go through the motions. He moved back to Janey Lucas and sat down next to her.

'You were on stage with the dead man, Miss Lucas, sitting next to him,' Vogel began. 'May I ask, was there anything about Mr Harding which gave you cause for concern before his fatal collapse? Perhaps made you think that he could be very ill?'

'Not really,' replied Janey. 'Well, not until almost immediately before he stood up so dramatically and then fell to the ground, just as Delia and Carolyne have described it to you. I could see he was a bit hot and bothered, but it's very warm in the marquee, and these panels are harder work than they look. Takes a lot of effort to keep the audience engaged. I certainly didn't think he was about to drop dead, if that's what you mean.'

Janey looked a tad askance at her own words, as if aware that she might sound insensitive.

'I mean . . . well, I didn't really think about it. I did see him, just before his collapse, pause, stop more or less mid-sentence, I think, and lean back in his seat, and I did think he looked a bit uncomfortable. But then an audience member asked Delia a question and I turned to look at her whilst she was answering. She was on her second question when I heard the crash of James's chair falling over, obviously as he rose suddenly to his feet, and the sound of his juice bottle breaking when he knocked it off the table. But by the time I turned around, he was standing up and clutching his chest with both hands. Then he screamed. Well, cried out. Maybe not quite a scream. He may also have made some sort of noise in his chest, too – I'm not sure. He just dropped to the floor. Like a stone. I'm pretty sure he was dead before he hit the ground. It was so sudden. Just horrible, horrible.'

'I'm sure it was,' empathized Vogel.

This sounded more and more like a heart attack. He really wanted to get back to his abandoned family. And he could almost taste that plum crumble with clotted cream.

There would be a post-mortem at some stage, of course, as was always the case in the UK, except with people of great age or a serious underlying health condition, although it would not be considered a matter of any urgency. Vogel had already learned that at fifty-eight Harding was younger than he looked, and had been well enough, or considered himself well enough, to travel the world in the pursuance of his craft. He had apparently flown into Bristol from Netflix production meetings in Los Angeles to attend the Appledore Book Festival. Vogel suspected that his schedule would not have been helpful to a man who had a weak heart. But, of course, he may not have known he had a weak heart.

The paramedics were still at work when the police patrol team finally arrived. Vogel told the two uniforms they needed to stay until the paramedics had finished and the body had been removed. Meanwhile, he saw no reason why he shouldn't leave them all to it. He was by now definitely worrying more about his daughter and his plum crumble than anything else.

Vogel was used to death in almost all its forms. And he had no personal feelings about James Harding. He'd never met the man. The screenwriter's passing had not ruined Vogel's Sunday. But if he didn't get back to the Seagate in time to rejoin his family and tuck into the waiting crumble, that really would.

ELEVEN

The sudden death of James Harding had made Delia completely forget the disturbing notes that had been delivered to her hotel room. She may have detested the man, but although she had behaved with her usual cool aplomb, this was the first time anyone had suddenly dropped dead before her eyes, or very nearly, and she had been just a little shaken.

Also, she had earlier very nearly resigned herself to handing over her books pretty much carte blanche to Harding in order neither to rock the Netflix boat nor to set herself at loggerheads with the screenwriter, even though his threats had never worried her as much as he thought they had. Now that whole scenario would be up in the air again. His death was not entirely unwelcome in that regard. She just had to hope that Netflix were not so completely committed to Harding's input into her work that they would withdraw their offer of a series of adaptations. She would probably be presented with another co-writer, and whatever her personal views on Harding, she had also known that the man could do the job, perhaps not the way she liked it, but certainly the way Netflix liked it. By and large, however, she could not pretend to be anything other than relieved to be rid of him. That is, she couldn't pretend to herself, but she would pretend to other people.

Due, he said, to the confusion surrounding Harding's death, her driver Michael wasn't waiting for her at the festival site. When she called him, he apologized profusely, explaining that the police hadn't let him drive in, and he'd been led to understand that it was unlikely that Delia would be free to leave for some time. He said he'd been worrying about an unusual noise coming from his electric motor and had decided to make the most of the opportunity to take the car to be checked out at the garage he had bought it from which opened on Sundays through the summer, albeit primarily for sales.

'They've just told me the problem is only a loose connector – they're fixing it now – and I'll come straight to you as soon as they've finished,' he said. 'But I'm bound to be at least half an hour.'

Delia was frustrated. She could call for a local taxi, but goodness knew how long that might take. She could complain to Carolyne Smedley, but that seemed a little insensitive under the circumstances. She could complain to Michael, but that would be unkind and counterproductive. He already sounded more than a tad upset about the situation, which, in any case, really hadn't been his fault. Michael had been trying to do the right thing. So she did none of those things.

It was a beautiful day. Perhaps she should take the opportunity to enjoy it. A little fresh air might clear her head. She was not going to admit to anyone else that she had been shaken up by the afternoon's events, but she felt distinctly wobbly.

'It's all right, Michael,' she told him. 'I'm going to take a walk into Appledore, clear my head. Perhaps you'd call when you get to the village and pick me up outside the Seagate.'

'Of course, Miss Day,' said Michael.

Delia walked briskly along the main road until she reached the village, then turned off towards the Torridge estuary and along Irsha Street. She didn't know the way, exactly, but she had been driven via Appledore to the festival site three times now, so she just followed her nose in order to reach The Quay. She was glad that, realizing the festival site would still be sticky after the downpour on the opening night, she had again chosen to wear trainers rather than heels. The Quay was busy.

The fine weather on a June Sunday had brought the crowds out. Delia kept her head down and resolutely avoided eye contact. It was an old trick. With a bit of luck, even if people recognized her, they might at least hesitate to approach. She had planned to buy herself an ice from the cream-and-red Hockings van parked opposite the Seagate. She had been told Hockings ice cream was something of a local delicacy, but there was a big queue. She wandered towards the quayside and stood looking out over the water towards Instow, a predominantly white line of seaside urbanization bathed in the still-warm afternoon sunshine.

A small dog on a long lead ran towards her, threatening to wrap itself and its lead around her legs, but was thankfully reeled in by its owner before it could do so. There were children playing, young lovers walking arm in arm and an elderly couple walking hand in hand. All contributing to a hum of chatter and laughter. Possibly a good backdrop for a book sometime, she thought idly.

And then it happened. Delia became vaguely aware of some-body approaching, closer than anyone else had come to her. But she experienced no sense of impending danger. She remained standing, looking across the river towards Instow. She was completely untroubled by the close proximity of another human being. She didn't even turn around.

Suddenly, she felt a push in the small of her back. Gentle at first, but then firmer. Enough to knock her forwards and completely off balance. Fast, too. She never had a chance to see who had sent her flying. Instead, she rocketed forward into the riverbed.

The tide was out. There was a fifteen-foot drop, and Delia fell head first. She was at once knocked unconscious, having hit her head on a stone or some other piece of debris lying semi-exposed in the thick mud below. Concerned onlookers rushing forward found themselves looking down at a woman lying absolutely still, face down, and with at least one arm twisted at an unnatural angle.

Two young men climbed down one of the long ladders set into the wall a hundred feet or so along the quay and waded through the mud to get to her, their feet sticking in the goo.

More than one person called the emergency services. Appledore was keeping them busy that day.

And all the while, Delia Day, the world's most celebrated romantic novelist, dressed as usual in a variation of her trademark colours, lay face down in the mud. Perfectly still.

TWELVE

Vogel had finally just finished his plum crumble. It was getting on for five o'clock, and he and his family were about to leave after the much-delayed conclusion of their lunch when he became aware of the commotion outside the Seagate, which spread inside when a clearly shaken group of young women on a hen weekend made their way into the bar, discussing what they had just seen in loud voices.

The DCI had left the festival site soon after Delia. But unlike her, he had been driving his car, so it had taken him only three or four minutes to make the short journey. He had got there even more quickly because he had been answering an emergency call and had thrown caution to the wind, but Vogel was naturally a painstakingly slow and careful driver. Although he was in his late forties, he had only just passed his driving test. In that achievement alone surprising most people who knew him, including his wife. As a Londoner, formerly in the Met, and having previously lived all his life in the heart of the capital city, Vogel had never felt the need to learn to drive and, to the annoyance of his superior officers, had continued to avoid doing so even after making the move to the West Country several years earlier. Until he relocated from Bristol to North Devon – there, the total lack of any form of public transport worthy of the name had finally frustrated him into submission.

The landlord, Peter Carter, stepped outside at once, closely followed by Vogel, who could not stop himself. If there was any sort of incident anywhere near him, on duty or off, Vogel just had to find out what was going on. If there was the slightest chance that a crime had been committed in his vicinity, it was a matter of honour that he should be first in line to investigate and try to solve it. He did not know, of course, that he was already involved in this incident. Not yet.

Holding his warrant card aloft and calling out, 'Move aside, please. Police!' Vogel pushed forward through the small crowd gathered at the quayside until he was able to look down at the scene below.

He could clearly see the victim lying in the mud. Motionless. Perhaps unconscious. Or even dead. And he could see that the victim was almost certainly a woman. She was lying on her side, and two young men were crouched in the mud alongside her. He could not see the victim's face, which was obscured by one of the young men who was bending over her.

However, he could see her purple and silver hair, and the colour of her clothes – the jacket purple and the trousers white. Or once white. In spite of the mud covering much of her body, he quickly realized that this was almost certainly Delia Day. She had been dressed so distinctively that even Vogel had noticed when he'd met her for the first time back at the festival.

He was just assimilating the possible significance of this when one of the two men moved slightly away. He could see then that it was Delia all right, lying on her side, angled towards the quayside, in the recovery position into which she'd presumably been placed by the two young men, judging from the mud on her face and the parts of the front of her body that were visible to him. Suddenly, she appeared to move, perhaps attempting to sit up. She was alive and, momentarily at least, conscious. But she was obviously having difficulty breathing, and her attempt at movement, particularly of her left arm, caused her to cry out in pain. She slumped back into the mud and lay still again.

At that moment, Vogel heard an ambulance arriving. A paramedic quickly exited from the passenger side and ran across the pavement towards Vogel, who recognized her at once from earlier in the day. It was Aniya Amin. Clearly, the same team had been diverted from the festival site where there had been little more they could do once they had pronounced James Harding dead.

'Over here,' Vogel called, and Aniya hurried to his side, making her way nimbly through the crowd which parted obligingly for her.

'She's down there, and she seems to be quite badly injured,' said Vogel.

The paramedic leaned somewhat perilously forward and peered over the quayside.

'Hello there, I'm Aniya. Come to help you all,' she called down. 'How's the patient?'

'She's been out cold, suffered quite a bash on the head, but she's coming around on and off now,' one of the men shouted back. 'We put her in the recovery position.'

'I see that. Well done. Can you see any other obvious injuries?'

'We think she might have broken her arm. She seems to be in quite a lot of pain.'

'Can you hear me, lady? How are you feeling?' called Aniya. 'We'll be with you in just a jiff.'

Vogel thought Delia may have shifted slightly to look up at the paramedic, then her head dropped yet again, and he thought her eyes had closed. Certainly, she made no attempt to reply.

'She's drifting in and out of consciousness,' the second man called up. He was older and broader. But like the first man, he seemed pretty calm under the circumstances. Both men had sunk well up to their ankles in the mud.

'What should we do now?' the second man continued.

'Talk to her. Keep talking to her. Just try to keep her with you until we get down there. Also, do your best to stop her from moving. We'll be as quick as we can.'

Aniya turned to Vogel.

'Do you know the best way for us to get down there, with a stretcher and all the other equipment we need, Mr Vogel?' she asked. 'And for us to get the patient out of there.'

'I'm afraid not,' Vogel began. 'I'm not local, but maybe somebody—'

He was interrupted by a tall, burly man, with a shock of white hair, who stepped forward purposefully.

'There's a ladder just over there,' he said, gesturing to the point a hundred feet or so along the quay where the two men already down on the riverbed had descended. 'But you'd have a hell of a job to get your stuff down it, and then you've got a fair stretch of mud to go over, and even more of a problem trying to get the poor woman back over the mud and up the ladder. You need to get her out pretty quick, too. The tide's coming in. Fast.'

He gestured again, this time at the incoming water.

'But there is a way. I'm Brad Powis, I'm lifeboat crew,' he continued. 'I'll get the boys and girls called out and I'll take you round to our station, over on Irsha Street. We can transport you up-river in our boat. We've got an inshore Atlantic 85; that's a rigid inflatable, so we can bottom her on the riverbed, and we can make sure we keep you safe whilst you're down there and get everybody out of danger as quickly as possible.'

'Sounds good to me,' responded Aniya, who most likely hadn't been looking forward to wading through a hundred yards or so of clinging mud. 'Come on, we'll give you a lift.'

She headed off at speed towards the parked ambulance, Brad Powis, already speaking in an animated fashion into his mobile phone, following close behind.

Vogel turned to face the little crowd.

'Did anyone here see what happened?' he called out.

Several people stepped forward.

'I did.' A man holding a small dog on an extending lead was the first to speak out.

'I was getting an ice cream – I was in the queue just over there. I heard a scream, and I looked over and I saw this woman just topple over the edge. She very nearly kept her footing, I think. It was a close thing. People are saying she's a famous writer – is that right?'

'I'm afraid I can't reveal any information of that nature at the moment,' said Vogel. 'Did you see what caused her to fall?'

'No. Well, not exactly. I suppose she must have tripped or something. That's what I thought anyway. I mean, what else could it have been?'

Vogel's mind was racing in circles quick as a spooked pony. He could think of all manner of possibilities. None of them anything but deeply disturbing, and all of them leading him to curse himself and his preoccupation with plum crumble. And with his daughter and her lost cat. Although that was rather more excusable. Delia Day had already been in close proximity to a sudden death that day, sitting on a platform just feet away from a man she knew well, who Vogel had merely assumed must have had a heart attack. Because he was of a certain age, had a florid complexion and was overweight. And there had been no obvious sign of anything else – certainly not of any foul play. There had been no physical attack on the man. He hadn't been shot or stabbed or hit over the head with a heavy object. But Vogel was beginning to wonder if he may have been quite wrong to so quickly accept that James Harding had died of natural causes.

'Did you notice if there was anyone close to the woman when she fell?' he asked.

'Well, you can see how busy it is on the quay today, but I wasn't really looking in the right direction until I heard the scream. Then people started to move further towards the quay-side to see what had happened. Do you think somebody might have knocked into her, causing her to fall?'

'We will be investigating all possibilities,' remarked Vogel obliquely.

He was approached then by a young man wearing a smart grey suit and looking rather out of place amidst the casually dressed Sunday-afternoon seaside crowd. He introduced himself as Michael Souch, Delia Day's driver.

'Is . . . is that Delia down there?' he stumbled. 'Uh . . . I've just come to get her . . .'

Vogel confirmed quietly that it was indeed Delia.

Michael looked stricken.

'I was l–late to pick her up from the festival,' he continued, his speech still halting. 'She said she'd walk into the village and meet me here. This could be my fault . . .'

Clearly, the man had seen nothing. Vogel muttered vague reassurances and moved on to question several other bystanders who had stepped forward to say they had witnessed the incident, but none of them really had, it seemed. All spoke of being alerted by the sound of Delia Day calling out, screaming according to the man with the dog. No one seemed to have seen exactly what caused her fall.

Suddenly, Vogel's attention, and that of everyone else, was attracted by the sound of Appledore's Atlantic 85 lifeboat powering up the river. Vogel didn't know a lot about boats of any sort, but he could understand just from looking at her how she could be safely beached on a riverbed. The coxswain steered her sharply right towards Delia and her two helpers, and gently bottomed her on the soft mud. Two lifeboat crew assisted the paramedics, whom they must have provided with the rubber thigh boots they were now wearing, out of the boat and across the mud to Delia. Their equipment had been loaded on to a kind of raft which one of the lifeboatmen towed behind him.

The paramedics worked fast. In just a few minutes, Delia, wrapped in a foil survival blanket, had been strapped on to a stretcher and loaded aboard. The two men who had rushed to Delia's assistance followed. They were covered in wet mud, and even though it still felt like a warm day up on the quay-side, they looked as if they might be suffering both from exposure and a kind of delayed shock. One of them was visibly shaking. Both had been given foil blankets to wrap around themselves.

Vogel watched as the crew pushed the lifeboat out again – the incoming tide had already lifted it off the bottom – and take off downstream on the short journey back to the Irsha Street station.

He took some names and addresses of onlookers who might be regarded as witnesses, in case he needed to get in touch again, then returned to the Seagate where he apologized once more to his wife and daughter.

He told them what had happened, and that it was Delia Day, romantic novelist extraordinaire, who had fallen, very nearly to her death, off the quay into the riverbed.

'We need to investigate obviously,' said Vogel. 'Nobody seems to know what happened to make her fall.'

'Couldn't it have been an accident?' remarked Mary reasonably. 'Accidents do happen, David, particularly where there's water combined with a steep drop.'

'It could, of course,' responded Vogel. 'And James Harding may well have died of natural causes, as I and almost everybody else initially thought. But that's one eminent writer, an invited guest at the Appledore festival, dead, and another seriously injured in a somewhat freakish incident. Both on the same day. And less than a couple of hours apart. Could be coincidental but—'

'But you don't believe in coincidences,' Mary interrupted.

'No.'

'Coincidences also do happen, David.'

'Once in a blue moon. I operate on the principle that they don't happen, as you well know. Not when I'm investigating the possibility of criminal violence. Therefore, I'm already inclined to believe that these two incidents could well be linked and be part of something extremely sinister. I suggest you take the car and drive home with Rosamund, darling. I'm getting Saslow over here. She can drive me. I'm really sorry, but I may have a lot of work to do.'

'OK.'

Mary stood up from the table. She rested one hand lightly on her husband's arm.

'Are you aware that James Harding used to live locally?' she asked.

'Vaguely. Do you think that's significant?'

Vogel knew his wife well, as he should after almost a quarter of a century of marriage. She rarely made even the most casual-sounding remark about anything concerning his work without good reason.

'I've no idea,' Mary continued. 'It's just . . . well, if his death does prove to be suspicious, to be murder, isn't it likely that there might be a reason for him having been killed in such a public manner at a book festival in the very place where he used to live?'

Vogel was stopped in his tracks.

'What, actually here? He lived in Appledore?'

'Yes, Irsha Street, the original arty street. Still full of writers and painters, but only rich ones nowadays. It's been gentrified. Harding moved away six or seven years ago after his first marriage broke up, largely thanks to the affair he was having with the woman who became the second Mrs Harding.'

'How do you know all this?'

'Magazine article – a profile following up a news item. He's quite big news, you know. Cornered the market in screen romances. Always book adaptations, not original work, but he puts his stamp on it. One of the novelists took umbrage a while back, and there was a rather public row.'

'Not Delia Day?'

'No, not Delia. From what I've heard, she'd be far too canny to let any such feelings show in public. Bet she has them, though. I mean, wouldn't you?'

Vogel could not imagine even the remotest possibility of his writing a work of romantic fiction, let alone getting involved in a rumpus over it.

He handed over the car keys and walked Mary and Rosamund to the door, apologizing to his daughter again and giving her an extra big hug. Which he suspected made up for nothing.

'You have asked about Storey, haven't you, Dad?' Rosamund enquired.

Vogel kicked himself.

'No news yet, Rossy,' he replied obliquely. 'But everybody's still looking. We won't give up.'

He stood in the doorway for a few seconds, waving his wife and daughter goodbye, then he asked Peter Carter if there was anywhere private he could go in order to set up an enquiry. The landlord ushered him into a small back room without windows.

'It's a storeroom really,' said Carter apologetically. 'Best I can do, I'm afraid. We're packed out because of the festival.'

As well as piles of boxes and crates of beer, there were two chairs, a small table and a couple of electricity points. And the Wi-Fi proved to work. It was good enough.

First Vogel phoned Saslow. Detective Sergeant Dawn Saslow. They had worked together for some years now. He could no longer imagine conducting a major enquiry without her.

'Sorry to call you out on a Sunday—' he began.

'Course you are, boss,' interrupted Saslow.

Vogel couldn't help smiling. They were easy together nowadays, he and his favourite DS. He ignored her interruption and continued.

'Afraid I need you pronto. We've got a curious one. Might still be nothing to concern us, but I'm beginning to think it could turn into something pretty big.'

He gave Saslow a quick rundown on the death of James Harding and the apparent accident that had befallen Delia Day.

'What do you want me to do, boss?' asked Saslow.

'I want you to get over here to me at the Seagate,' he instructed. 'I've had to send Mary and Rosamund home in the car. I've some setting up to do, and then you and I need to make a plan. I'll fill you in with more detail when you get here.'

They ended the call. He immediately dialled again. This time he dialled the number of the regional Home Office pathologist, Daisy Dobbs. She also picked up on the second ring, to Vogel's relief. If roles were reversed, he wasn't sure he would pick up to a DCI on a Sunday. Not quite so quickly, anyway.

'Hope I haven't interrupted anything,' he began.

'Just an orgy of ancient TV – a *Dad's Army* box set, followed by *'Allo 'Allo!*' Daisy replied. 'In bed, obviously. And on my own.'

Vogel found himself smiling again.

Professor Daisy Dobbs, the youngest Home Office pathologist in the country, with her outlandish streetwise style of dress and feisty manner, did not seem the sort of person who would spend Sunday afternoon in bed with vintage TV comedy. Nor, come to that, did she seem like the type of person who would spend Sunday afternoon in bed on her own! But, a bit like Saslow, Daisy had never ceased to surprise Vogel since they'd first met a year or so previously. Perhaps that was why he liked them both so much.

'There was a sudden death at the Appledore Book Festival this morning, suspected heart attack,' he told her. 'James Harding, the screenwriter. His body has been taken to the morgue at the North Devon District Hospital, and there would be a post-mortem eventually, obviously. But I want it fast-tracked. I now have serious doubts that he died of natural causes. And I need to know one way or another as quickly as possible.'

'I see. Are you saying you think it could be murder?'

'I'm saying I need you to tell me whether or not my suspicions are correct . . .'

'But what exactly *are* your suspicions?' Daisy persisted. 'Do you have any evidence to suggest the man may have been murdered?'

'Not exactly,' said Vogel.

He decided it might be best not to relate Felicity Smythe's assertion that the manner of James Harding's death had closely resembled the passing of one of her fictional victims who'd been poisoned by serum taken from a killer spider.

'But I'm now investigating two serious incidents connected with the festival, one resulting in death and the other in serious injury, both of which have happened on the same day,' Vogel continued. 'As you know, Daisy, I don't believe in coincidence.'

Daisy agreed that she knew that well enough. Vogel gave her a brief rundown on what had happened to Delia Day.

'Right, I'm on it,' said Daisy. 'Let's just hope I don't end up doing two post-mortems in a hurry.'

'Indeed,' said Vogel.

He then called Detective Superintendent Nobby Clarke, head of Devon and Cornwall Police's Major Crimes Team and his immediate superior – a woman with whom he shared quite a past, some good, some bad.

'I thought I should alert you straight away, although I don't really know where we are going with this yet, boss,' he said.

Clarke, not an officer who liked to stand on ceremony, preferred everyone, including the men and women under her command to address her by her nickname, Nobby. Certainly not Ma'am, and certainly not by her real Christian name, which was a closely guarded secret. But Vogel had never been entirely comfortable with that, particularly after the case a few years previously which had caused something of a rift between them. Whilst he had from the beginning acquiesced to her wish for the M word not to be used, she had almost always been 'boss' to him, and now would remain so. Their one-time close friendship had broken down irretrievably over that unfortunate case, to the regret of them both, Vogel suspected. And he was aware that, since then, she had stopped even trying to get him to call her Nobby. They continued to operate a good working relationship. But that was all. And sometimes even that seemed a little strained to Vogel.

'I'm happy to make enquiries with Saslow, calling in the wooden tops if we need help, until the post-mortem is done or we unearth something which gives us cause to step things up,' he continued. 'But my gut feeling is that we could soon be forced to launch a full-scale murder investigation.'

There was silence at the other end of the phone. Vogel did not break it. He knew that Clarke would take his 'gut feeling' opinion very seriously. Vogel was not a fanciful kind of policeman. He didn't do hunches as such. There were already several aspects concerning the two incidents connected with the festival which gave him very real cause for professional concern. And Clarke would be well aware that he would not have bothered her – at any time, let alone on a Sunday – were that not so.

'OK, Vogel, I'll go along with you on this,' she said eventually. 'You and Saslow get stuck in. The quicker we know exactly what we are dealing with here the better, but I don't have to tell you that. How about CSI?'

'I've no idea if it will be worth it, boss, Harding died several hours ago. Nobody – including me, I'm afraid – seriously considered anything but natural causes. Except for the rather excitable crime writer who called it in, which is why I was contacted. At the time, her assessment seemed pretty laughable. Not anymore. Albeit more by luck, or bad luck, than judgement. No doubt the scene has been contaminated over and over again since then, but I was going to ask you if we could give it a go.'

'If we have a team available, I'll get them over there ASAP – you never know,' responded Clarke. 'And I'll get Ricky Perkins on side to help you out straight away, or as soon as

I can get hold of him. Good lad. Keen. You've worked with him before, haven't you?'

Vogel agreed that he had. And he remembered DC Perkins well. An earnest young man who wore a more or less permanently anxious expression on his long, thin, overly pale face. Clarke was right. Perkins was an excellent detective.

'I'll have a Major Crimes Team ready to slot in if this does turn into a murder enquiry,' Nobby Clarke continued. 'We'll need an incident room. Do you have anywhere in mind?'

'I've headed up two murder enquiries before around here,' Vogel responded. 'And each time we used the old police station at Bideford.'

'Good idea. No doubt they'll be thrilled to welcome you and your lot back again.'

Vogel thought he detected a hint of a chuckle in the super's voice. It was well known that specialist major crime units were never welcomed with open arms in police stations anywhere. Generally, they were regarded by the grass-roots coppers who staffed the regional stations as 'flash gits'. Certainly no more likely to solve a high-profile crime on their patch than they were. Indeed, often less likely, it was frequently mooted.

The setting up of a murder enquiry and its staffing was a slightly different matter. The local boys and girls, uniform and CID, would know only too well that they needed all the help they could get, and the staffing levels required by such enquiries demanded an influx not only from their own force's specialist units but also often detachments of officers from other forces.

'No doubt they will, boss,' he repeated, deadpan.

'Make sure you keep me informed, that's all,' Clarke continued.

'I certainly will, boss,' said Vogel. 'As soon as we end this call, I'm going to check on just how badly hurt Delia Day is. If she's well enough, I'll make sure I interview her today, even if it's later tonight. But I've no idea either way yet. It's possible she might not even survive. She looked pretty rough when she was carried on to the lifeboat. Meanwhile, Saslow should be here any moment, and unless anything else happens, I want us both back at the festival site soonest. I did some interviews there before, but I wasn't really focused . . .'

He paused. No, he hadn't been focused. There were considerable mitigating circumstances, but he had been rather more preoccupied with having abandoned both his family and his plum crumble than anything else, and he was somewhat ashamed of himself. He was a senior professional murder investigator, for goodness' sake. And he had barely investigated at all.

'Not as much as I should have been, I'm afraid, boss,' he continued honestly. 'Even the paramedics thought Harding had suffered a heart attack, and I just took it all at face value. Like everyone else.'

'You're not infallible, Vogel, none of us can always be perfect,' responded Clarke.

There was a distinct edge to her voice, Vogel was sure of it. *None of us can always be perfect.* Perhaps a reminder of what had happened between them on that other job, that other enquiry which was always going to be close to the surface for both of them.

'I'm certainly aware of that,' he replied mildly.

'Yes, well, I hope so,' she responded obliquely. 'I'll leave you to get on with it, then. Just one thing, though: remember it was you who may not have conducted your earlier interviews at the festival with enough intent, and therefore not necessarily the fault of the people you interviewed. I'm just saying, don't come down on them like a ton of bricks, Vogel. The festival is an important entry in the North Devon calendar, brings a lot of tourists in and has become quite prestigious. Let's exercise discretion until or unless it becomes impossible to do so. OK?'

Vogel's shoulders tightened. She was doing it again. She'd never been like this back in the day, when they'd been in the Met together and she had plucked him out of nowhere to become her number two in MIT. Nowadays, all too often, when he had a conversation with her, he was left thinking that she had an agenda other than the only one he ever had – which was a fervent desire to chase down criminals and make them pay for their crimes. All too often, he ended up convinced that politics lurked behind so much of Clarke's dialogue. He felt that again now. And he didn't like it, even though this was probably a fairly innocent example from the super, expressing concerns most top cops would have over the area they policed. But she had more or less given him the go-ahead to launch whatever investigation he saw fit. And that was all he wanted from her. For now.

'Of course, boss,' he said levelly.

Saslow arrived within a few minutes of the call ending. Vogel was extremely pleased to see her. Although any onlooker would not necessarily have guessed that. He barely said hello. His first words to her were purely business, without even the most perfunctory greeting.

'Right, then, let's get out to the festival site and this time give the third degree to anyone who can give us any clue at all as to what really happened to James Harding,' he began.

He supposed that was pretty much the approach Clarke had warned him against, but he didn't care. Vogel only knew one way of conducting any investigation. His way. He also knew he was only very rarely bombastic in his approach. Nor was Saslow. She would not be his favourite sergeant if that were the case.

'I'll brief you fully on the way,' he told her.

His phone buzzed before he could say any more.

It was Nobby Clarke already. She'd managed to get hold of Ricky Perkins who was now on standby. Vogel called him at once and dispatched him to the North Devon District Hospital, both to find out exactly how Delia Day was and to keep as close a watch over her as possible. The DCI didn't want any more 'accidents'.

As soon as he'd finished, Vogel addressed Saslow again.

'Where's your car,' he asked.

'Right outside, double-parked,' she told him.

He would have expected no less.

Jenny was on duty at reception at the Imperial when she heard of Delia Day's fall from Appledore Quay. And she heard even before the news was posted on social media.

Ian the concierge told her. His wife, the Bideford girl he had moved from London to marry, had been walking their dog along Appledore Quay when Delia fell. Ruth didn't actually see the incident, but she had moved closer to find out what had happened just as the paramedics arrived, and heard the mutterings about the victim being Delia. And, of course, she'd called her husband at once, because he had told her that Delia was staying at the Imperial.

Jenny was shocked to the core.

'How badly hurt is she?' Jenny asked straight away.

'It's pretty bad. Ruth said she seemed to be unconscious at first and looked to be quite badly knocked about. Apparently, she'd regained consciousness a bit before they took her off to hospital.'

'Oh, good,' said Jenny, hoping she didn't sound as absurd as she felt.

There was nothing good about it at all. But her first reaction had been immense relief that Delia Day wasn't dead. Jenny was in turmoil. Jenny had agreed to do something, something that was totally against her nature, something she never should have done. But she'd felt that she had no choice. Nonetheless, she couldn't quite believe she'd done it. It not only went against all her principles but was quite unforgivable for a person in a position of trust. A position she took very seriously. Jenny was not ambitious in any way. She had no desire whatsoever to leave North Devon. She was one of those who thought she was immensely lucky and privileged to have been born in such a wonderful place. She knew she was no academic genius – barely average, in fact – and had never wished to go to university or college. Neither had she ever desired to be a high flier in business, not even locally. The job of receptionist at the Imperial suited Jenny absolutely. She was working in what she regarded as the best hotel in the area, amongst people she liked and was comfortable with. She was related to several of them, knew them all quite well and was friends with most of them. The height of Jenny's ambition was that she might become head receptionist, and perhaps, one day in the distant future, an assistant manager. Unless she was lucky enough to meet the right man and marry, of course. And maybe have children. Even in that regard, Jenny was not ambitious. If it happened, it would be lovely. But if it didn't, she had the job which meant so much to her, amidst all those people who were so important to her.

Or she had until this business had started. Suddenly, all of it was in jeopardy. It felt to Jenny as if her entire life was in jeopardy.

Now Delia Day had been seriously injured and taken to hospital, and there was a distinct possibility that Jenny was involved. However remotely. That's how she saw it, anyway.

'So, how did it happen?' she asked Ian, trying not to show her anxiety.

'Nobody seems to know – not exactly, anyway,' the concierge replied.

'Well, I mean, presumably it was an accident, wasn't it?'

Ian looked puzzled.

'Yes. Of course it was an accident. What else would it be? Ruth said there was a big crush of people on The Quay today, and someone might well have bumped into Delia, caused her to stumble. But nobody seems to know for certain.'

'Well, if there were so many people there, how come there aren't any witnesses?'

'I expect there are witnesses. How should I know?'

'Are the police involved?' asked Jenny, her heart racing.

'I don't know. Why are you asking all these questions?'

'Oh, sorry,' said Jenny. 'It's just with her staying here and everything, I feel kind of responsible.'

'What for, for God's sake?'

'N–nothing. I expect I'm just being silly. But, um, I'm wondering, are there people we should contact?'

'Well, I was about to tell Bob. That's up to him really, isn't it?'

Bob was the general manager.

'Of course,' said Jenny, managing what she hoped was a bit of a smile rather than a grimace.

Ian headed off in the direction of Bob's office.

Then he turned back.

'Are you all right, Jenny?' he asked. 'Is something bothering you?'

'Of course not. I'm fine,' Jenny lied.

THIRTEEN

Vogel called the festival director upon arrival at the site and told her he needed to talk to her again as a matter of urgency.

Carolyne Smedley emerged at once from the main marquee where, James Harding's body having been removed and the initial police presence departed, the festival was continuing pretty much as planned. So far. She hurried towards them, looking anxious.

'Is something wrong, Detective Chief Inspector,' she asked.

'Apart from one of your principal contributors dropping dead on stage, you mean?' Vogel enquired.

He couldn't help himself. He had encountered this sort of response before when conducting an enquiry into a suspicious death. Murder could be so darned inconvenient.

'I'm sorry, I mean, yes, of course, I know, it's just, uh . . .'

Carolyne seemed to run out of words. She was flustered, aware that she could well be accused of having made an extremely insensitive remark. Vogel didn't dwell on it.

'Well, yes, I fear something might well be very wrong,' he told her. 'Do I take it you haven't heard about Delia Day?'

Carolyne shook her head, looking even more anxious.

CSI, the Crime Scene Investigators, had yet to arrive, assuming that Nobby Clarke had even managed to raise a team to check out what had initially been dismissed as a death by natural causes. And doubtless the festival created its own bubble, within which the contributors and all concerned existed during their participation, largely unaware, for a relatively brief period, of what was going on in the outside world. It was perhaps not surprising that Carolyne had yet to hear the news, although Vogel already knew that he wasn't the only person who at least thought they had recognized Delia at the quayside, even if she was lying partially covered in mud. She was so distinctive, and it was also possible that there had been people looking down at her on the riverbed who had recently seen her at close quarters at the festival.

'Delia Day fell over Appledore Quay an hour or so ago and has been injured, perhaps quite badly,' he told Carolyne.

Her jaw dropped. It really did.

'Oh my God,' she said. 'I don't believe it.'

'Indeed, that's two grave incidents involving festival delegates on the same afternoon,' Vogel continued. 'First of all, I want to go over again with you in detail everything that happened leading up to James Harding's collapse and death. Absolutely everything you know. Is there somewhere we can talk in private?'

Carolyne suggested the tent which served as a green room.

'It won't be used by anyone else today now. The crime panel in session at the moment, which we had to postpone earlier, is our last of the day.'

Vogel thought that he was likely to make sure it was the last for some time, the way things were going. But he did not say so. Instead, he introduced Saslow properly to Carolyne as she led the way to the green room.

As soon as they were settled, Carolyne began to relate the part she had played in the Harding/Day panel.

'I looked after them until they went on stage,' she said. 'Then Janey Lucas took over, of course. She introduced Delia and James, then began to ask questions designed to lead them into the sort of animated conversation we were all hoping for. And it did just that, building up into an excellent event. The audience was really into it. They listened keenly and were eager to take part, to ask questions, as soon as they were invited to do so. Delia has an enormous following, as I'm sure you know, and James was very well known, too, with a number of high-profile TV series to his name. He used to live locally, too. It was all going so well. Until James collapsed, rather dramatically, as you know. And suddenly. There was no indication before of anything amiss. Really there wasn't.'

'Are you absolutely sure of that, Miss Smedley?' Vogel persisted. 'Was there nothing that was even very slightly out of order, not as it should be? Sometimes in situations like this, all of us, including police officers, fail to register the significance of minor anomalies.'

'Well, no, everything was as it should be. Oh, except that the two participants sat down in the wrong chairs, behind the wrong name cards. So I sort of followed them on stage, and while they were settling into their chairs and the audience was applauding them, and Janey was still doing introductions, I moved the labels around, whilst at the same time pouring out some apple juice for them, so it didn't look conspicuous. Or I hoped it didn't. But there couldn't be any significance in that, surely?'

Vogel looked at her in amazement.

'I think it could be highly significant,' he said, keeping his voice as calm as he could manage.

Carolyne stared at him in silence for a moment or two.

'Oh my God,' she said eventually. 'You don't think James Harding had a heart attack, do you? You think he may have been murdered? Just like Felicity said, but we all thought, didn't we, that—'

'I don't know, Miss Smedley, and I am keeping an open mind,' Vogel interrupted, not wanting the festival director to get too carried away. 'But I *will* know. There is now going to be a post-mortem examination of Mr Harding, sooner rather than later.'

'And if he didn't have a heart attack, if . . . if someone did something to him, something to cause his death, then it could have been a mistake because James was sitting behind the wrong name card,' Carolyne continued, almost as if Vogel hadn't spoken. 'The target could have been someone else – could have been Delia. And then they had another go. On the quayside. Somebody pushed her over. Is that what you now think happened, Mr Vogel?'

'That is a possibility we will be investigating,' Vogel agreed. 'But, as I told you, I am keeping an open mind for the time being. I have to say, though, Miss Smedley, I am rather surprised that you didn't think to mention the name-card incident when we spoke earlier. And neither did anyone else. People in the audience must have noticed it, surely?'

'It was hardly an incident. Or it didn't seem like it at the time. I don't think Janey noticed; I think she was looking down at her notes whilst I put it right. And James and Delia were probably concentrating on what was coming next. Of course, it seems likely that at least some members of the audience would have noticed, but I don't expect they would have thought anything of it. As I didn't. Not a particularly unusual thing to happen, I can assure you, Mr Vogel. And everyone was convinced James had suffered a heart attack; even the paramedics from what I recall. It certainly looked like a heart attack . . .'

'Sometimes we see what we want to see, or, even more commonly, what we expect to see,' responded Vogel. 'What we have to do now is look at the facts and study any evidence that might still be retrievable. I'm hoping a CSI team will be here later this evening.'

'CSI? Crime scene investigators? Here? Really?'

'Uh, yes—'

'What sort of evidence are you hoping might still be retrievable?' interrupted Carolyne.

'Well, certainly CSI would want to do tests on the apple juice bottles which were on the table in front of the panellists and the moderator – in particular the broken one which Mr Harding had drunk from, obviously,' replied Vogel. 'And the glasses they would have been drinking from. Or would they have been washed up already?'

'Oh, no,' exclaimed Carolyne. 'We use disposable plastic glasses. You may not have noticed – they look quite good. We have no proper kitchen facilities, so I'm afraid it's hygiene over ecology . . .'

She paused abruptly.

'For goodness' sake, what are you saying now, Mr Vogel? Are you suggesting James might have been poisoned? Just like Felicity Smythe said. In the middle of an event at our festival? In front of hundreds of people? In spite of all those potential witnesses?'

'Well, as you partially explained yourself, maybe *because* of that,' responded Vogel. 'I just don't know. Not yet. But I will. I've already promised you that. Now, what will have happened to those juice bottles and plastic glasses? Are they retrievable?'

'They'll have been binned,' said Carolyne. 'Along with all the others used today and yesterday. We have several commercial wheelie bins on site, which are emptied daily, but not today because it's Sunday. They'll be full to the brim, I'm afraid. Glass and plastic are separated, of course, as best we can. But a lot of the bottles will have broken as they were tossed into the bins, so the one James Harding knocked off the table will just be one of many broken bottles, I'm sorry to have to tell you.'

Vogel experienced a sinking feeling. He had noticed a Devon Glory stall alongside the main marquee, selling bottles of the sponsor's apple juice to all and sundry. In addition, of course, to the bottles supplied to all the participants in the various events. He dreaded to think how many bottles and plastic glasses there would be in those bins. Amongst goodness knows what else that might have been disposed of, whether it should have been or not. But there was nothing he could do about that. He turned his attention back to what he could do that might move the investigation forward.

'Miss Smedley, you mentioned that the event in session at the moment is a panel of crime writers. I wonder, is Felicity Smythe involved? I'd like to talk to her again.'

'Yes, she is.' Carolyne glanced at her watch. Vogel knew it was nearly eight p.m. 'And the panel should be ending now. Felicity will be taken backstage to have her microphone removed and so on. I'll go and find her for you.'

Vogel thanked Carolyne and asked her if she could also request that anybody who had been at the Harding/Day event, or had any connection to the two writers, would kindly wait behind.

Carolyne agreed that she would do that then asked, albeit a little hesitantly: 'I—uh wonder, do you think there's any chance of Delia recovering by tomorrow night? She has another event, you see; she's supposed to be introducing a screening of Love's Dream Eternal . . .'

The programming of her festival clearly remained Carolyne Smedley's primary concern in spite of one sudden death and another near death. Vogel was struck again by the woman's insensitivity, although he did not let it show.

'I should think that is highly unlikely,' he remarked evenly.
By then, it seemed that the crime writers' panel had indeed
ended. The audience was pouring out of the marquee into the
field, several of them talking animatedly to each other and
poking at their mobile phones. Vogel guessed that the news
was out on social media about Delia Day's fall, just as he had
expected it to be. Probably on Twitter or Facebook, or both.
He'd been right. That distinctive hair and Delia's unique style
of dress would have been enough for it to be likely that she
would be recognized by the somewhat voyeuristic group at
the quayside. Mud or no mud. Plus the incident that had led
to Delia being hospitalized had occurred at the heart of the
village staging the festival at which she had been on public
display for three days.

Two young women suddenly detached themselves from
the throng spilling out on to the grass and ran across the
field towards Vogel and Saslow. They had to be twins,
identical twins, thought the DCI. They were alike in every
way, including the flowing cotton dresses they had both
chosen to wear that day and the big floppy sun hats, which
they were each holding on to their heads with one hand
as they ran. With the other, they were waving frantically.
They presented an unusual sight, not least because they
were both in floods of tears. And they were weeping not only
copiously, but also noisily.

They were, of course, the Tucker twins.

'Are you the police – you are, aren't you?' they cried in
unison, struggling to get the words out through their sobs.

Strange how a uniform was so often not necessary for police
officers to be spotted, thought Vogel, not for the first time.
Even when those doing the sobbing were very nearly hyster-
ical. Of course, the two women may already have seen him
earlier in the day. He agreed that he and Saslow were indeed
the police.

'We want to know how Delia is. Please, please tell us.'

Vogel explained that he could not give out any information
at this stage, beyond telling them that she had been taken to
hospital, and asked them who they were.

'I'm Tilly Tucker, and this is my twin sister, Tina, and

we are Delia Day's greatest fans, her super-fans, though actually . . .'

'. . . much more than that. We are her friends, very good friends . . .' Tina continued.

'. . . she even drove us to our digs on the first night . . .'

'. . . in the rain. She always has time for us, we've known her for years, we go everywhere she goes . . .'

'. . . so we are frantic with worry . . .'

'. . . I mean, she's not dead is she?'

'. . . it says on Twitter that she could be dead . . .'

'. . . she isn't, is she? Please tell us she isn't . . .'

'. . . she can't be, she just can't be . . .'

Vogel was more than a little overwhelmed. He began to blink rapidly behind his round-rimmed, heavy-lensed spectacles, something he always did when he felt awkward or embarrassed. He had no idea how best to deal with these two, even though he realized they could probably be quite useful, in spite of their bizarre appearance and behaviour. Saslow stepped in smartly to the rescue.

'Just take it easy, ladies,' she said. 'We can't tell you much, but we can tell you that Miss Day is very much alive. And being well cared for.'

The twins hugged each other, emitting little squeaks of joy and relief. Saslow shot Vogel an enquiring look. He nodded very slightly, clearly indicating that she should continue.

'She is in hospital, as Mr Vogel said, and we understand that she is conscious and doing well . . .'

'Oh, thank you, thank you . . .' interrupted the twins excitedly.

'. . . it's just such a relief . . .'

'. . . we couldn't bear to lose her . . .'

'. . . she is so important to us, you see . . .'

'Yes, I do see,' said Saslow, who didn't see at all. She had no understanding whatsoever of fan culture. But she did see, just as Vogel had, that Tilly and Tina were likely to be useful.

'And I'm sure you would like to help Miss Day, wouldn't you?' Saslow continued.

The twins agreed in enthusiastic chorus that they would.

'Right. I have some questions for you. I presume you were

at the event with Delia and James Harding when Mr Harding died?'

'Oh, yes, of course, we never miss any of Delia's events,' said one twin.

'Never, not ever, we're always there,' said the other.

'Perhaps you could describe to us exactly what you saw.'

The twins did so in their usual peculiar duet. Vogel continued to find them quite disconcerting for reasons he could not fully explain. Their account matched exactly almost every other he had so far heard, including Carolyne Smedley's. But they made no mention of name-card swapping.

'Are you sure you didn't notice anything unusual before Mr Harding collapsed?' Vogel asked.

They both said that they hadn't.

'Didn't you see that Miss Day and Mr Harding sat in the wrong seats, and that the festival director changed their name cards around?'

The twins looked at each other.

'I don't think we noticed, I mean . . .' one of them began.

'. . . we were just watching Delia . . .' continued the other.

'. . . we wouldn't need to look at her name card, would we?'

'. . . or his . . .'

'. . . no, certainly not his.'

Vogel's ears pricked. Had he perhaps picked up on a little edge there?

'. . . we may have noticed somebody moving things around on the table . . .'

'. . . not sure, and certainly we didn't take much notice.'

'OK, so could you describe please exactly what you saw happen when Mr Harding collapsed,' Vogel asked.

The twins did so, in detailed unison, and their account matched almost exactly what Vogel had been told already by the principal witnesses.

'So what did you do after the event was over?' Vogel enquired.

'Well, we left when we were told everybody could go, should go even – except Delia, of course, and the moderator, Janey Lucas. And Felicity Smythe. She'd come right forward when it happened, and we heard her call the emergency services. She seemed to know exactly what to do. Do you think that's because she's a crime writer?'

Vogel stifled a groan. He said he had no idea.

'Didn't you wait for Delia outside?' he asked. 'From what you say, I would have thought you might have wanted to check she was all right.'

'We did . . .' began one of the twins.

'. . . we waited for ages, but we were outside the main entrance to the marquee. We were waiting for her driver to turn up there. That's what happened before. But he didn't come, and when we next looked inside, after the paramedics had arrived, and you'd left, Delia wasn't there . . .'

Of course. That made sense. Vogel already knew from Delia's driver that she had arranged to walk into Appledore to meet him there. And she had presumably left the marquee through the backstage entrance. The DCI had not really taken that on board.

'. . . so we hung around for a bit, in case she was still around somewhere, peeped in the green room and so on, and then, well, when we realized things were still going on in the second marquee, we thought we might as well join in . . .'

'. . . yes, that woman who writes those self-help books about getting published and all sorts of things, Mary Carmichael, was doing a workshop, and we like her, don't we . . .'

'. . . though not as much as Delia obviously . . .'

'. . . nothing like as much as Delia . . .'

'. . . but we like her . . .'

'. . . then when the main marquee opened up again, we went into the crime writers' panel, because George and Felicity Smythe were on it . . .'

'. . . and we already had a ticket . . .'

'. . . because we like them, too . . .'

'. . . though, of course, not as much as Delia.'

'. . . we don't like anyone as much as Delia.'

Vogel reckoned the twins were veering off-piste. Even by their own obscure standards. And he didn't feel that he and Saslow were likely to learn anything more from them. Not anything constructive, anyway. He thanked them and sent them on their way, first assuring them, in answer to their continued anxious requests for information about Delia, that he would be keeping Carolyne Smedley informed of Delia's progress, and that they should check with her.

The two women began to walk off, all the while chattering to each other sotto voce. After a few steps, they turned back.

'Do you think we might be able to go to see Delia?' asked one of them.

'No,' said Vogel abruptly. He was beginning to run out of patience with the Tucker twins. He had other matters to concern him.

But he relented slightly.

'Even the police can't see her at the moment,' he continued.

'It is important,' said the twins, partly in unison again and partly speaking alternately.

'Yes, we have something to tell her . . .'

'. . . something that she needs to know . . .'

'. . . so we really need to see her . . .'

'. . . as soon as possible, yes.'

By then, they had at least attracted Vogel's full attention again.

'So let me get this straight. You are saying that it is a matter of urgency for you two to see Delia, because you have something important to tell her that she needs to know – is that right?'

'Yes, that's it, that's right,' said the twins.

'In that case,' countered Vogel. 'You'd better tell me what it is, hadn't you?'

The twins looked at each other, panic in their eyes.

'Oh no, we couldn't do that,' said one.

'Oh no,' said the other.

'Really? Well, then, I shall have to arrest you for withholding information which might be pertinent to a very serious police investigation,' said Vogel, who had absolutely no intention of doing any such thing. It wasn't just that he wouldn't; he really couldn't.

A look of total panic once more passed between the two young women.

'Oh, it's nothing really . . . nothing to do with anything here . . . no, just something personal between us and Delia . . . it's

not urgent, no, not really . . . don't know why we said it was
. . . we just want to see her . . . it can wait . . . obviously.'

The twins spoke almost together as they so often did and
were both gabbling.

'Are you quite sure of that?' asked Vogel.

'Oh yes, quite sure,' said one twin quickly.

'Yes. And we're so sorry to have bothered you both,' said
the other.

'Don't take any notice of us, we always get things wrong . . .'

'. . . yes, that's right, don't take any notice of us. Nobody
else ever does . . .'

'. . . no, and we need to go now, we need to go to the loo . . .'

'. . . yes, that's right, we need to go to the loo . . .'

A rather strange and somewhat disconcerting use of the
plural pronoun, thought Vogel, as the twins began to back off,
looking rather as if they expected him to stop them. He didn't.

'That's all right, isn't it?' they asked.

'I think it's going to have to be,' muttered Vogel resignedly.

The twins then turned, linked arms and hurried off in the
direction of the ladies' toilets.

'What on earth do you make of that, Saslow?' asked Vogel.

'I think they're barking mad, boss,' replied Saslow. 'You
only have to look at them . . .'

'Which, of course, could be the intention.'

'What do you mean, boss?'

'Well, looking and behaving the way they do, I would
imagine they can do pretty much what they like at these events
and nobody bats an eyelid.'

'Possibly. But so what? Personally, I think they just like
drawing attention to themselves. Everything about them points
to that. The way they dress and look. Even their talking double
act. They just want to seem different, special, important even.'

'You could be right about that, Saslow,' Vogel agreed. 'But
I somehow wouldn't rule out them being important. To our
investigation anyway.'

'Really, boss?'

'Really, Saslow. They may well know something significant
that they don't want to share with us. I certainly don't think
they are quite what they seem.'

'Well, I suppose that makes sense,' said Saslow. 'How could anybody really be how those two seem?'

'Who knows? They may be just slightly mad and don't know anything of any importance to anyone. I'd like to know more about them, though. Get on to Barnstaple and ask them to put someone on it, will you?'

Saslow took her phone from her pocket and was about to call Barnstaple nick when she suddenly stopped, tapped the screen with both fingers to enlarge an image and passed her phone to Vogel.

He found himself looking at a surprisingly clear image of Delia Day lying on the riverbed at Appledore. Her face was muddy but the picture was pin sharp. Her identity could be in no doubt.

'There are more,' murmured Saslow.

Vogel scrolled sideways, displaying further images of Delia, including one of her being carried across the riverbed on a stretcher, and another of her being loaded on to the Appledore lifeboat.

'Well, that should start a media frenzy,' Vogel commented.

'Yes, boss,' agreed Saslow. 'And anybody at the Harding/Day event this afternoon who didn't know about the Delia incident certainly does now, I reckon.'

Vogel agreed with her.

'I just can't believe that Carolyne Smedley failed to mention the name-card swapping thing,' he remarked. 'And Felicity Smythe didn't mention it either, which is peculiar, because you would have thought she would have come forward straight away to tell us about anything that might have looked remotely suspicious.'

He glanced across at the main marquee and saw that Carolyne was walking around it from the backstage area at the rear, bringing Felicity with her.

He walked towards them. Felicity was looking rather pleased with herself.

'I understand my suggestion that James Harding may not have died of natural causes is no longer being ridiculed, Detective Chief Inspector,' she began.

'There was never any question of ridicule,' responded Vogel

evenly, taking Felicity to one side and gesturing to Saslow to follow. 'I always told you that his death would be appropriately investigated. But the police can only ever be guided by evidence, and whilst we continue to investigate, we still have no direct evidence pointing towards anything other than natural causes.'

Felicity looked slightly less pleased with herself. But only slightly.

'Meanwhile, I have one or two more questions for you,' Vogel continued. 'I wondered what sort of a view you had of Mr Harding's panel with Delia Day, and where in the marquee you were sitting?'

'I wasn't. I wasn't in the audience.'

'You weren't in the audience? But you earlier described to me, in some detail, exactly what happened to Mr Harding.'

'Yes. George and I were backstage getting ready for the crime writers' panel, which was scheduled to start next. I was in the wings, as it were, peeping through, but I was actually only a few feet away from James, and I had an excellent view of what happened, if that's what you are getting at.'

'Did your husband also witness James Harding's death?'

'No, he didn't. George was chatting to the sound man, Billy. They're old chums. He didn't see anything. He heard the commotion and stepped forward to see what was going on, but James was already lying dead on the ground by then. It happened so fast.'

'So I understand. May I ask how much of the event you actually saw, Mrs Smythe?'

'Oh, only about five minutes or so, then James collapsed, and that was that.'

'So you weren't in the marquee for the beginning of the event, when Mr Harding and Miss Day were introduced by Janey Lucas?'

'No, I don't think we'd even arrived at the site. The panel had been going for about forty minutes before we got there. We would have been earlier – it was a panel we wanted to see, obviously. But we got delayed by an old friend of George's who'd just arrived. Couldn't get away.'

So that would explain at least why Felicity didn't mention seeing Carolyne switch the name cards. Vogel thought he would mention it anyway, just to see what her reaction would be.

Felicity looked amazed.

'Of course, I had no idea that had happened,' she said. 'How could I have? But that brings a whole new perspective to everything, doesn't it?'

Vogel could see that Felicity Smythe's crime writer's brain was about to go into overdrive again. He wasn't sure that he could take much more of that.

But he was not to be spared.

'You didn't mention poison, Mr Vogel. I've been thinking about it. If it wasn't a heart attack, what else could it be except poison? And now that you've told me about the swapping of the name cards, well, it's obvious, isn't it? Delia must have been the target. The murderer poisoned the bottle of apple juice that had been meant for her, and then—'

'I need to remind you, Mrs Smythe, that we don't even know whether or not we have a murderer,' interrupted Vogel a little curtly. 'And I shan't know the answer to that or any other of the points you have made until there has been a post-mortem examination.'

'Oh, yes, of course, but you will keep me informed of any new developments, won't you, Detective Chief Inspector?' asked Felicity.

'I can assure you, Mrs Smythe, that you will be the first on my list of people to contact,' said Vogel, deadpan.

Saslow stifled a giggle, with obvious difficulty.

Vogel also wanted to talk to Felicity about Delia's fall from Appledore Quay, primarily to ascertain, if only as a matter of routine, and as casually as possible, her whereabouts. It had occurred to him that it was somewhat curious that Felicity Smythe hadn't mentioned anything, or asked him anything, about that. The two women were supposed to be friends too, were they not? Mind you, it was possible, if unlikely, that she did not yet know of the incident. She had only just walked off stage, after all.

As soon as he mentioned it, he realized that was indeed the

case. She looked shocked to the very core. And when she spoke again, she couldn't quite get her words out properly.

'Oh my g–g–good God,' she stumbled. 'Is Delia all right? N–no idea. I had no idea. Whatever h–happened?'

Vogel said that nobody seemed to know exactly what had happened, just that Delia had fallen. Felicity certainly didn't look pleased with herself anymore, that was for sure.

'Oh my g–good God,' she said again. 'She's in intensive care, you said? That's–s–s–so awful. We must go to her.'

Another one, thought Vogel.

'No visitors, yet, I'm afraid,' he said.

'Ah. Y–yes. Of course.'

Felicity still sounded very shaken.

'I'm just a little surprised that you hadn't become aware of Delia's fall before now, Mrs Smythe,' he commented.

'I can't think why you're surprised,' countered Felicity, rather more sharply than Vogel would have expected. She was a quick recoverer, it seemed.

'Our panel has only just finished, and Carolyne brought me straight over to see you. Come to think of it, I'm surprised she didn't tell me. Perhaps she wanted to leave it to you.'

Vogel thought that was quite likely. From what he had seen that afternoon, Carolyne Smedley's only abiding concern was to keep her festival going, if at all possible.

He quickly established that Felicity had little or nothing useful to add to the information he had already gathered. Until it came to his final question.

'Do you know of anyone who might wish Delia harm, Felicity?'

Her eyes widened. 'Wish Delia harm?' she queried. 'So you don't think her fall was an accident, then, do you?'

'I am keeping an open mind,' said Vogel, for what felt like the umpteenth time.

'Well, there's always James Harding.'

Vogel was intrigued.

'Why would you say that?' he asked. 'He and Delia were successful writing partners, weren't they?'

'Yes, of course,' said Felicity quickly.

Rather too quickly, thought Vogel.

'I've no idea why I said it, silly of me,' she continued. 'In any case, he was dead when she fell, wasn't he?'

'Indeed he was.'

Felicity looked flustered.

'Um, I wonder, can I go?' she asked. 'We're supposed to be signing books, and, uh, George is waiting for me.'

Vogel considered pressing her further but didn't think he would get anywhere. Not yet. He'd let her stew a while. Clearly, something was going on, something was bothering Felicity Smythe, but it could just be writers' politics.

'Yes, you can go, Mrs Smythe, and thank you for your help,' he said. 'That's all I want to ask you, for the time being. But we will probably need to speak to you again.'

'Right, yes, of course,' muttered Felicity as she hurried away.

The two detectives moved across to the smaller group of people still standing outside the main marquee, most of whom, it turned out, had been part of the audience at the Harding/Day panel, and had stayed behind as Vogel had requested. They were still gossiping and looking at their phones. He and Saslow addressed them as a group, asking if there was anyone present who thought they might have further information, or know something that might shed any light on what had happened. Some of those who had been present had noticed that the two writers had sat down behind the wrong name cards and had been aware of Carolyne Smedley changing the cards around, and some hadn't. Just as Carolyne had suggested would be the case. She had also been right in her assumption that none of those who had noticed had attached any import-ance to it. Not even after James Harding had died so dramatically. They had all assumed that he had suffered a heart attack and had continued to believe that until the news of Delia Day falling off Appledore Quay had raised certain doubts. But in spite of that, it seemed that most of them still thought James Harding had died of natural causes.

Just as Vogel had decided there was nothing more to be gleaned from any of the audience members, CSI arrived. Nobby Clarke had worked the oracle it seemed. Well, one thing hadn't changed about the detective superintendent over the years, thought Vogel. She usually got her way.

He explained the sequence of events to the team leader, primarily concerning the delay in calling CSI in.

'I've no idea what evidence, if any, will remain uncontaminated,' he said. 'But I would suggest the principal items of interest would be the apple juice bottles and the plastic glasses provided to the panellists.'

'Were they kept aside?' asked the man.

'I'm afraid not, no,' Vogel told him.

'So where might we find them?'

Vogel explained. The team leader regarded him with a distinct lack of enthusiasm.

'So both the relevant bottles and the plastic glasses are somewhere amongst dozens if not hundreds of others which presumably look identical, and one of the bottles was broken, along, doubtless, with many others. Is that it?'

'Afraid so,' agreed Vogel.

'I shall enjoy telling the lab all that,' said the CSI man.

Vogel wished him luck, then turned to Saslow.

'I think we've probably done all we can here for today, Saslow,' he said. 'Time to find out how things are with Delia. I wonder if Perkins has made it to the hospital yet . . .'

As if on cue Vogel's phone rang. And the caller was Perkins, checking in from the North Devon District Hospital. He seemed to have already gathered a considerable amount of information. Vogel knew that the young man lived in Barnstaple; nonetheless, he had clearly moved at commendable speed.

'Delia is still in A and E being fully assessed,' Perkins related. 'I'm told she does seem to be gradually returning to normal consciousness. But, apart from the bang to her head, which is the biggest cause for concern, several other injuries already detected include a broken arm and at least two cracked ribs.'

Vogel was relieved to hear that Delia was continuing to slowly recover consciousness, and not at all surprised to learn of the other injuries she had sustained, particularly the broken arm. That had seemed pretty obvious to him as he had looked down on her as she lay in the mud below the quayside.

'Well, that's news that could have been a lot worse,' he said. 'Do you know what the prognosis is?'

'It seems likely she's going to be OK and will make a full recovery,' Perkins continued. 'But they're going to admit her as soon as they can find a bed, because they're afraid she may still have some concussion. She was quite badly knocked about altogether, boss. They let me peep in and have a look at her, on condition I didn't try to interview her. Not that there was much chance of that. She was still pretty much out of it. Nasty bruise just above one eye where her head was banged. They want to keep her in overnight for observation . . .'

Vogel had heard enough. He was in a hurry now.

'Have you asked when we can talk to her properly?' he interrupted.

'Yes, of course, boss. They said possibly later this evening, as long as she continues to improve.'

'Right, Saslow and I will be there in about half an hour. We need to see Delia as soon as possible. Meanwhile, make sure you keep an eye on her wherever she is in the hospital. If I'm right about all this, she could still be in grave danger.'

'Really, boss?'

'Really, DC Perkins.'

FOURTEEN

Vogel and Saslow left for the hospital straight away then. They had to cope with considerable holiday traffic heading back to various destinations after a weekend by the seaside. It was getting on for ten o'clock when they crossed Barnstaple Bridge, on their way to the N.D.D.H. out on the Braunton road.

Vogel called Perkins upon arrival and learned that Delia had now been moved to a general ward. Perkins had made it clear to all concerned that Vogel and Saslow needed to interview her ASAP, but he had also been told that whilst there had been further improvement in her cognitive powers, she was not considered to be fully recovered from her concussion yet, and they would have to wait until she had been seen again by the duty doctor. The DC was sitting in the lobby area outside Delia's ward, keeping an eye on all comings and goings, as instructed by Vogel. And when the DCI and Saslow joined him, he was able to tell them that the duty doctor had just arrived and was in the ward.

Twenty minutes or so later, the doctor stepped outside and informed the three officers that he considered Delia was now well enough to be interviewed.

'Only, please make it as brief as you can, and I can't allow three of you in,' he added. 'Miss Day is a very strong woman, but she's been through a lot today.'

Vogel and Saslow left Perkins on sentry duty. The nurse in charge greeted them as they entered the ward and guided them to a curtained-off area.

Delia was sitting propped up in her bed, arm in a sling, the bruise on her head vividly prominent. Vogel knew exactly how badly knocked about she'd been, and she looked the part. But she seemed reasonably lucid and was considerably improved from when Perkins had been allowed a glimpse of her.

'Twice in one day, Mr Vogel,' she said. 'I'm honoured. Can't think what I could have done to deserve it.'

Vogel smiled.

'I think you probably can,' he murmured. 'How are you feeling, Miss Day?'

'Delia, for God's sake. How do I look as if I'm feeling?'

Vogel smiled again. He did not bother to respond directly. The doctor had already remarked on Delia's strength. Vogel did not doubt that she was one tough cookie. He admired the woman's spunk, but he just wanted to get her version of the day's events. As quickly as possible, just as the duty doctor had requested. Also, he had been advised that she might still be suffering from a degree of concussion, and Vogel was well aware that this was a condition which manifested itself in many different ways.

'Detective Sergeant Saslow and I need to ask you some more questions, Delia,' he began, obeying her request to use her Christian name, whilst not inviting her to use his. He almost never did that.

'We will be as quick as we can,' he continued. 'More than

anything, I'd like to know how much you remember of what happened at Appledore quayside this afternoon?'

'I remember almost everything, I think, right up to when I tumbled over the side,' she replied. 'After that, it all gets more than a tad hazy.'

'I'm sure it does,' said Vogel. 'So, do you remember what caused you to fall?'

'Oh, yes, absolutely. I was pushed.'

Vogel did a double take. He hadn't expected Delia to be this definite about anything!

'Are you sure?' he asked.

'Of course I'm bloody sure,' she replied sharply. 'I have concussion. I haven't gone potty. And I'm not saying it was deliberate. Not for a second. There were a lot of people about. Quite a crush by the quayside. I just felt a push in the small of my back, and then – there I was. Down! And out, I'm told. Probably just someone behind me who was pushing their way through the crowd, lost their balance a bit, I expect. Don't you?'

'Perhaps, Delia. But we are still investigating in order to attempt to find out the truth about both of today's unfortunate occurrences connected with the festival. All I know for certain is that we have had a sudden death during an event and an incident leading to the serious injury of a second participant in the same event, both in the same afternoon. You and someone you were close to.'

Delia raised both eyebrows.

'Ah, yes, me and James Harding?'

'Obviously. Yes.'

'I wouldn't say close, exactly,' she said.

Vogel studied her with interest. Delia didn't look good, and he suspected she was in considerable pain, but it seemed to him she had recovered better than might have been expected from her concussion. And he was remembering Felicity Smythe's earlier remark about Harding.

'Well, you certainly worked closely with him, did you not?' he countered.

'Yes, but that was all, other than the work we were contracted to do we had no contact at all,' she responded curtly.

'Did you have a problem of some kind with Mr Harding?' he asked bluntly.

'No problem at all. I just couldn't stand the man.'

It was Vogel's turn to raise his eyebrows. He hadn't expected this either. Not so directly, anyway. He remained silent, hoping Delia Day would continue to speak. She didn't disappoint him.

'Look, why the leading questions about James?' she asked. 'He had a heart attack, didn't he? What else could it have been?'

'We are awaiting a post-mortem, then we will know exactly what killed Mr Harding.'

'But do you now think he could have been murdered? Is that it?'

'I'm keeping an open mind for the time being.'

'Are you, Detective Chief Inspector? Clearly, you believe that is a strong possibility. So, am I a suspect? Do you think I killed James, then threw myself off Appledore Quay in order to throw you off the scent?'

'No, Delia, I don't, actually.'

'Well, what do you think, then? I feel sure you have a theory of some sort.'

'Delia, did you realize that you and Mr Harding sat down on stage this afternoon behind the wrong name cards?'

'No, I didn't. It happens. Is it significant?'

'Possibly. Did you notice Carolyne Smedley change the name cards around, so that they were in front of the right people?'

'No, not really. I was mostly looking at our interviewer, listening to her completing her introductions and getting myself ready to speak. I was aware of Carolyne faffing about doing something, pouring out apple juice mostly. But nothing more specific than that.'

She paused.

'I've got it now, Mr Vogel,' she continued. 'You think James was killed by mistake, instead of me, because he was sitting in the wrong seat, after drinking poisoned apple juice, or some such nonsense. Then the perpetrator had another go at me on the quayside. Is that it?'

'I told you, I am keeping an open mind. But that is a possibility which we might consider. A lot depends on the result of Mr Harding's post-mortem.'

'Oh, my dear Detective Chief Inspector, you're creating a conspiracy theory. And I don't believe in 'em. By and large, the vast majority of people one encounters wouldn't be capable of making any sort of conspiracy work. Not for a moment.'

Vogel smiled. In his experience, too, Delia was probably right. By and large. But there were exceptions. Sometimes quite extraordinary exceptions.

Delia had spoken in an animated fashion, hoisting herself up into a more upright sitting position on her remaining good elbow. Suddenly, an expression of mild concern crossed her features, and she rested back on the pillows, before speaking again, considerably more quietly.

'Look, there is something – something I probably should have told you before. But when James collapsed and died, well, to tell the truth, I didn't connect it at all. Not for a second. And everything else just went right out of my mind . . .'

'What is it, Delia?' pressed Vogel.

'Um, I've received a couple of notes you might be interested in.'

'What kind of notes?'

'The not very nice kind, I'm afraid. Look, they're both in my bag, if you can bear to delve into it. It's in that cupboard.' She gestured towards her bedside cabinet. 'Inside a hospital plastic bag. Bit muddy, I'm afraid. Rescued from the riverbed along with me.'

'Go on then, Saslow,' instructed Vogel.

'Of course, sir,' said the DS, with exaggerated courtesy.

She extracted the shoulder bag and gingerly removed the two notes from within, which she passed at once to Vogel without reading them.

They were, of course, the threatening letters Delia had received in her room at the Imperial. Vogel read them quickly before passing them back to Saslow. Then he addressed Delia quite sharply:

'You're dead right you should have told me about these

before,' he said. 'I need to know exactly when you received them and how they were delivered to you.'

Delia responded immediately with the precise details of their arrival under her hotel room door, within the time frame of which she was aware.

'Do you have any idea who might be responsible for them?'

'None at all. Obviously, it could be somebody local, or a visitor to the festival, I suppose, and I barely know anyone here. Except one or two of the other writers.'

'Right, give me the names, please, of anyone whom you would regard as more than a casual acquaintance.'

There were only really the Smythes. But Delia also mentioned the Tucker twins.

'I don't know them very well – they are just what people nowadays call super-fans, but they could almost be regarded as stalkers, I suppose,' she said.

Vogel reckoned that was a fair assessment, although it didn't seem to make sense that they would wish to harm Delia.

He asked her how well she knew Carolyne Smedley.

'I only met her for the first time at the festival's opening night,' Delia replied.

She then mentioned James Harding again.

'I wouldn't put it past him to have done something like this to upset me, but, on the other hand, I'm not sure that it would have been his style,' she said. 'I don't think he would have threatened me or anyone else anonymously. His ego was too big. Of course, he was pretty desperate to get me to sign that new Netflix contract . . .'

Saslow wrote everything down in her notebook. Vogel couldn't help being a little irritated by Delia Day's revelation, and the manner of it. He was feeling more than a tad frustrated.

'You do realize Delia, don't you, if you'd mentioned this when I first spoke to you after James Harding's death, the distinct possibility that he hadn't died of a heart attack, which everyone accepted so readily under the circumstances, might well have occurred to me,' he said. 'Then we would have launched a proper investigation straight away, a post-mortem would have been fast-tracked at once, and CSI would have been called in before almost all the evidence has probably been destroyed. I don't understand why you kept it to yourself. Why did you? And please tell me the truth.'

The DCI really was quite angry and hadn't been able to conceal it. Even though he was dealing with a quite seriously injured woman lying in a hospital bed. He very nearly shouted the last few words.

'I already have told you the truth,' said Delia. 'It didn't occur to me for a moment that James Harding collapsing at the festival could possibly have anything to do with me – or those notes. Why on earth would it? It is also true that it more or less stopped me from thinking, let alone worrying, about those notes for a bit. It was the first time anybody had dropped dead in front of me, for a start, and I suppose I found that something of a distraction.'

She laughed in a rather strangled sort of way, then started to cough.

'I mean to say . . .' she began before her coughing got the better of her and she fell back on the pillows. Vogel thought her face had turned a rather unnatural colour.

'Go find a nurse, Saslow,' he instructed. Vogel was already regretting his out-of-character outburst.

Delia's coughing eased almost as suddenly as it had started, but she still looked very poorly. She closed her eyes just for a second or two, then opened them again, before shaking her head as if trying to clear it.

Vogel thought she had probably overstretched herself, and there was little doubt that he was responsible for that. Clearly, he must back off, for the time being at any rate. The hospital had described Delia Day as having suffered a severe concussion. He knew this was a condition that could come and go, and sometimes affect the sufferer quite badly hours and occasionally days after its infliction, even if they seemed to have fully recovered. This was why concussion checks in sport, particularly contact sports like football and rugby, were now so meticulously conducted. And why it had been decided to admit Delia Day and keep her in overnight – not a move taken lightly by hospital authorities in the post-Covid days of crisis-level pressure on the NHS. There were still fears of a possible relapse.

'Delia, I think you should rest,' he said. 'I didn't mean to upset you, and I apologize if I have. But I also think you should consider what I've said. And until we have at least clarified the situation, we're going to have someone here keeping an eye on you. I certainly don't want you attempting to leave this hospital without our knowledge. Is that clear?'

Delia's gaze was perhaps a little hazy, but her voice was clear enough when she spoke again.

'Perfectly, DCI Vogel,' she said, pushing herself up on one elbow again. He was well aware, in spite of everything, of the slight note of sarcasm in her voice.

'Delia, I need you to take me very seriously indeed,' he told her quietly. 'I sincerely believe you could be in great danger.'

'Oh, really,' she replied.

But when he said goodbye and wished her a swift recovery, and she lay back on her pillow, he thought he may have once more caught just a fleeting glimpse of very real concern in her eyes before she closed them again.

Vogel instructed DC Perkins to stay at the hospital on sentry duty until he could organize relief.

As he and Saslow stepped outside, and he was discussing with her what should be their next course of action, particularly in view of Delia's revelation of threatening letters, he received the phone call he had been waiting for – from pathologist Daisy Dobbs.

'Yes, professor,' he greeted her eagerly.

'I have a PM slot booked for seven tomorrow morning,' she said. 'Couldn't persuade the coroner to let me do it tonight, I'm afraid. Seems everybody except you still thinks James Harding's death was almost certainly down to natural causes.'

'That'll have to do, then,' he said. 'I reckon they may all be changing their minds. We already have new evidence.'

'OK, do you want to be present when I do the deed?' she asked, just a hint of playfulness in her voice.

Everyone who had ever worked with Vogel knew how he hated the sight of blood. Not entirely good news for a leading murder detective. Post-mortems were a kind of torture for him. But he knew this was one he must not miss. It was entirely down to him that it was happening at all, as quickly as this, anyway.

'I'll be there,' he said. 'Seven a.m. sharp.'

'Right, I look forward to it,' responded Daisy, just a tad obscurely. 'See you in the morning.'

Vogel turned to Saslow, confirming what she doubtless had already guessed, that the PM was fixed.

'So I don't see there's any more we can do tonight, Dawn,' he said. 'Perhaps you could give me a lift home and then get yourself home. Pick me up about six thirty?'

'Of course, boss.'

Vogel might have passed his driving test, but whenever possible on duty he much preferred to be driven by Saslow. They were likely to get to their destination a lot more quickly, for a start. Driving just seemed to come naturally to her. He doubted it ever would to him. And Saslow had accepted chauffeuring Vogel about as one of her duties from when they had first worked together in Bristol, and he had co-opted her from uniform. His finally passing a driving test had not changed things much. Taking Vogel back to his Fremington home and then picking him up in the morning meant quite significant detours for Saslow, who lived on the right side of Barnstaple for the hospital. But she did not demur.

On the way home, he texted Nobby Clarke to give her a brief progress report, then called Control at Barnstaple nick to ask for a uniform to be sent to the hospital by midnight at the latest to relieve Perkins. He didn't want the young man to fall asleep on the job, nor to be out on his feet the following day.

FIFTEEN

When the phone rang, it seemed a long way off. In a way, it was a long way off. Vogel was playing in an international backgammon tournament on a Greek island, and he was doing rather well. As was his wont. Certainly in his dreams. He was in the semi-final and had his opponent in a bit of a corner. One more decent throw could have the poor chap terminally trapped behind a prime.

Then he woke up.

The caller was DC Perkins. In a panic. His breath was coming in short, sharp gasps, and he seemed to be having difficulty getting his words out.

'Boss, thank God. I thought you weren't going to answer . . . I uh . . . it . . . I'm just so sorry, boss . . .'

'All right, Perkins. Take it slow and easy. Just tell me what's happened.'

'It's Delia Day. She's been attacked again. Some bastard put a pillow over her face. She . . . she's . . .' His voice tailed off.

Vogel swung his legs over the edge of the bed and sat up straight. He was suddenly very awake.

'She's what?'

'She's in intensive care . . .'

The DCI breathed a small sigh of relief. At least Delia wasn't dead. Not yet, anyway.

'Did you see who attacked her?' he asked hopefully.

'I didn't see anything boss. I – uh – I'm so sorry boss. I must have fallen asleep. I was struggling . . .'

Vogel glanced at the digital clock on his bedside table. It was three forty-five a.m.

'Didn't anybody send a relief for you?' he asked, aware even as he spoke that this was an unnecessary question.

'No, boss.'

'You should have called me.'

'I didn't want to wake you up, boss.'

Vogel was angry. Not with Perkins. He was a diligent young officer, but he wasn't Superman. He'd been called out in the middle of a day off, and he couldn't have been expected to stay awake and alert all night. Which is why Vogel had asked for a uniform to be sent to relieve him.

'Yes, well, it seems like you should have done,' the DCI muttered. 'I'm assuming nobody was caught.'

'No boss. A nurse interrupted whoever it was when she walked past on the way to another patient who had rung her call bell. The nurse cried out. They dropped the pillow and ran.'

'They? Are you being woke, Perkins, or couldn't the nurse even tell you the attacker's gender?'

'No, boss, she couldn't. Apparently, the attacker was dressed in full PPE, complete with mask and hood over the head.'

Personal protective equipment. Not the first time that, or certainly surgical masks, had been used as a disguise by a wrongdoer since the onset of Covid, thought Vogel. And, of course, still not an uncommon sight at hospitals throughout the country, so Delia's attacker wouldn't have stood out at all making 'their' way through the wards in search of her. But when they were very nearly caught in the act and took off at a run, surely that was a different matter.

'Isn't it a little surprising that nobody spotted this person as they presumably ran through the hospital in the middle of the night?' Vogel asked Perkins.

'It's an odd one, boss,' replied the DC. 'The nurse's cry woke me up. I rushed straight into the ward and even caught a glimpse of the attacker departing at speed through the door at the far end. I took off after them, not even waiting to find out exactly what had happened, though I already had the gist. Thing is, even though I started off quite close, they sort of disappeared. I'd yelled to the nurse to alert security. But nobody saw anything or anyone suspicious. And whoever it was almost certainly didn't leave the hospital by any of the main public exits, or they would have been seen. Or you'd think so, anyway.'

Perkins had calmed down and was quite lucid now.

'Could they still be in the hospital?' asked Vogel.

'Yes, that would be possible, obviously, and the whole place is on red alert now. But the trouble is we don't know what we are looking for. We don't know their gender, race, age range, anything, if they're still wearing the PPE, or what they might be wearing under it if they've taken it off. The nurse said if it was a woman, she thought it was a very tall woman. But that's it, boss.'

'Not even colour?'

'The nurse thought probably white, there was a bit of flesh exposed around the eyes. But everything happened so fast she couldn't even be sure of that.'

Hidden in plain sight, thought Vogel. Arguably, the most effective way for anyone ever to hide. And if the nurse was right, and the attacker was white, so, he would guess, was more than ninety-five per cent of the population of North Devon.

'I'm on my way to you, Perkins. I'll be with you in less than half an hour. Meanwhile, call it in. And tell Control you need back-up urgently.'

This was one of those occasions when, albeit with considerable reluctance, Vogel opted to drive himself, in order to save the time it would take for Saslow to come and pick him up. He called her on his hands-free on the way, one of the few extras in his car that he could work. She answered as groggily as he would expect at that hour in the morning.

'Get to the hospital as fast as you can,' he ordered bluntly. 'There's been another attack on Delia Day. I'll meet you there.'

He hung up then, barely giving Saslowa chance to say anything beyond 'hello'. Vogel was uninclined to speak on the phone whilst driving, even using hands-free. He felt that he needed every iota of concentration he could muster to transport himself, and anyone else reckless enough to ever travel with him, from A to B.

He did, however, risk one more brief call. To Control, to ensure that suitable back-up was finally dispatched for DC Perkins. And he delivered his message in no uncertain terms to the unfortunate operator who picked up his call and seemed uncertain whether or not DC Perkins' request had been dealt with. The rollicking he intended to issue to whoever had ignored or simply failed to put into action his own earlier request for relief for DC Perkins could wait. As could alerting Nobby Clarke. But not for long.

Two patrol cars arrived at the hospital at the same time as Vogel. He had a reputation for being quiet and mild-mannered in his approach. But he was also capable of being just the opposite. And his highly assertive approach to Control only a few minutes earlier had clearly worked.

Each patrol car was crewed by a pair of uniformed constables; there were three men and one woman. Vogel recognized two of them as officers he'd worked with before, and rather liked – PCs Docherty and Lake, the team looking into the frequent disappearance of cats in the area. He gathered them together and swiftly briefed them, on a need-to-know basis.

'Right, you lot, I want every possible entrance and exit to this hospital covered, and everyone leaving or entering stopped, their identity checked. That's everyone you see. It's not long past four a.m. There won't be that many people moving about. But nobody passes you without being challenged. Have you got that?'

The four officers affirmed that they'd got it and took off, spreading across the hospital complex.

Vogel realized that the horse may already have bolted, of course, and feared it was almost certainly too late for the attacker to be caught at the scene. But you never knew. Hospital security had been put on the lookout already.

Saslow had also just arrived, and she and Vogel made their way together to the intensive care unit, where Perkins was waiting for them in the corridor outside.

'I'm so sorry, boss,' he said again.

'You're not Superman,' said Vogel, voicing his thoughts of earlier. 'You can't stay awake all day and all night. You should have been relieved.'

'Yes, but all the same—'

'That's enough, Perkins. We move on. Is that clear?'

'Yes, boss.'

'Right, so what's the latest on Delia? How bad is she?'

'Well, her attacker tried to suffocate her with a pillow, as I told you. Primitive, but effective. She very nearly didn't make it. She stopped breathing, albeit only for a minute or so, I understand. The nurse who disturbed the attacker started CPR at once and had more or less brought her back to life even before the resus team arrived.'

'But they moved her back to ICU?'

'Well, yes. Technically, she died. So I think it was automatic for her to be moved here. They had her hooked up to oxygen and all manner of things. I followed her in as soon as I could, but they wouldn't let me stay.'

'Was she conscious?'

'It was hard to tell, boss. It wasn't even clear to me whether or not she could breathe unaided.'

'Did you ask when we might be able to talk to her again?'

'Not exactly, boss. Didn't seem any chance of it. They were pretty much still fighting to save her life.'

Vogel checked his watch. It was not quite five a.m.

'All right, Perkins, you take yourself off home and get some sleep,' he instructed. 'But before you go, find one of the uniforms who've just arrived and send them up here to take over from you. Preferably the woman – PC Docherty. Might be better under the circumstances. Seem a bit less heavy-handed.'

As he spoke, Vogel realized he had probably been voicing sentiments no male officer should give voice to any more, particularly not a senior officer. He shook his head at his inability to fit into the modern world sometimes. He was never going to be woke, was he? However hard he tried.

He watched Perkins take off in search of Docherty. The DC made no comment. For a fleeting second, Vogel wondered what he was thinking. But there were rather more important issues demanding his attention.

He considered calling Nobby Clarke then, in order to get the enquiry stepped up to attempted murder status. He wasn't worried about waking her, not any more. Not after an attempted murder. But he would very much like to be able to speak to Delia Day before he did so. He had felt all along that Delia's show of bravado was just that, and possibly concealing certain information she did not wish to share with him. Or at least, until now she hadn't wished to share with him.

A senior nurse passed by, probably the nurse in charge, Vogel thought. He introduced himself and asked when he and Saslow could see Delia.

'It's vital that we question Miss Day as soon as possible,' he said. 'Ideally, I would like to see her straight away.'

'I'm afraid the answer is no at the moment, Detective Chief Inspector,' responded the nurse. 'Miss Day very nearly died, as I expect you know. We need to be sure she is out of danger and functioning properly before we can allow her to be interviewed by the police. She is actually only barely conscious.

So in any case I doubt you would get much out of her right now. I'm running this ward until the day shift come on at eight, and there'll be doctors' rounds soon after. I'm sorry, but I certainly couldn't permit you to talk to her until then.'

'I'll respect that for the moment,' responded Vogel. 'But I must insist that a police officer sits right by Miss Day's bed and keeps watch over her. After what happened earlier, I'm sure you would agree to that.'

'Yes, of course,' said the nurse. 'As long as they don't try to talk to her.'

'They won't—'

Vogel was interrupted by the arrival at the ward, with excellent timing, of PC Morag Docherty.

'Reporting for sentry duty, sir,' she said, by way of greeting.

'Right, Docherty, please do not move from Delia Day's bedside until you are relieved,' instructed Vogel. 'It is quite likely she is still in danger.'

'Yes, sir, of course, sir,' said Docherty smartly.

Vogel knew that Morag Docherty was an experienced constable, with a reputation for having a brain that was every bit as sharp as the way she looked and spoke. It was good to have her around, and her presence also meant he could fulfil his promise to his daughter.

'Before you get settled in, Docherty, any news at all on the missing cats? I suspect I would have been told if you'd found my Rosamund's Storey?'

'Yes, indeed, sir. And I'm afraid we only have bad news. It's just been reported that another cat went missing on Friday night. From Northam. Went out before bedtime as usual, and hasn't been seen since.'

'Damn it. No leads at all, still?'

'Not really, sir. In any case, we've been taken off it at the moment because of the festival—'

'Yes, of course, Docherty,' interrupted Vogel.

He called out to the nurse who was on her way back into the ward.

'Nurse, I would very much like you to let PC Docherty know as soon as we can talk to Miss Day. I can't stress too much how important this is.'

The nurse agreed that she would. Vogel turned to Docherty again.

'Call me as soon as you have any news at all,' he instructed. 'Most importantly, when we can talk to Delia, of course, but also anything else that you notice – a change in condition, however minute. And watch out for anyone not obviously medical staff who tries to approach Delia. Is that clear?'

Docherty said it was crystal clear.

Vogel checked his watch again. They still had more than an hour and a half to kill before heading for the post-mortem. There was little point in leaving the hospital and attempting to move the investigation forward elsewhere.

'How do you fancy some breakfast, Saslow?' Vogel asked. Saslow asserted that she would very much fancy some breakfast, and suggested the Costa situated just behind A and E. It was, however, closed. Which was not surprising at that hour. After all, it was still the middle of the night, more or less, thought Vogel. Only it seemed neither of them had given that a thought.

'Funny, if you are up and about, how you just assume everyone else is too, whatever the time, don't you think, Saslow?' remarked Vogel somewhat philosophically.

'Yes, boss,' agreed Saslow obligingly.

They had to make do with coffee and biscuits from a vending machine, which they carried to a row of empty chairs just off the main corridor on the way to orthopaedics.

Once settled there, Vogel called Clarke. She didn't question the time of call, and neither had he expected her to. She would know perfectly well that he wouldn't call her at that hour without a sound reason.

He told her briefly and succinctly about the attack on Delia as she lay in her hospital bed. An attack that could only be regarded as an attempt on Delia's life, he remarked.

'Almost certainly the second attempt by the same perpetrator, boss,' he continued. 'I have no doubt that we are investigating two cases of attempted murder. And I think we should set up that incident room and an investigation team accordingly.'

Clarke didn't respond directly.

'What about a post-mortem on James Harding? Do we have that set up yet?'

'Yes boss, it's scheduled for seven this morning.'

'And you are hoping that the post-mortem will discover that James Harding did not die of natural causes, after all, are you not?'

'I don't know about hoping, boss. But I'm pretty certain that will prove to be the case. Even more than I was when we last spoke.'

He also told her about Harding and Day sitting down behind the wrong name cards at the beginning of their panel.

'I see. So you now think that Harding was killed by mistake, is that it?'

'Well, boss, I do believe that is what could have happened.'

'So how exactly was he killed? Nobody approached either of the panellists on stage, did they? Nobody was shot or stabbed or strangled, were they?'

'No, boss. And if they had been, the killer would, in the first place, almost certainly have been apprehended at once, and, in the second place, wouldn't have been very likely to kill the wrong person. I think there may have been a less immediately obvious MO.'

'Oh, Vogel, for God's sake, you don't really believe Harding was poisoned, do you?'

'I strongly suspect it, boss. There were bottles of apple juice put out for each participant. I think our perpetrator spiked the wrong one – the bottle placed where Delia Day should have been sitting. But that bottle of juice ended up being in front of James Harding. And he drank it, or a considerable quantity of it, I understand. And, as you point out, boss, no third party inflicted any sort of injury on Harding, so I've pretty much come to the conclusion that poison is the only reasonable alternative to natural causes in this case.'

'Reasonable? You must be aware that poisoning is a thoroughly unfashionable murder method in the twenty-first century. Far too easily detected with modern forensics.'

'Yes, well, maybe we don't have a very modern murderer. And if I'm wrong, and James Harding was the intended victim, well, he was a perfect candidate for a heart attack, and

– without what has happened since – there may not even have been a post-mortem. Not straight away anyway. I have to admit that he does have a history of heart trouble. A dodgy valve, apparently. We've already checked his medical records.'

'But even that didn't make you change your mind?'

'No, boss . . .'

'As intransigent as always. I would expect nothing other. Tell me, Vogel, have you ever actually investigated a poisoning?'

'No, boss. But I'm well aware of more than one very high-profile case in recent times. As I'm sure are you. The Skripals, father and daughter, only narrowly survived after being poisoned in Salisbury by the nerve agent Novichok, and then there was Alexander Litvinenko who died in a London hospital after being poisoned—'

'Vogel, you know perfectly well these were people linked with international espionage, who were believed to have been targeted by Russian assassins,' interrupted Clarke. 'I doubt there are too many wannabe murderers in North Devon this weekend who can get their hands on Novichok, or even have a clue what it is or what it does.'

'Fair enough, boss. Doesn't rule out a more readily available poison, though. Anyway, we'll know soon enough. Saslow and I are attending the post-mortem, and I'll contact you as soon as we have any news.'

'Good. Meanwhile, I'll get it cleared for you to move into Bideford nick. Are you happy with Janet Peters as your deputy SIO and office manager?'

'More than,' replied Vogel.

He had worked with DI Peters on two previous cases. On the first occasion, he had not been entirely impressed, perhaps because she was relatively new to the task, and he'd been still hankering after DI Margot Hartley, the experienced deputy he had worked with during his time in Bristol with the Avon and Somerset. But Janet Peters had just seemed to get better and better. She was quick, clever, indomitable and fiercely loyal. He was delighted to have her on board again.

'I'll send an MCT presence over straight away, also get some local officers on board,' Clarke continued. 'And if your hunch is right, Vogel . . .'

She paused. Vogel knew that she was aware how much the suggestion that he was following a hunch would annoy him. That wasn't how he saw it at all. Vogel believed that he had studied the facts and carefully deduced the most likely conclusion.

'And if your hunch is right,' Nobby Clarke repeated, to the DCI's further annoyance, 'then we'll be launching a full-scale murder enquiry today, probably before half the country sits down to its breakfast. Then I'll ship in teams from stations right across the two counties to bring you up to full strength.'

'Thank you, boss,' said Vogel levelly. He'd got what he wanted. It wasn't the time to be small about it.

SIXTEEN

Vogel and Saslow, kitted up in PPE, entered the mortuary on the far side of the hospital complex just a few minutes before seven.

Daisy Dobbs was already there. So was James Harding, or Vogel assumed it was James Harding, as the body on the table dedicated to post-mortem examination – which was more or less a large tray with a raised edge, on legs and slanted so that blood did not spill on to the floor – was covered entirely by a sheet.

Daisy's assistant, Raoul, whom Vogel had met before, was laying out the required instruments on a smaller adjacent table. These included a powered bone saw, primarily used to cut open the chest cavity, a knife closely resembling a domestic bread knife, and usually called by that name, which was used to shave off slices of organs for examination, special scissors for opening up the intestines, a hammer with a hook to remove the cap of the skull, and a Hagedorn needle, used to sew up the body after examination. There was also a set of rib shears, used to get at important organs inside the ribcage. Some pathologists believed that shears gave them more manageability in certain instances than a power saw. When Vogel had been in the Met, he had worked with a pathologist – even more eccentric than, in Vogel's opinion, they usually were – who liked to use a set of garden shears which he insisted were better suited to the job than any specialist implement he had been supplied with.

Vogel took it all in at a glance. The very sight of the body on that awful table, and the instruments being prepared to summarily dissect it, was enough to have already made him feel slightly nauseous.

'Morning David, Dawn,' Daisy Dobbs greeted them cheerfully.

It was Vogel's experience that pathologists always seemed to be cheerful. As well as eccentric. Vogel responded in kind, as much as he could manage. Unlike him, Saslow never seemed concerned on these occasions.

'Right, so as we're all here, we may as well begin,' Daisy continued. 'You all set, David?'

Vogel ignored her. He just wished people would leave him alone to cope with his various inadequacies.

First came the external examination, which even Vogel could cope with easily enough. Daisy scrutinized Harding's entire body, back and front, removed hair samples, head and pubic, and also took samples of saliva, ear wax, and mucus from inside the nose. She photographed everything step by step and gave a recorded running commentary.

She paid particular attention to Harding's face and mouth, eventually making a remark which put Vogel on red alert.

'There is some swelling of the mouth and tongue and discolouration of the skin around the mouth which could be consistent with the presence of a toxic substance,' she said.

The internal examination began as usual with the dissecting of the subject's ribcage, or, as all pathologists were inclined to say, the unzipping. This was the bit that caused Vogel the biggest problem. He could instantly feel the bile rising in his chest and throat until he could taste it at the back of his mouth. You really would think he'd have got used to it by now, the number of post-mortems he'd attended. But he hadn't. He did what he always did, bowed his head slightly, shut his eyes and hoped nobody would notice. Though he was fairly sure that the people who worked with him regularly, like Saslow and

Daisy Dobbs, were perfectly aware of what he was doing. And he could still hear the crunching sounds of the chest breaking open and the slurping squelching noises as Daisy delved into the organs within the cavity.

When he thought the worst was over, he opened half an eye. Daisy was harvesting various biological fluids and tissues, no doubt for toxicology tests.

She paused in her recorded commentary and addressed Vogel and Saslow directly.

'We're going to start with presumptive tests,' she began. 'Primarily of stomach contents, urine, and blood.'

Vogel had a fair idea of what she was talking about. Saslow looked blank, which Daisy Dobbs obviously noticed.

'Colour tests, Dawn,' she said. 'The substances I have collected will be tested by a reagent which will effect a colour change if any of the specific compounds, or classes of compounds, which we may be looking for are present. In this case, dangerous toxins or poisons. The emphasis for colour tests, which are quick and easy to perform, is on indication. Such tests do not provide confirmation of identity. Almost certainly, we will have to complete further more complex and specialist forensic tests, which will take a little longer.'

'But will these tests give you a pretty good idea, more or less straight away, of whether or not James Harding has ingested or otherwise absorbed a poisonous substance?' asked Saslow.

'They will indeed,' Daisy replied.

Vogel was aware that Raoul was already beginning the analysis process of the substances extracted from James Harding's body. He was preparing slides, rather as Vogel remembered from school, but beyond that, this was a whole new world of science. In modern pathology, analysis is primarily digital. Both Daisy and her assistant were now studying computer screens linked to a high-tech unit into which the slides were inserted.

Vogel made himself wait in silence for Daisy to speak again.

After just a few moments, Daisy stood up and moved closer to Vogel and Saslow.

'Almost all of the biological fluids we have removed from

James Harding's body contain a significant level of toxins,' she announced. 'Indeed, a catastrophically high level. To such an extent that I think you can safely assume that your theory is right, David. James Harding has been poisoned.'

'Wow!' said Saslow.

'Right,' said Vogel. 'But do I take it that you can't tell us at this stage what poisoned him or how it was administered?'

'No to both of those. These colour tests can often indicate the nature of a specific poison, or indeed a drug, but, in this case, there is nothing we have been able to recognize so far. Raoul here thinks it's something neotropical. He's a bit of an expert in that field – before leaving India, he worked for a while at the subcontinent's answer to Porton Down.'

'Porton Down? That's where they research chemical warfare, isn't it?' Saslow blurted out.

Meanwhile, Vogel was wondering if his conversation with Nobby Clarke concerning fatal and near-fatal attacks with rare and deadly poisons by secret service agents or the like might turn out not to be as far-fetched as she had suggested.

'Not entirely, it also involves research into toxic and poisonous substances for all kinds of reasons,' interjected Raoul. 'As indeed was the case at the laboratory where I was employed in India.'

'So are you going to be able to find out exactly what did kill Harding, and how long will that take?' asked Vogel bluntly.

'Oh yes,' said Daisy. 'Particularly with Raoul's specialist knowledge. And within hours, rather than days, I would hope.'

SEVENTEEN

Vogel was just wondering whether to await developments in the hospital or pay a visit to the newly emerging incident room at Bideford Police Station when he felt his phone vibrate in his pocket.

PC Docherty's name was displayed on the screen.

Vogel turned to step outside the mortuary, gesturing for Saslow to follow him.

'You're not going to believe this, boss, but Delia is insisting on seeing you,' she began excitedly. 'Right now.'

'Good, that's just what we need,' commented Vogel levelly.

'Yes, boss. The medics aren't too happy, but she's just swept them aside. She still looks awful, and most of the time I've been here, she's been asleep, or drifting in and out of consciousness, I'm not sure which. Could be medication, I suppose. Anyway, during one of her awake moments, she spotted me. She just stared at me. I said nothing, like you and the charge nurse told me. But then she asked if you were around. So I answered her, didn't I? I said you were still at the hospital. And she asked me . . . well, told me really – she's like that, isn't she? – to get you to come to see her. Said she wanted to talk to you straight away.'

'Excellent, well done, Docherty. We'll be right there,' said Vogel.

'You should know, boss, that same nurse is still around – seems her shift's been extended – and she had a right go at me, said I'd been told not to speak to the patient. But do you know what happened then, boss? Delia Day told her in no uncertain terms to leave me alone, that she needed to see you, she had asked me to arrange it and she wouldn't have any interference. Sent her packing.'

'Ah, yes, I can see that happening, Docherty,' commented Vogel, who could indeed imagine it vividly. 'Tell Delia I'll be there in a few minutes, and don't leave her side until I get there.'

Delia Day had propped herself up on the pillows and was no longer wearing an oxygen mask or connected to any life support machines by the time Vogel arrived at the ICU. Nonetheless, he could see that this was a very different woman from the one he had talked to the previous day.

The attack on her during the night had clearly taken its toll mentally as well as physically. She looked weak to the point of frailty, she was sweating, and there was an air of real anxiety about her.

'Good morning, Mr Vogel,' she said, and he thought she was struggling to sound as normal as possible. 'We meet again.'

'Indeed, Delia, and under even more distressing circumstances. I am so sorry about what happened.'

'Yes, well, these things are sent to try us . . .'

It was a strange remark, under the circumstances. And her voice tailed off. Vogel found that he was quite shocked by her appearance. Her hands were trembling, and she was unnaturally pale. She was still trying to present the same confident front, to maintain her professional persona, the image she liked to show the world. But she wasn't succeeding that well.

'I need to thank you for seeing me so quickly after such an awful incident,' Vogel continued. 'It's just so important, because I suspect only you can throw any light on what happened.'

'I will try, Mr Vogel, but I am puzzled,' Delia responded.

'Are you really, Delia?' persisted Vogel. 'You have just been attacked at very close quarters. Somebody tried to smother you with a pillow and almost succeeded. You must have seen them fairly clearly, didn't you?'

'Well, I had a pillow over my face most of the time.'

'Yes, of course, but didn't you see them when they approached your bed before they tried to smother you?'

'Yes. But they were wearing full PPE, including hood and mask. I wouldn't have recognized my agent, for God's sake. I didn't even register the gender – no idea whether it was a man or a woman.'

Delia had unconsciously echoed the words of the charge nurse. That much about the attack seemed beyond doubt. But it was also completely unhelpful.

'Do you not have any idea at all who might want to attack you, or why?'

'No, I don't, not a clue,' responded Delia, still trying to maintain a relatively light note. 'But look, Mr Vogel, I asked your constable to contact you, to get you here to talk to me, because, well, I have to admit it now, don't I? You were absolutely right last night. I'm in very real danger, aren't I?'

'Yes, you are Delia. Quite clearly.'

'And I spend most of my life playing some sort of particularly silly superwoman, but it's just an act. And one I certainly can't keep up at the moment. I'm frightened, Mr Vogel, I have to admit that. Very frightened.'

'Delia, you'd be stupid not to be frightened. And you are certainly not that.'

Delia managed a small, strained smile.

'That's not what the critics say.'

'But your readers don't agree, I presume.'

'No.'

'And there are many millions of them, are there not?'

'Yes.'

Vogel had hoped that by allowing the conversation to swing off at a tangent, he would encourage Delia to open up. Instead, she had turned monosyllabic. That would not do at all.

'I am glad that you seem now to be rather more realistic about the situation you are in, Delia. You see, I feel fairly certain that I need to know *why* you are being attacked before I can find out *who* is attacking you. Can you help me with that?'

'Perhaps, but I'm not entirely sure,' remarked Delia.

Vogel noticed that she was looking around her. The IC unit, which housed probably eight or ten beds, seemed to be full to capacity. There was a curtain surrounding Delia's bed, but it was only half closed. A nurse could be seen tending a patient in a bed just a few feet away. Vogel stood nearest to Delia's bed, studying her closely. Docherty and Saslow, notebook in hand, were standing just behind Vogel.

'I will try, though,' Delia continued, perhaps unexpectedly. 'But I will only talk to you, Mr Vogel. Alone. And off the record.'

Vogel was growing more and more confident that he would soon be heading a murder enquiry. To interview someone at the heart of that enquiry, someone who had very nearly become a murder victim, without another officer as a witness and taking notes, would be highly irregular. As was any suggestion of the interview being off the record. Also, he wasn't in the habit of making promises he couldn't keep.

'Delia, I would like to accommodate you, but we are dealing

with a very serious matter here, and what you are asking is totally against police procedure,' he said. 'I need at least to have DS Saslow with me. And "off the record" is something you ask journalists to agree to. Not police officers.'

Delia stared at him in silence for a few seconds, the strain of the last few hours showing even more clearly on her face. Her hair was a mess. Her face and arms looked clean, but she had been so far unable to wash her hair since her fall on to the riverbed. Not properly anyway. There seemed to be many more streaks of mud in it than streaks of purple. She looked as if the strength and confidence that were so much a part of the persona she so resolutely adopted had finally left her. But when she spoke again, although her voice remained weaker than usual, it was with more than a flash of her usual assurance.

'Take it or leave it,' she said.

Vogel took a moment to consider his options. If he refused Delia's demands point blank, he was quite sure she would stick to her guns. She would clam up. He doubted he would get another relevant word out of her, however hard he tried. And he remained quite certain that Delia Day held the key to the events of the night and the previous afternoon. He had to break through her front and get this woman talking. But if he accepted her demands as they stood, he could compromise not only his own position but the entire operation. However, he did not consider Delia a suspect in any regard. Initially, it had indeed been remotely possible that she had been responsible in some way for the death of James Harding and had then thrown herself off the quay as a diversionary tactic. But he had never thought that was very likely. She could have been killed, and, indeed, very nearly was. Her fall could also have been both a coincidence and an accident. He'd never thought that was likely, either. Now, following the attempt to suffocate her, there was surely no doubt that Delia was the target of a killer who was unlikely to give up until they had succeeded in doing away with her. Vogel thought that gave him grounds to attempt a compromise. He hoped so, anyway.

'All right, Delia, I will go along with you – up to a point. I will talk to you alone . . .'

He paused. Saslow was standing facing him. He was very aware of her disapproving stare.

'. . . but there will have to be certain conditions,' Vogel continued. 'I am prepared to keep what you tell me in confidence between us, unless and until it becomes imperative for the integrity of this investigation or the safety of anyone involved, including you, to go on the record with it. And I will need to record our conversation, just in case—'

'No way,' interrupted Delia. 'I'm not allowing a recording.'

'I was going to say just in case you were no longer with us, in case the person who has now tried to kill you twice finally succeeds, and you are dead,' said Vogel bluntly.

'Ah,' said Delia.

'Ah, indeed. It is perfectly clear that you are in grave danger. It would be irresponsible not to have everything you say to me recorded. But I will keep your confidence if at all possible. You have my word on that, and it may well prove that whatever it is you want to tell me ends up having no bearing on the case. That quite often turns out to be the way, in spite of what those involved think. Please trust me.'

'Trust you, Detective Chief Inspector? I barely know you and I don't like your compromise, particularly as it seems to be almost entirely on my side. But I want to stay alive, and it appears that you want to keep me alive, so I suppose I am going to have to trust you.' She made the comment grudgingly.

'A wise choice, if I may say so,' said Vogel.

He waved Docherty and a reluctant Saslow out of the cubicle and pulled the curtains fully closed behind her.

'OK, Delia,' he said. 'We're as alone as I can make us. So shall we begin?'

'Come and sit close to me, Mr Vogel,' she instructed.

He did so, pulling up a chair as close as possible to the top end of Delia's bed.

'Under the circumstances, why don't you call me David?' he muttered, more than a little awkwardly. 'It might make things easier.'

Delia smiled faintly. 'Thank you, David,' she said.

Vogel then took his phone from his pocket, put it into record mode and placed it on the bedside table.

'This is DCI David Vogel interviewing Delia Day at the North Devon District Hospital. Delia, would you please confirm that you consent to this interview being recorded?'

Delia remained silent for just a few seconds, but it felt longer. Vogel was afraid that she was about to change her mind.

'I confirm my consent,' she said eventually.

'Thank you,' said Vogel. 'Delia, you have indicated that you have something you want to tell me. Perhaps you would like to start now.'

Delia nodded.

'I am not what you think I am,' she began in what, for her, was a very small voice. 'Delia Day is a pseudonym, and her persona is an invention, you see.'

Vogel saw all right, but pseudonyms were common enough among writers, and he had always suspected that living up to some kind of assumed persona was common amongst people who lived in the public eye. Delia seemed to be waiting for him to say something. So he did, telling her more or less exactly what he'd been thinking.

'Rather more than that in my case,' she responded. 'It's a matter of record that my career began when I was twenty-two years old and I entered a writing competition, which I won. The prize was that the short story I had submitted would be published in a national magazine. Then the magazine asked for another one, and another one. Somebody suggested I should write a novel. I did so and it was taken up by a major publisher and became one of those first-novel sensations. Everything I did seemed to bring instant success. All of that is a matter of record. Every time I appear at a book festival or any kind of event, or just give an interview, this is the story I tell. Almost as if my life began with that competition and its aftermath. With becoming Delia Day. And in a way, it did.

'But there was a life before Delia Day that I never talk about. A life I am not at all proud of, that I have managed to keep secret. You see, I was in prison when I won that writing competition. Serving a five-year sentence.'

'Prison?' Vogel blurted the word out.

'Yes. And as far as I know, there is nobody alive who knows that. Except you, now, David.'

Vogel had no idea what he might have expected Delia Day to tell him. But not this. Not in a million years.

'Why were you in prison?' he asked.

'I hurt someone, very badly,' answered Delia quietly. 'And I am deeply ashamed.'

EIGHTEEN

Vogel was still trying to take this in when the curtains around Delia Day's bed were wrenched open. An extremely angry-looking doctor approached, accompanied by a nurse who immediately began taking Delia's temperature, testing her blood pressure and oxygen levels, and so on.

Delia didn't look pleased. But neither did she protest.

Meanwhile, the doctor rounded on Vogel, who immediately stood up to face him.

'John Garvey, senior registrar, do you mind telling me who the hell you are and what the hell is going on here?' he stormed.

'DCI David Vogel,' responded Vogel, his voice calm but icy. 'I am heading an investigation into a suspicious death, and no less than two attempts on the life of your patient. I am conducting a very important interview with Miss Day who I believe to be in possession of vital information pertaining to these three grave incidents.'

Garvey did not appear to have listened. Or, if he had, he took no notice at all of Vogel's explanation.

'I can't believe what's going on,' Garvey continued. 'We don't pull curtains around beds in ICU unless a doctor or nurse is attending the patient. Nor do we allow police interviews here, except in the most exceptional circumstances, and—'

'These are exceptional circumstances, Doctor,' Vogel interrupted, making a real effort to remain calm but sounding even more dangerously icy than before. 'I have just tried to explain these circumstances to you. I have reason to believe that I am now conducting a murder enquiry.'

Even as he spoke, Vogel regretted his phraseology. Which

he feared had summarily lost him the high ground. He had no idea why he'd put it like that.

The doctor picked him up on it at once.

'Reason to believe you're conducting a murder enquiry, eh?' he enquired, still blazing with anger. 'Well, not in my ICU you're not. I'm about to re-examine Miss Day, and she may then be moved to a general ward until we see fit to discharge her. Your interview will have to wait until then, I fear.'

Vogel was about to launch into a further and, he hoped, better-presented argument for continuing the interview when Delia chipped in.

'I asked Mr Vogel to come to see me, Doctor,' she said. 'It was my decision.'

'Not a decision I can allow you to make at the moment, I'm afraid, Miss Day,' said the doctor. 'You are in my care, and I will decide what is best for you.'

Delia looked as if she wanted to challenge Garvey on that, as Vogel would expect, but she didn't seem to have the strength.

Dr Garvey turned to the nurse and asked her what readings she had.

'Blood pressure one hundred and forty over ninety,' she replied. 'Oxygen level ninety-two per cent, temperature thirty-nine point one degrees—'

'Well, that's that, then,' interrupted the doctor. 'Afraid you won't be moving out of here for a bit, after all, Miss Day. Those are all unsafe readings. Putting you in danger of a stroke or a heart attack, and quite frankly, either of those is now probably considerably more likely than another attack by some lunatic.'

Vogel reckoned he had no argument left after that. So frustrating, when Delia had been beginning to open up at last.

'All right, Doctor, of course I wouldn't want to put Miss Day at any greater risk,' he said. 'But please don't underestimate the danger she is already in from, as you put it, "some lunatic". There have already been two attempts on her life. Therefore, I must insist on police protection for Miss Day. PC Docherty here will continue to stay with Miss Day for the time being. And that is not negotiable, Doctor.'

Vogel had determined that it was time to assert a little of

his own authority. Saslow had followed the doctor into the curtained-off area around Delia's bed and had been watching Vogel with a certain degree of surprise, he thought. She probably hadn't expected him to agree so readily to abandon his interview with Delia. Particularly when faced with a tirade from a medical professional on a scale that was likely to infuriate any police officer heading a major investigation. Even the usually mild-mannered Vogel. But the DCI had felt he had no choice. Apart from the more human side of things, it would be totally against the interests of his investigation if Delia were to die. And not only had he picked up a fair bit of medical knowledge over the years, through his work, but there was a history of high blood pressure in his family. Both his maternal grandparents had died of strokes brought on by high blood pressure, in the days before such conditions were monitored and medicated as they are today. This did not affect Vogel directly, as he had been adopted as a boy, but he was very aware of just how suddenly such a condition could kill.

The doctor agreed, albeit with not particularly good grace. Vogel gave Docherty her instructions, and he and Saslow made their way out of the ICU.

Just as they stepped out into the corridor, Vogel received a phone call. It was from Professor Dobbs. Vogel answered it eagerly.

'Are you still in the hospital?' she asked.

Vogel confirmed that he was.

'In that case, would you care to come back to the mortuary? I have some news for you.'

'Already?' queried Vogel rhetorically. 'That was quick!'

'Yes, well, seems we asked the right questions straight away. Sometimes in life, you get lucky.'

Vogel was beginning to get to know Daisy Dobbs very well. She was as sharp as the needles she used to zip up her cadavers. And he knew that she held young Raoul, he of the specialist knowledge of noxious substances, in extremely high regard. Vogel doubted luck came into it.

Daisy and Raoul were sitting side by side in front of their computers when Vogel and Saslow arrived. They turned to greet the two officers. They both looked rather pleased with themselves, but also a little puzzled.

'As you will have guessed, we have managed to isolate and identify the toxic compound which killed James Harding,' Daisy Dobbs began. 'There were aspects to our initial findings, and variations in the colour tests we had already undertaken, that led Raoul, with his experience of such matters, to suspect a certain substance, although it seemed so unlikely that I must admit I was sceptical. However, Raoul was quite right. As usual.

'We found in Mr Harding's body a significant presence of batrachotoxin.'

The pathologist stopped speaking very suddenly, as if for dramatic effect. Or maybe she was waiting for applause. Which didn't come, primarily because neither Vogel nor, he felt sure, Saslow had any idea what batrachotoxin was.

After just a moment, Daisy Dobbs spoke again.

'Batrachotoxin is a toxic cardio- and neuro-steroidal alkaloid. For perspective, it is one thousand times more potent than cyanide. Just a small amount of it, the equivalent of two grams of table salt, is enough to kill a person. Which it does by destroying the body's sodium channels – the means by which our nerves communicate with each other. This causes paralysis, and since you need your nerves to breathe and for your heart to beat, it will result in cardiac arrest and respiratory failure. Plus, there is no antidote, even in the unlikely event of the presence of batrachotoxin being detected in a person whilst they are still alive. Because if you get it in your system, you are likely to be dead in just a few minutes.'

'Wow,' said Saslow.

'So where does this poison come from, and how would Harding have absorbed it?' asked Vogel. 'Is it soluble? Could it have been dissolved in the apple juice he drank just before he died, as I've always suspected something might have been.'

'I think those are questions for Raoul,' Daisy Dobbs replied. 'Particularly where this little beauty comes from. He's the expert.'

Raoul swivelled his chair around so that he was directly facing the two detectives.

'It is soluble, and it could have been dissolved in the apple juice consumed by the deceased,' Raoul began. 'But whoever put it there would have had to be an expert in handling the stuff. You can actually absorb it through touch. Anyone trying to dispense it would have to be wearing protective clothing, certainly at least gloves. In laboratory conditions, it is normally kept in small vials which open if pressure is applied at the correct point, allowing for the toxin to be emptied out. Then, of course, the vials have to be disposed of safely, and they are obviously classed as hazardous waste. In this case, extremely hazardous waste.

'As for where batrachotoxin comes from, well, that is the extraordinary part of all this. Indeed, the most extraordinary.'

He paused. Vogel wanted to tell the young scientist to get on with it. He knew better than to do so. Instead, he waited patiently for Raoul to continue. Which he did after just a few seconds. Although it felt longer.

'*Phyllobates terribilis*,' said Raoul.

'What?' queried Vogel.

'*Phyllobates terribilis*,' repeated Raoul. 'Colloquially known as the golden poison dart frog.'

'What?' said Vogel again.

'The golden poison dart frog,' repeated Raoul. 'A quite fascinating creature. It lives in the untamed Western Pacific lowland rainforests of Colombia in one very small region about the size of New York City. It's bright yellow so that it stands out dramatically in the forest undergrowth, a dramatic colouration which is a kind of aposematism. A warning, advertising with bright colours that the frogs are toxic. In fact, if ever you see extremely brightly coloured creatures of this kind in the wild, it's an indication that they're highly toxic, or possibly mimicking something highly toxic, like those little pretend wasps you get in the UK, and so on—'

'Raoul, thank you,' interrupted Vogel. 'That's all fascinating, but I'm trying to understand exactly how James Harding died. Are you telling me the man was killed by a poisonous frog with a ridiculous name from Colombia? The golden poison dart frog, for heaven's sake? How did it get its name? And most importantly of all, how did it get here?'

'Uh, yes of course,' responded Raoul. 'I'm sorry, Mr Vogel. This is just such a fascinating subject I am inclined to get carried away. There are more than two hundred species of little frogs that live in the neotropics that are collectively called poison frogs. The yellow-coloured *Phyllobates terribilis* is the most potent of these frogs and produces secretions of such toxic intensity that the indigenous hunters of days gone by used to make a lethal concoction from dead *Phyllobates terribilis* to dip their blow darts in. And so it became known as the golden poison dart frog.

'If disturbed, it will secrete its lethal compounds from glands in its neck and on its back. A single specimen measuring two inches long can produce enough venom to kill between ten and twenty grown men.'

'I see,' said Vogel, although he didn't really. He remembered how only the previous day Felicity Smythe's ramblings about James Harding possibly having died after being poisoned by spiders had seemed laughable. Not so laughable now.

'All right, but how on earth would any of these little monsters get to North Devon?' he continued. 'Or are there people out there mad enough to keep them as exotic pets?'

'Probably,' replied Raoul. 'However, not necessarily that mad. These frogs only produce their deadly toxin within their native habitat. In captivity, they quickly become completely harmless. As are any bred in captivity. Unless, of course, they are fed a particular diet and given certain supplements.'

'Isn't that just a little far-fetched?' interjected Saslow.

'The whole darned thing is far-fetched if you ask me,' muttered Vogel.

'You can't argue with science, David,' responded Daisy, with a wry smile.

'Wouldn't dream of it,' said Vogel. 'So come on, Raoul, how did this lethal poison get from a frog that can only produce it in Colombia into our dead man?'

'I didn't say that the frog can only produce the poison in Colombia,' responded Raoul quickly. 'I did already mention that this could be produced under certain conditions. Probably only laboratory conditions. And only when given access to certain food sources, particularly Choresine beetles. The most famous UK research complex of this nature, and the most controversial, would be the one Daisy mentioned earlier – Porton Down – where they experiment with all manner of toxic compounds, both naturally generated and deliberately manufactured by man, all in the interest of national security. But there are others. It could also have been harvested from a frog in its natural habitat and brought into this country in dedicated containers. Although that would be highly illegal. And most dangerous. Either way, the most likely option would seem to be that it was administered at the festival from a vial of some kind.'

'How long does this substance remain deadly poisonous?' asked Saslow. 'Do its powers lessen eventually?'

'I'm not an expert on batrachotoxin,' admitted Raoul. 'But it is generally believed that toxins, left to their own devices, do not lose their powers. Which is why they, and anything that has been in contact with them, come into the highest category of hazardous waste. Their disposal is highly specialist. And I'm afraid there is no doubt that it can be transmitted by touch.'

Vogel was struggling to control a blinking fit. This whole case was beginning to turn into a nightmare. Indeed, thought Vogel, what could be more the stuff nightmares are made of than death by poisonous frog?

'So, Raoul,' he began. 'If we're right about the way this toxin was administered, even the broken bits of the apple juice bottle and the plastic glass James Harding used could prove lethal if anyone touched them. Is that so?'

'Well, hopefully not,' Raoul replied. 'Batrachotoxin, once diluted in the apple juice, would probably not prove lethal to touch. And also might take a little longer to kill than a neat sample if ingested, as with James Harding. Still pretty effective, though.'

'But there is at least one contaminated vial involved, which contained the venom in its original state, and which may or may not have been disposed of properly,' Vogel continued. 'Probably not, I would assume.'

He paused whilst assimilating the thought that had just occurred to him.

'This is frighteningly reminiscent of the Salisbury poisonings, isn't it?' he commented. 'And a woman called Dawn Sturgess, with no connection at all to the perpetrators or their intended victims, died when her partner found the discarded fake perfume bottle which had contained Novichok in a rubbish bin. He gave it to her, she sprayed the remaining contents on her wrist, was taken ill in fifteen minutes and died a few days later. Her partner was also taken ill but survived, as did a police officer who had attended the pair when they collapsed on a park bench.'

'Oh my God,' said Saslow. 'This has immense ramifications, doesn't it, boss? All sorts of people could be at risk. We could be at risk. We were at the festival site.'

'Don't worry about it, Saslow; if we had come into contact with the stuff yesterday, it seems we'd be well dead by now,' commented Vogel drily. 'Isn't that so, Raoul?'

'Indeed, Mr Vogel,' said Raoul.

'Can this stuff ever be rendered harmless if it is sufficiently diluted, Raoul?' Vogel asked suddenly.

'Yes, it can. Eventually. In large quantities of water.'

'I was thinking of the sea,' said Vogel. 'After all, the festival site is right by the sea. Could just about the best we could hope for be that the perpetrator threw the container he used to transport this toxin into the sea?'

'It probably is, and we would also need to hope that the container was either swept out to sea or washed clean by the time it drifted back to shore.'

'But anyone who sets out to poison another human being is not likely to have a great deal of respect for life,' commented Vogel. 'They may well have just dumped the thing, and possibly their gloves and any other connected paraphernalia, into a rubbish bin.'

'Just like Salisbury,' commented Saslow.

'Just like Salisbury,' repeated Vogel.

His mouth felt dry. He could feel knots of tension forming in his shoulders. Less than twenty-four hours earlier, he had been called to a sudden death that he and everybody else thought had almost certainly been caused by a heart attack.

Now he was dealing not only with a murder, and two

attempted murders, but also with a situation involving one of the most toxic substances on earth, the release of which could threaten the lives of hundreds of innocent people. Perhaps thousands.

NINETEEN

Mayor Roberts had not been present at the festival when James Harding died.

His official presence was only required for the opening and closing ceremonies, and he had no wish to be there at any other time. Particularly not this year.

When his wife had come into his home office to tell him the news, having seen it on Facebook or Twitter or some such thing, the mayor had been sitting at his desk, worrying.

He had quite a lot to worry about. When he'd heard that Harding was dead, his first thought was that his biggest worry of all had been removed. That his position in the world, his status as mayor of Bideford and, indeed, his freedom were no longer at risk.

But as the chain of events which followed Harding's death had unfolded, particularly those leading to Delia Day being seriously injured, the mayor realized that his troubles were far from over.

It was also his wife, again alerted by social media, who had told him about the first incident concerning Delia, how she had fallen off Appledore Quay on to the riverbed. Mayor Roberts had been enjoying a glass of rather good claret at the time. It may have been only late afternoon, and he watched his drinking carefully nowadays, but it was Sunday, and he'd thought he might have something to celebrate. Not that Jeremy Roberts would ever celebrate the death of another human being, of course. Or not in such a way that anyone else might become aware of it, not even his wife. But he could surely be allowed to celebrate the lifting of the cloud that had been hovering over his head for so long.

At first, Harding's death was considered to have been an accident, of course. Publicly, at any rate. But Mayor Roberts had immediately had his doubts. He was a bit like Vogel in one regard at least. He was deeply suspicious of coincidence.

He'd made a call to a long-standing police contact, an old chum, and enquired as casually as possible, in his mayoral capacity, how the incident was being treated by the force. He'd been told that a preliminary investigation had begun, already involving the Major Crimes Team and headed by DCI Vogel, but no conclusions had been drawn yet about what may have happened to Delia Day. And it was still believed that James Harding had died of a heart attack. What else could it have been?

Mayor Roberts also asked his chum how Delia was. When he'd placed the call, he hadn't even known for sure that she was alive. It seemed she was very much alive, but quite poorly with concussion and possibly several broken bones. It was all very disconcerting for the mayor. He asked to be informed of developments, concerning both the investigation and Delia's condition, in case of any significance or consequences concerning his civic duties, he said. Then he tried not to worry. There was, his father had always told him, no point in worrying. It helped nothing. A homily which invariably made little difference. If you were worried, you were worried.

A couple of hours after their first conversation, his police chum had called to tell him that it was understood that Delia Day had recovered consciousness and was believed to be out of danger. Which brought him some relief. Whatever it was he may have become inadvertently involved in did not seem, any more, to be murder.

He was, however, still worrying when he went to bed.

The mayor – only he hadn't been the mayor then, not even in local government at all – had first met James Harding when the writer had bought his cottage in Irsha Street back in the noughties. Harding had been on the crest of a wave back then. In demand as a scriptwriter at the highest level. And he had captivated Jeremy Roberts with his tales of glamour and celebrity. Jeremy had not led an exciting life. He had worked for his father since leaving school, but following his father's death Jeremy had been ready to step out on his own into rather more adventurous territory, areas where the risk might be bigger but the returns were likely to be far greater. At least he had that to tell James about.

Meanwhile, James Harding's career hit a bad patch, and his marriage hit the rocks, largely thanks to his philandering. His drinking had been reaching dangerous levels, too. And it was when Jeremy found himself joining James one night in a drinking session far beyond anything he could cope with that the trouble began. The mayor's tongue was loosened by alcohol and his brain numbed. James was an engaging companion when he chose to be. The legacy of that night continued to plague Jeremy.

In the morning, when he woke after a sleepless night, things had got even worse. His chum phoned again with the news of Delia being attacked in the hospital during the night. Which, of course, had not yet been made public.

When he took the call, the mayor was just about to tuck into a breakfast of four-minute boiled eggs and soldiers, sliced precisely into equal sizes the way he liked them, perfectly prepared by his wife. Jeremy Roberts liked his food, to which his girth, jowls and complexion bore witness, and he particularly liked to start his day with boiled eggs.

The more he listened, the more worried he became, and the more his appetite waned. Somebody had tried to smother Delia with a pillow. He had never heard of such a thing. Not in his beloved North Devon, anyway. And this was the second attempt on her life. That much was surely now abundantly clear.

The mayor pushed his untouched breakfast to one side, ignoring his wife's anxious scolding.

Somebody local, or at least connected with the festival, was trying to kill Delia Day, it seemed. His first thought would probably have been James Harding. He couldn't imagine what motive Harding might have as Delia would seem to be the goose laying his golden egg, although Mayor Roberts could believe almost anything of that man. Harding was probably the most awful, despicable, contemptible human being he had ever met in the whole of his life.

However, Harding had died before either of the attacks on Delia occurred.

And there was another problem. One that caused Jeremy Roberts to break out in a muck sweat. He may not have pushed Delia Day off the quay, he may not have tried to smother her in her hospital bed – not personally – but he was involved. And he could only imagine what part in it all his own actions might have played.

TWENTY

V ogel was in a decisive mood as he and Saslow left the mortuary.

'The first thing we have to do is close down this damned festival before someone else gets badly hurt,' he told the detective sergeant, as they hurried out of the hospital heading for Saslow's car. 'God knows where traces of that toxin might be lurking. You get on to DI Peters straight away, tell her what's happened and that we need the festival site cleared and nobody allowed in or out until further notice. Hopefully, it won't have got going yet today. And tell Peters we're on our way to Bideford. I need to run things from the incident room. I'm going to call Carolyne Smedley and get her on side.'

The festival director was bewildered and distraught.

'But why?' Carolyne asked. 'I thought James Harding died of a heart attack? I don't understand.'

'No, I'm sure you don't, and I'm afraid I can't tell you any more at the moment. There will be an announcement soon, and then you will understand. I promise you that.'

'But, Mr Vogel, I have several more authors arriving in Appledore today, two of them very big names indeed. What am I going to do? I mean, what can I say? I can't stop them coming now . . . no, you can't expect me to do this. Really, I can't. I don't even know what it's all about . . .'

'Carolyne, if you don't want to stop more authors coming

to Appledore, or are simply unable to do so, that is one thing, but there will very soon be a large police presence in the village making sure that the festival is halted and that no member of the public goes near any of the venues. The more cooperation you can give us, the better it will be for all concerned. But this is happening whether you like it or not. And now I'm running out of time. I have to go.'

He ended the call abruptly just as he and Saslow reached her car. She was clearly nearing the end of her call to DI Peters when Vogel asked her to pass her phone to him.

'Just one last thing, Janet,' he said. 'Obviously, the public health aspect of this and the need to keep people safe now overshadows everything. And finding James Harding's murderer is a big part of that. But I don't want us to lose sight of Delia Day's involvement. We don't even know how she is involved, but we do know there have almost certainly been two attempts on her life. I'd also like you to organize a top-level background check on Delia. Everything that is known about her past life, possible criminal record, any court appearances or convictions, time spent in prison and so on.'

'Right, boss,' said DI Peters, sounding surprised. But she knew better than to question Vogel.

'Oh, and there's someone else I'd like to get checked out. A woman called Penelope Peabody-Jones who sat on a panel with Delia yesterday and was at the event today when James Harding died. She left the scene in floods of tears, and I just wondered if there was anything going on there. Not that I can imagine her having much to do with South American poison dart frogs, but just get it checked out, will you, Janet? I'll text over her contact details.'

'Right, boss,' said DI Peters. She still sounded surprised.

But not as surprised as DS Saslow sounded when she spoke next.

'Is that what Delia told you?' she exclaimed. 'She has a criminal record, she's been in prison? Is that what she was saying when Doctor Grumpy interrupted?'

Vogel had already decided that the promise of confidentiality he had made to Delia Day could not extend to Saslow.

'Yes, but almost certainly not under the name Delia Day,'

he said. 'And now I seem to have lost the opportunity to even ask the woman what she was called before she became Delia Day. For the time being anyway . . .'

Once he and Saslow had set off from the hospital, and content that the obvious first course of action had been taken, to arrange for the festival to be shut down, Vogel made what was undoubtedly the most important call of all. To Detective Superintendent Nobby Clarke. So much of what had to be done now could only be put into motion at her level. Vogel was a senior officer, but he did not, by and large, have direct contact with the Home Office. And authority for the kind of action he felt sure would now be called for would probably have to come from government.

Clarke answered Vogel's call at once. She almost always picked up when he called, and quickly, even since their relationship had become a tad strained.

Vogel decided that the best thing he could do would be to condense all the information he had gathered in the last few minutes into one concise outpouring. So he went for it.

'James Harding died of poisoning after ingesting a lethal toxin excreted by a rare neotropical frog native to Colombia, known as the golden poison dart frog. It kills in minutes and there is no antidote, and, most scarily of all, we have no idea exactly how it was administered nor what may have happened to any container it was transported in or anything else it was in contact with. This toxin can be absorbed by touch, so we have a potential major incident on our hands, boss,' he almost blurted out.

There was silence for several seconds.

'Are you absolutely sure of all this, Vogel?' asked Clarke, her voice sounding as calm and controlled as ever.

'Yes, boss, the post-mortem revealed it. We had one stroke of luck: Daisy Dobb's assistant, a young Indian scientist, is something of an expert in this field, or we mightn't have got there quite so quickly. Daisy's putting together a full report, which I've asked her to send to you as well as to me. Oh, and I'm in the process of getting the festival closed down. DI Peters is dealing with the mechanics of that, and

I've warned the festival director and given her instructions on what she must do to assist. Saslow and I are on our way to the incident room now. We're going to need all the help we can get, boss.'

'You certainly are, Vogel. As am I! Funny that you mentioned the Salisbury poisonings last night and I told you off for being fanciful, isn't it?'

'I'm not surprised you did, boss. I never for a moment thought we had anything like that on our hands . . .'

'I know you didn't, Vogel, and let's hope we haven't. All the same, we need specialist assistance straight away and I'm about to get on to it. We also need to make a public announcement. Pronto. And I think it should come from us both. Get Peters to organize a press conference and find us a room at Bideford nick . . .' There was a brief pause as Clarke checked her watch, Vogel thought. 'For twelve noon,' she continued. 'I'll leave here as soon as I can and you, me and Peters need a meeting before the conference. Good luck, Vogel.'

'Thanks, boss,' said Vogel. 'Good luck to you, too.'

Clarke, Vogel and Peters were now, between them, running a mammoth operation.

Clarke arrived at Bideford nick just after eleven a.m. She didn't want an office of her own, preferring to muck in with Vogel and Saslow and be out on the floor of the ops room with the team. Which was typical of Nobby Clarke. She had already dealt with much that had to be done at government level. She'd explained the situation to the Ministry of Defence on her journey from her Exeter HQ, and asked for a specially equipped military task force to be deployed, just as after the Salisbury poisonings.

The first army vehicles bearing military personnel in camouflage-style protective clothing, and equipped with breathing equipment, trundled over the Torridge Bridge shortly after the detective superintendent's arrival.

DC Perkins, back on duty after the minimum amount of sleep required to keep him upright, was a local boy, born and bred. He was perhaps the most shocked of all.

'I can't believe I'm seeing this on the streets of Bideford,' he told Saslow. 'How long do you think it's going to take for them to clear everything, Sarge?'

Saslow was in a state of shock, too. She had been ever since learning that Harding had been killed by a lethal toxin excreted by a South American frog. It all sounded straight out of science fiction to her. And the invasion of Bideford and Appledore by soldiers in full PPE and wearing breathing equipment also seemed like science fiction to Dawn Saslow.

'It took them a year to clear Salisbury after the Novichok incident,' she remarked grimly.

'Oh, yes, but this is nothing like that, is it?' asked Perkins. Saslow moved closer to him.

'I don't know, Ricky,' she said. 'I have no idea what this is like. Except it's like nothing you and I have experienced before. Nor the boss, either.'

There had so far been no other reports of people collapsing suddenly, or unexpectedly suffering a dramatic heart attack. The North Devon District Hospital, however, was on standby for a major incident. As were all other major hospitals in the South West. And the three police officers in charge, Clarke, Vogel and Peters, were on tenterhooks.

Representatives of DEFRA were on their way from London. The incident room phone lines and email were inundated with queries from press nationwide and even some overseas, as the news of a possibly very strange major incident spread far and wide. The internet, of course, mostly in the form of social media outlets, was alive with speculation.

But – rather to the surprise of the three officers leading the investigation and monitoring the health and safety operation – the news that James Harding had not died of natural causes, but had been killed by the venomous secretion of a toxic South American frog, had still not leaked when the press conference began.

In spite of that, Vogel reckoned that everyone in the room was aware that something dangerously big was afoot. They already knew, of course, that the book festival had been suspended and that specially equipped military personnel were all over the village of Appledore, and they also knew by then that there had been two attempts on Delia Day's life. They did not know, however, if the latter was connected with the former. Vogel suspected they would believe that it was. In some yet-to-be-revealed way. As, indeed, did he.

Nobby Clarke took the lead, as she had to in such a critical situation, and stepped up to the podium at twelve minutes past twelve, just a few minutes late, which Vogel regarded as something of an achievement under the circumstances.

Her expression was grave as she introduced herself. You could have heard a pin drop in the room. The air of expectancy was almost palpable.

'Good morning, ladies and gentlemen,' she began. 'No doubt you will have realized already that we have a major emergency here in North Devon. A critical situation has presented itself, of a severity that I personally have never experienced in over twenty-five years of policing.

'We are now investigating two attempted murders and a murder.'

There was a collective murmur of surprise from those in the room. They had no knowledge of any murder, nor a second attempted murder. The first incident concerning the world-famous Delia Day, the military presence in the area, the closing down of certain parts of Bideford and Appledore, and being told that Detective Superintendent Clarke, the head of MCT, would be leading the press conference had been quite enough to draw an extremely large and expectant media turnout.

Just wait until they hear what's to come, thought Vogel.

'James Harding, who died suddenly at the Appledore Book Festival on Sunday, did not die of natural causes as was first thought,' continued Clarke. 'He was murdered.'

She paused. The murmurs and mutterings in the room grew a little louder and more prevalent.

Then Clarke dropped the bombshell. Two bombshells.

'Mr Harding was poisoned, by person or persons unknown,' she announced first.

Which in itself was enough to set the room buzzing even more.

'He died because he absorbed the venom of a toxic neotropical frog.'

The room erupted.

There had been discussions at government level concerning whether or not the manner of Harding's death should be made public. And there had been differing opinions, ranging from old-school need-to-know to the more modern leaning towards transparency. Or, at least, appearing to be transparent, Vogel always thought.

The latter course of action had ultimately been decided upon, largely due to the necessity for the public to play a part in its own protection. People needed to be told why certain extreme measures had already been taken, starting with the closing down of the festival, so that they would cooperate fully and not put themselves in unnecessary danger. Clarke and Vogel had both pressed strongly for this alternative because as police officers they believed that the safety of the public should always be their first priority.

Clarke gave as full a description of the golden poison dart frog and its immense toxic capacity as she was able and answered the initial barrage of questions, many of which echoed the questions Vogel had asked Raoul at the mortuary.

One topic, raised by the *Daily Telegraph*'s representative, had been expected by all involved in staging the press conference.

'Detective Superintendent, we have all seen the specialist units moving into the district today and you have confirmed the security measures that are being put in place, and I'm sure I'm not the only one present who has noticed the similarity with the aftermath of the Salisbury poisonings,' he began. 'Can you tell us whether you believe we are dealing with a situation of that gravity, and do you suspect the involvement of agents operating under the authority of foreign powers?'

'I cannot comment on just how grave this situation might be in terms of public safety at the present time, nor do we know yet who might be responsible for having used this toxin against Mr Harding,' responded Clarke. 'But we hope that by acting as swiftly and as comprehensively as we have, we will continue to control the situation without any further endangerment to human life.'

'What about the two attempted murders you mentioned? Are we to assume that Delia Day was the target of at least one of them and that you now consider her fall off Appledore Quay to have been an attempt on her life?' asked the young woman from *The Sun*.

'That is correct,' responded Clarke. 'We have concluded that not least because Delia was also the target of the second attempted murder.'

She then explained how Delia had been attacked in her hospital bed – Clarke deliberately didn't mention which hospital, although she knew that wouldn't take a lot of working out in North Devon – by an unknown assailant who had attempted to smother her with a pillow.

There was a collective gasp in the room.

The detective superintendent added that Delia was believed to have recovered full consciousness and had been described as comfortable but was still in intensive care.

'Do you consider the murder of James Harding and the attempts on the life of Delia Day to be in some way connected?' continued *The Sun* reporter.

'I'm going to call on DCI David Vogel, who is heading this investigation and who has been on the spot ever since James Harding's death, to answer that,' said Clarke.

'We don't know but we are investigating every possibility,' replied Vogel, who was, of course, almost certain that they were.

'And do you know what that connection might be?'

'No,' replied Vogel honestly. 'We know that Mr Harding and Miss Day worked together and knew each other well. But at this stage, we cannot confirm anything more than that. We have no information concerning the motives for these attacks or the possibility of links between them.'

He did not, of course, mention that Delia Day, it seemed, was a woman with a past; he saw no need to break his confidence on this scale. In any case, it had yet to be learned exactly what her past was, and if it had any direct relevance to the case.

'We also know that Delia Day has received two threatening notes since her arrival in North Devon, both of them anonymous,' Vogel continued. He had the two notes with him, read them out and then held them up to be seen and photographed.

'Do you suspect that the same perpetrator was responsible for all three attacks?' asked a local radio reporter.

'Obviously, that is something we are investigating,' said Vogel obliquely. 'But until we have made an arrest, or indeed arrests, we continue to fear for Miss Day's safety, and she is under police protection.'

This caused another buzz around the room.

Vogel answered several more questions, gave a further update on Delia's condition, as best he could, and explained in as much detail as possible the nature of the investigation he was heading. He did not mention certain aspects, such as the switching of the name cards before the panel during which James Harding died. He did not want to encourage the obvious speculation that Harding had been killed by mistake and that the killer had intended Delia Day to die. Not yet.

As he spoke, he became starkly aware of how little he could say. So far, the investigation had discovered absolutely nothing to indicate who might be responsible for the shocking chain of events that had engulfed the district.

TWENTY-ONE

I t wasn't until she turned up for her next shift at the Imperial, just before noon on the morning of the press conference, that Jenny learned about the second attack on Delia Day.

Again it was Ian who told her about it. His sister-in-law was a nurse at the North Devon District Hospital. She and Ian's wife, Ruth, were inclined to chat on the phone several times a day. So, of course, she had mentioned the attempted suffocation of such a famous novelist. And as soon as she did so, Ruth texted Ian with the news. After all, he worked at the Imperial, where Delia had been staying. It was almost a family affair.

Jenny felt a cold chill spread through her body from the base of her spine. It made it difficult for her to function.

Eventually, she managed some kind of response to Ian, who

had delivered the news as if it were just the most delicious piece of gossip. Which, she supposed, to many people it would be. But not to her.

Fortunately, she was approached by a guest seeking information, which gave her time to compose herself a little.

It was Jenny who had delivered those two notes to Delia Day's room. She had not opened the envelopes. She had been told not to. In any case, it wouldn't have occurred to her to do so. People's mail, whether delivered by hand or by Royal Mail, was private. Their business. Not hers.

So she'd had no idea what the envelopes had contained. She had told herself, of course, that it was quite possibly just fan mail. Or perhaps more likely, considering the person who had asked her to deliver the notes, some sort of business proposition. And she supposed she had been encouraged to believe that. But now she had terrible doubts. Had those envelopes contained threats against Delia? And had attempts since been made to execute those threats?

Jenny was distraught. Bob the manager was passing through reception. She went to him at once.

'Bob, I'm so sorry, I feel really ill, I've been sick,' she lied. 'I don't think I'm going to be able to work.'

Bob was immediately sympathetic.

'Of course not,' he said kindly. 'You must go home at once. Would you like me to get someone to drive you? We can sort out your car tomorrow.'

'No, no, I'll be fine.'

'Well, all right, if you really think so. Maybe some fresh air will help . . .'

'Yes, yes, I'm sure it will,' Jenny called back over her shoulder. She was already half out of the hotel.

Bob liked her. And respected her. Jenny knew that. She couldn't believe what she was doing. Lying to an employer who had always treated her well. Abandoning her post. And, of course, what she had already done was even worse. She was complicit in two attempts on Delia Day's life. Isn't that what the police would say? She ran to her car, tears trickling down her cheeks. She felt like scum. She was a wreck.

However, she had no intention of going home. She was

going to see the person who had landed her in this mess. The person she had been beholden to for so long, and who had always made her very aware of that. The person who had told her coldly when asking her to deliver those notes that it was payback time. The person she now believed might be responsible for those attacks on Delia. And she was going to confront that person.

The thought occurred to her that this could be a dangerous course of action. She didn't care. Jenny was quite religious in her way. A Baptist. She didn't go to church every week, or anything like that, but she believed in God and considered herself a Christian. She always tried to live a Christian life and believed totally in the concept of sin. She now almost welcomed retribution. The person she was going to see was not going to get away with what they had done. Not if Jenny had anything to do with it. And whatever the consequences might be for her, well, she deserved everything she got.

But gradually it became apparent to Jenny, as she approached Bideford, that she was going to have problems completing her short journey. Something was very wrong indeed. There was a strong military presence. She found herself in an unexpected traffic jam. It seemed that the road ahead which led to her destination was blocked.

She switched her car radio from the music channel she usually listened to on to the local news station. Her timing could not have been more apt. A special news bulletin covering the press conference at Bideford Police Station was just beginning.

As she listened, Jenny grew more and more distraught. James Harding had been murdered, she learned. And by an exotic deadly toxin, traces of which could still be a public risk. Much of the district was trapped in a kind of siege situation. The two attempts on Delia's life were mentioned. As were the notes Jenny had delivered. And they were both highly threatening, as she had come to suspect.

Jenny was horrified. She could have unwittingly played a part in all of it. Even James Harding's death and the use of the deadly toxin.

She had to confess; she had to tell the authorities everything she knew. She no longer intended to even try to reach the person who had forced her to deliver those notes to Delia.

She was going to the police. As soon as this traffic jam moved, she would drive to Bideford Police Station which was, she had heard on the radio, the headquarters of the entire investigation. And she would tell them everything.

She had to. Whatever the consequences.

The Tucker twins knew nothing of any events beyond James Harding's death and Delia Day having fallen from Appledore Quay until they too tuned in, by chance, to news reports of what was regarded as a quite sensational press conference, on the TV in their Airbnb.

The twins were a little late on parade as the shock of all that had happened the previous afternoon had led to them consuming even more cannabis and whisky than they would on a normal night. Theirs had been a slow start, and they had decided not to bother with the late-morning panel at the festival for which they had already bought tickets. It was not of particular interest to them. Indeed, nothing was of particular interest to Tilly and Tina unless it featured Delia Day. Neither had they yet bothered to look at their phones. They didn't even know that the festival had been suspended.

They watched the coverage of the press conference in total horror. They had previously told themselves that Delia's fall must have been an accident. Any other possibility had been unthinkable to them. Also that James Harding's death was not in any way connected.

Now they had learned that there had been two attempts on Delia's life, that James Harding had been murdered – by a deadly toxin derived from a killer Colombian frog – and that all three violent incidents could well be linked. Also that their beloved Delia was probably still in great danger.

'We have to go to her,' said Tilly.

'Yes.'

'We have to tell her now, we must,' said Tilly.

'I told you we should have told her, before,' said Tina.

'No, you didn't. I told you that,' said Tilly.

'You didn't.'

'I did,'

'It was me.'

'No, it was me.'

'Look, we mustn't quarrel.'

'We never quarrel.'

'We're quarrelling now.'

'No, we're not.'

'Yes, we are.'

There was a pause.

Tilly spoke first.

'All right, look, all that matters is what we should do now.'

'I agree with that,' said Tina.

'We both agree on that.'

'Yes.'

'So let's go to her.'

They were still in their pyjamas.

'We need to start getting ready,' said Tina.

'Yes, of course,' said Tilly.

She was looking at her phone.

'I've just googled, there's only one big hospital around here – the North Devon District Hospital in Barnstaple,' she said.

'She's probably in intensive care, though,' said Tilly. 'And she's under police protection. They won't let us see her, surely.'

'Well, we can try.'

'All right, let's try.'

'As soon as we're ready, let's call for a taxi and go to the hospital. That has to be the right thing to do.'

'Oh, yes, it has to be the right thing to do.'

Less than an hour after the press conference finished, Vogel felt his phone vibrate in his pocket again. The caller was DC Perkins. He had just arrived at the N.D.D.H to relieve Docherty on guard duty. And he'd walked straight into a crisis.

'Boss, Delia's much better. Her blood pressure, oxygen level and temperature are all normal. They want her out of ICU now, and they want to send her home. She wants to go back to the Imperial.'

'For God's sake, Perkins, only six hours or so ago, they

behaved as if they thought she was still at death's door and sent us packing!'

'Yes, boss, but they say she's recovering better than expected and is out of danger, and don't forget the hospital has just been put on alert for a major incident.'

'Well, there is that, I suppose,' muttered Vogel grudgingly. 'But she certainly can't return to the Imperial. I thought the plan was to move her into a general ward after ICU.'

'They don't have any beds, apparently. You know the state hospitals are in at the moment. Even without the major incident.'

'OK, OK, have you told them Delia is a special case, that she could still be in grave danger of attack – almost certainly is, in fact – and they really must keep her until we have sorted something out.'

'Yes, boss, the doctor I've been dealing with is called Garvey, and I understand you had a bit of a run-in with him this morning. When I said he really mustn't discharge Delia until I'd at least reported back to you, he said, "I don't take orders from DCI Vogel, even though he seems to think I do. In this hospital, I give the orders." He just won't listen to reason.'

'That sounds like him all right,' said Vogel glumly. 'Look, every Tom, Dick and Harry will know Delia's been staying at the Imperial, including whoever attacked her and the entire great British press corps, I should imagine. We haven't done a very good job of protecting her in hospital; it would be considerably more difficult in a hotel. We have to find an alternative. We could put her in a car back to her home in London, but whatever Garvey says, from what I've seen of her, she wouldn't be up to the journey, and I need to talk to her properly before she leaves our patch. Stall as much as you can. We need to go over this idiot doctor's head. Don't worry, Perkins, I'll sort this out somehow, and get back to you soonest. But if necessary, keep Delia in a bloody corridor. Do not let her out of that hospital until we've organized somewhere for her to go.'

'Right, boss,' said Perkins. He really was a stalwart, thought Vogel.

The DCI quickly explained the situation to Clarke and asked her if she would approach the hospital at the highest level. She was extremely good at that sort of thing. Always knew somebody at the top, and always seemed to get her own way. Arguably, her greatest talent, thought Vogel.

Clarke started making calls immediately. Vogel thought she was rather enjoying herself.

He turned to Saslow, who had overheard both his half of the phone conversation with Perkins and his subsequent conversation with Clarke.

'We need to move Delia somewhere we can protect her, Saslow, and quickly,' he said.

'Yes, boss, what about another hotel, somewhere a bit smaller and more discreet?' queried Saslow.

'Wouldn't do,' responded Vogel. 'She's too readily recognized, and once the press we've just been talking to have done their damnedest all over every possible form of media, if anybody gets even the smallest glimpse of her, it'll spread like wildfire. She's bound to be spotted in a hotel.'

'A safe house then, boss?' Saslow suggested.

'A safe house?' repeated Vogel. 'This isn't Moscow in the 1960s, Saslow. And you and I aren't Burgess and Mclean. This is Bideford in 2023. And we're a pair of English coppers.'

Saslow giggled.

'Yes, boss, sorry, boss,' she said. 'What about an Airbnb, then?'

'Still too public. Delia would still be likely to be recognized, wouldn't she?'

'Not if we get a self-contained flat or a studio,' countered Saslow. 'I could book it and arrange payment and pick up the keys and all that sort of thing. We just have to take her in discreetly.'

'All right, Saslow, that could work. Well done. Do you think you'll be able to find somewhere for tonight?'

'You often can, boss.'

'OK. Get on to it, will you?'

'Straight away.'

'Good. And I'll let Perkins know. We'll keep him on nursemaid duty for as long as possible, I think. Just one last thing, Saslow . . .'

'Yes, boss.'

'Good luck with the "discreetly".'

TWENTY-TWO

Within the hour, Delia Day was moved into a side ward. Dr Garvey, who had been so curt with Vogel, and who she didn't think was her greatest fan either, was nowhere to be seen.

Perkins, whom she now called 'Shadow', but not really in a derisory way as she had taken quite a shine to him, hadn't moved from her side since coming on duty, and was still there, sitting very upright in a rather uncomfortable-looking chair.

'Well, that was quick,' she commented.

Delia had been well aware of the kerfuffle about what to do with her. Dr Garvey had a very loud voice which he seemed to use at full volume most of the time. Not ideal for a doctor, Delia thought, but she had rather enjoyed the cabaret.

Garvey had also shouted earlier at Perkins, who seemed to be an unflappable sort of chap, a quality Delia rather admired. Perkins had taken it on the chin and refused to budge, or allow Garvey to budge, until he had spoken to his superior officer.

And the superior officer – Vogel, she assumed, as she didn't yet know about Detective Chief Superintendent Clarke's involvement in anything – had not messed about. Obviously. It appeared that there would be no further suggestion of her being asked to leave the hospital until she could be relocated to somewhere the police felt she would be safe and where they could continue to protect her.

Delia hadn't protested the way she normally would have done. What had happened to her over the last twenty-four hours or so was, after all, totally abnormal. She had at first convinced herself that her fall must have been accidental, but there was nothing remotely accidental about being half smothered by a pillow. Whilst lying in a hospital bed, too. That had been exceptionally disconcerting. Nonetheless, she was still undecided about whether or not she would comply with what

Perkins had told her was now the police plan – that she should be moved to some Airbnb of yet-to-be-revealed quality. Or no quality at all, she feared. Or whether she would do her own thing, as she usually did, and get Michael to drive her back to her comfortable accommodation at the Imperial. With excellent room service.

She was still pondering this when her phone, which had been in her bag and had somewhat miraculously survived her fall, bleeped. It had run out of juice whilst she'd been in ICU, but, after Perkins found a charger, was now signalling its return to life. It then bleeped again, and several more times, indicating that she had received a number of news alerts.

Idly, she reached for the phone, put on her purple-framed glasses and began to read.

She nearly jumped out of her skin.

'Top scriptwriter killed by lethal poison dart frog.' 'Delia Day in murder riddle – is she too in danger from killer frog?' 'North Devon holiday hotspots closed down.' 'Devon in the grip of a terror attack?' 'One death already – when will the poison frog strike again?' 'North Devon in poison panic – is this Salisbury all over again?'

The headlines and slogans leapt at her off the screen.

There were numerous pictures of the poison dart frog, one captioned: 'He may look pretty, he may seem harmless – but is this the most dangerous creature on earth?'

There were also pictures of quite sinister-looking military men and women clad in camouflage gear and full PPE, including futuristic breathing apparatus, swarming all over Appledore.

'They look like invaders from outer space – but they're only here to help,' read one extended caption.

Delia dropped her phone as if it was too hot to handle. Which, metaphorically speaking, she rather thought it was.

'For God's sake, DC Perkins,' she cried. 'Poison frogs, terror attack, invaders from outer space, Delia Day in murder riddle? What the fuck is going on?'

Perkins coloured slightly.

'I don't think I'm supposed to talk to you about it, ma'am,' he said.

'Do you not, my dear boy?' enquired Delia, her voice dangerously gentle. 'Well, it's quite simple. Either you talk, starting right now, or I get up out of this bed and walk straight out of this hospital, and the only way you would be able to stop me would be by using physical force. Which would be police brutality. Or it would be by the time I'd finished with you. So it's up to you, DC Perkins. Talk or I walk. And you can explain that to your boss.'

Perkins talked.

Meanwhile, Saslow had arranged to rent a studio flat in nearby Braunton for three nights. She picked up the keys and drove there to check the place out.

The little studio was perfectly acceptable, although not, Saslow thought, anything like the standard of accommodation Delia was accustomed to. But at least there seemed to be a fairly good chance that she would not be attacked again whilst staying there.

It fitted certain non-negotiable criteria. It had its own front door, albeit accessed through a communal hall, and the land-lord did not live on the premises. Once safely installed, Delia would be reasonably hidden away from the world and hopefully not bothered by any unexpected callers.

Perkins called to say that Delia had asked if some fresh clothes could be brought to her from the Imperial. Everything she'd been wearing had been pretty much ruined by her fall to the muddy riverbed, and she was still clad in only a hospital gown. She wanted her laptop, too, of course, her hair-wand, some nightwear and her makeup bag. He also said he thought he'd got her on board concerning the move to Braunton, which would be one hell of an achievement in Saslow's opinion. In fact, Perkins still wasn't sure about that. And Delia, perhaps significantly, hadn't asked for all her luggage to be brought to her. It seemed she remained under the impression that she would be returning to the Imperial at some stage. The way things were going, Saslow didn't think that was very likely.

Saslow called Vogel, who cleared it with the hotel manager for Saslow to be let into Delia's room. The DCI also instructed his sergeant to have a good dig around whilst she was there.

Saslow couldn't imagine what she might find that would be relevant to the case. Surely nothing that might incriminate Delia. There could be no doubt now, could there, that she, just as much as James Harding, was a victim of the extraordinary scenario that Devon and Cornwall Police, aided and abetted by a substantial contingent of the British army, were now faced with.

Saslow was rather more anxious about what she was likely to find in Delia's wardrobe that wouldn't at once scream out to the world that this was Delia Day. Something inconspicuous they could ask her to wear if she did agree to be moved to Braunton.

To her relief, she quickly came across a plain dark-grey tracksuit – with a hood, which was a real bonus. In its pocket, there was a black beanie. And a pair of black gloves. And there were three pairs of trainers lined up behind the door – two pairs were purple and black with silver and white flashes, the Delia Day trademark. But the third pair was plain black with just a single white streak along each side.

The tracksuit, its accessories and the black trainers would do nicely, thought Saslow. You couldn't get anything much more inconspicuous. Fleetingly, she wondered if maybe, just maybe, Delia occasionally dressed in this ordinary and anonymous outfit in order to slip out into the world unnoticed. And if so, she couldn't help wondering, what would her motives be? Was she like the late Princess Diana and just wanted to occasionally go incognito in a crowd? To be a nobody for a few hours. Surely even Delia Day might enjoy a rest from being recognized sometimes.

Or did these clothes indicate something more sinister? Possibly something connected with the murder and mayhem which had just struck North Devon with a vengeance.

Saslow told herself that had to be nonsense. Delia had been attacked twice by an unknown assailant. There was no doubt at all about the second attack. It was indisputable. And there really could be no doubt now about the first.

It didn't seem very likely, either, that Delia would ever have had much of an association with poisonous dart frogs from Colombia and their lethally toxic venom.

Nonetheless, although pleased and relieved to find those dull, anonymous clothes among all Delia's usual vibrant choice of garments, Saslow had been very surprised.

And she still couldn't quite stop wondering . . .

Delia had listened carefully to everything that Perkins told her. She was non-committal at first. She continued to surf the internet after he had finished, and took a few minutes to take everything in.

Her conclusion was inevitable, however. This changed everything. She no longer had any intention of being tricky about police protection, whatever that might mean and wherever she might be taken to.

The whole scenario was unbelievable. The venom of a super-toxic frog had killed James Harding and caused much of North Devon to be closed down. Maybe even the frog itself was on the loose. And it seemed that she was considered to be at the heart of it all. She wasn't even entirely sure whether the police's determination to watch over her was entirely down to a desire to keep her out of danger, or whether there was still a lurking suspicion here and there that she might be a danger to others.

On the other hand, she could hardly have smothered herself with a pillow, could she?

The feelings of unease, which had plagued her ever since her arrival in North Devon, could not have been more justified, it seemed.

And when Perkins had told her of the plan to relocate her temporarily to an apartment that had been found in nearby Braunton, where she would be safe and under police guard, she had actually been immensely relieved. And even more relieved when Perkins told her that DCI Vogel would be coming to the flat to resume their interview as soon as she was settled in.

When she had begun – was it really only earlier that morning? – to reveal to David Vogel details of her life that had always been a closely kept secret, she had not been sure how far she would be prepared to go.

Now, she realized that it was vitally important that she

talked to Vogel again and told him pretty much everything. She did not know how relevant her story was, or even in what way it could be connected to the events of the last twenty-four hours or so. But suddenly so many unanswered questions had presented themselves. And so many lives could be in danger.

Perkins had stepped outside to use his phone. He was now back in the room. She put him out of his misery at once.

'I don't seem to have much choice, Ricky, do I?' she asked rhetorically. 'Braunton it is. Let's get ready to move.'

She raised a hand to her head. Her hair was still muddy. She asked Perkins to help her arrange to use a bathroom and have a shower. Not only would it make her feel better, but she thought there could well be streaks of mud on her face, too. She hadn't had an opportunity to look in a mirror since she'd been in the hospital. Not that she'd had any inclination to do so until now, either.

A bathroom was duly arranged. Delia emerged with a towel wrapped around her head, still wearing on her broken arm the waterproof cast protector provided by a helpful nurse who had also provided her with a clean hospital nightgown, just as Saslow arrived with the smaller of her two bags containing everything she had asked for. Or, as it turned out, almost everything.

'I'm very glad to see you,' Delia greeted the detective sergeant. 'Can't wait to see what you brought me. You've got my laptop, of course?'

Saslow looked stricken.

'Oh my God, Delia, I'm so sorry,' she said. 'It just went clean out of my mind; I was concentrating on finding the right clothes.'

Delia, who was, by and large, attached to her laptop rather more than most people are to their phones, could have cheerfully slapped her, but actually did and said nothing.

'Look, as soon as I can after we've moved you to Braunton, I'll drive back to the Imperial and get it, I promise,' Saslow continued.

'Well, that will have to do, then,' said Delia, trying hard not to let her irritation show. 'I wonder if you found my grey tracksuit and my beanie? I should have told you about them. Suspect they may be very useful . . .'

'I have them,' interrupted Saslow. 'And I agree, they will be useful.'

'Ah, good,' said Delia.

'I also thought you might occasionally use them as a kind of disguise, for reasons other than being stalked by a possible killer,' Saslow continued a little haltingly. 'Certainly very different to anything you would normally wear.'

'Indeed. Quite right, Dawn. I always carry something of that kind with me in case I ever want to go unnoticed. One good thing about being as instantly recognizable as I usually am is that it's extremely easy to make yourself unrecognizable. All you have to do is create something other than your usual somewhat flamboyant look. Almost anything, in fact.'

'Well, I'm glad to hear it,' said Saslow. 'I'm beginning to think that getting you to that Airbnb may not be as difficult as I feared.'

'Apart from my broken arm,' said Delia. 'I think I can cover the bruise on my forehead with makeup.' She touched her face gingerly. 'But the cast on my arm is a bit of a giveaway.'

She waved it weakly at Saslow.

'Do you like my giant condom?' she remarked. 'Thing's actually called a LimbO, I understand.'

Saslow smiled. 'So when you're dry and not wearing a condom, do you have to have that arm in a sling?'

'I'm supposed to. And it's less painful if I do. But, no, I don't have to.'

'Good,' said Saslow. 'I also found a couple of plain T-shirts, one black and one white, amongst your stuff, and I've brought them along. Do you think you could get into one of them all right with that arm?'

'With difficulty, yes,' said Delia. 'We may have to cut a sleeve to make it wide enough.'

'OK. So my plan would be that you put on the tracksuit bottoms and a T-shirt, and wear the tracksuit top unzipped over your shoulders, making sure it covers your broken arm. Do your fingers still work on that arm?'

'Just about,' said Delia.

'Good, you may have to hold the tracky top in place.'

'No problem,' said Delia.

'Result,' said Saslow.

'Right, so perhaps you two would step outside now while I get dressed.'

'Do you want any help drying your hair?' asked Saslow, eyeing the broken arm.

'I'll be fine,' said Delia as she removed the hair-wand from her bag. 'You only need one arm for this.'

She applied very little makeup, except over her bruise, and certainly no false eyelashes. She always carried nail polish remover in her makeup bag for repairs on the run, and she removed the distinctive purple nail varnish which was another of her trademarks.

It took a while, but once she was ready, having pulled on the beanie over her distinctive hair, she was highly unlikely to be recognized as Delia Day by anyone – possibly not even the Tucker twins. Just as she had assured Saslow.

'See,' Delia remarked as Saslow guided her through the hospital to one of the staff exits where Perkins was waiting in his car. 'I'm almost a human being.'

TWENTY-THREE

The two police officers transported Delia to Braunton with no incident at all, and without attracting any attention that they were aware of.

Vogel, having extricated himself from the endless administrative duties of being SIO of such a major and complex operation, arrived at the Braunton flat about an hour later. Coincidentally, at the same time as a young man in a smart grey suit, whom the DCI recognized at once as Delia's driver, Michael. They met on the doorstep.

'And what the fuck are you doing here?' enquired Vogel, who hardly ever swore.

'Miss Day asked me to go to the Imperial and bring her

laptop here,' said Michael mildly, holding up Delia's top-of-the-range MacBook Pro for Vogel to see.

Vogel almost snatched it from him.

'Do you realize nobody is supposed to know where Delia is?' Vogel enquired irritably.

'Uh, yes, well, I did assume that.'

'Right, so please do not tell anyone, anyone at all, that she is here. OK?'

'Of course OK,' said Michael. 'I wouldn't dream of it.'

Vogel asked Michael for his full name, address and phone number, which he jotted down in his notebook.

'Right, I'll take the laptop to Delia,' he said then. 'You just get on your way.'

'I'm going,' said Michael quickly. 'I was only doing my job.'

Vogel turned away. How many times in his life had he heard that?

He called the flat on the intercom. Perkins answered and buzzed him in. Vogel ran up the two flights of stairs. The DC opened the door for him.

Delia was sitting on one of two arm chair by the window.

'I want those chairs moved away from the window at once,' Vogel barked. 'Delia, please get up.'

She did so, although looking puzzled.

'I've just met your driver on the doorstep,' Vogel announced angrily, slamming down the laptop on the table. 'This is supposed to be a secret location, Delia. Somewhere safe for you. A place where we wouldn't need to move you away from the window in case some lunatic throws a brick in. Or something worse! What did you think you were doing?'

'I needed my laptop,' said Delia. 'Michael won't tell anyone where I am. He's rock solid, I'm sure of it.'

'Perhaps.'

Vogel glanced towards Perkins and Saslow.

'Where were you two when she contacted this Michael?'

'I texted him,' volunteered Delia. 'They couldn't have known.'

'It was my fault, boss,' said Saslow. 'Delia asked me to bring her laptop, and I forgot it.'

Vogel did not comment.

Delia sat down again on one of the two armchairs. Vogel sat in the other. Without her full makeup and wearing a plain grey tracksuit, she was indeed almost unrecognizable. Apart from the hair.

'I'm sorry, David, I know you have my best interests at heart.'

'We're just trying to protect you, Delia,' said Vogel. 'There have been two attempts on your life, you know.'

'I do know. Yes.'

'All right. Hopefully, no harm done. So let's move on, shall we?'

Delia nodded her agreement.

'I think we should begin where we left off then – do you agree, Delia?' he asked.

'I think we better had,' said Delia. 'But it has to be just you and me alone again, David.'

Vogel studied her carefully for a moment. The situation had changed dramatically since he had begun the aborted interview with Delia earlier in the day. He had expected this approach from her, and he knew he couldn't allow it. Not this time. Not anymore.

'Look, Delia, I'm afraid this isn't just about you now,' he began. 'Not even just about you and James Harding. We have a major incident on our hands in North Devon, potentially on a scale way beyond anything I have ever dealt with before. Not only do I need to record our conversation, but I need another officer present as a witness.'

'I understand where you're coming from, David,' countered Delia. 'But I don't see how anything I might tell you about me and my life could have any connection with what is happening in North Devon right now—'

'You're going to have to let me be the judge of that, Delia,' said Vogel. 'The goalposts have moved. Significantly.'

'Well, I'm not sure . . .'

'Look, I'm only giving you one choice,' interrupted Vogel. 'Either you talk to me here and now, recorded as before, on the terms I have just offered you, with just me and DS Saslow present, or you come to the police station where you will be interviewed formally. The only reason you are being offered an alternative is that you are recovering from serious injury, and I consider you still to be in very real danger of another attack. Therefore, it is in all our interests not to take you to a police station and thrust you into the public eye in the view, no doubt, of whoever has already attacked you twice. But have no doubt about it, Delia, that is what I will do if you do not cooperate fully. And if you should refuse to accompany us to the station of your own free will, then I will arrest you to facilitate that. Is that clear?'

Delia's eyes were open wide, in surprise as well as alarm, Vogel thought. People were almost invariably surprised when he decided to play it tough.

His gentle, usually amiable manner concealed a core of steel, which he only displayed when circumstances demanded it. The present circumstances demanded it, all right. And he just didn't have the time to argue the toss with Delia Day. He would have his own way. And that was that.

Delia, it seemed, recognized that.

'All right,' she said. 'You do indeed leave me no choice, David. And I suppose I have always known this moment would come sooner or later.'

'Good,' responded Vogel.

He asked Perkins to leave him and Saslow alone with Delia, and began a second recording, making the usual introductory announcements.

'You had just told me that you were in prison when your first book was published, because "I hurt someone very badly",' Vogel began. 'I'd like you to tell me now exactly what you did – when, where, and to whom.'

Delia lowered her head in her hands just for a few seconds, then looked up again at Vogel.

'It was forty-three years ago, when I was nineteen. I was alternately living on the street in central London – Covent Garden mostly – or in squats, and I was a heroin addict,' she spoke quickly, as if in a hurry to get the words out, to get rid of them perhaps.

Then she paused for a while. Vogel thought she might be summoning up the courage to continue. He looked at Saslow, and Saslow looked at him. They did not speak.

'One day, half off my head and desperate for more smack, I mugged an elderly woman on Endell Street. I grabbed her bag. But she hung on. I lashed out at her. She fell, and it was clear at once that she was badly hurt. Even stoned as I was, I was traumatized by what I had done. I remember I just stood looking for a moment or two, horrified. By the time I started to run away, a group of people had gathered, some of whom had seen exactly what had happened. Two of them were builders working just across the road. Big, burly men. They grabbed hold of me. I struggled, but I was never going to get away from them.

'The woman I knocked down suffered a broken hip and concussion. I was charged with causing grievous bodily harm and sentenced to five years' imprisonment, the maximum term for the offence. Unsurprising, I suppose, under the circumstances.'

Vogel tried not to let his shock show. Delia was arguably the most successful novelist in the world, certainly the biggest-selling; it didn't seem possible that she could have a past like this. He wanted to know the full story, from the beginning.

'How long had you been living like that, on the streets and in squats?' he asked.

'Three or maybe four years,' Delia responded.

'Since you were fifteen or sixteen?'

'Yes, fifteen, I think.'

'I'd like to know what led to this, what came before and how you ended up in such a state?'

'I thought you might,' said Delia. 'It's a long story, though, so I shall give you an edited version. I never knew my parents. I was told I was abandoned at birth. I spent most of my childhood, as far as I can remember, in and out of children's homes and in the care of a series of foster parents, never with any of them for long. Largely because I became an unruly, unpredictable child, most unpleasant to have around, I should think. I was, of course, deeply disturbed, but this was back in the sixties and seventies, when young people with those kinds of difficulties, now usually regarded as mental health issues, were inclined to be punished, often locked away, rather than helped and cared for.

'Needless to say, my childhood bad behaviour became more serious and destructive as I entered my teens. I sought out the company of young people equally as disturbed as I was. I experimented with drugs, the usual. I started by smoking dope, ended up hooked on smack. It was the usual progression. I stole from my various foster parents, then would be returned to a children's home, where I stole from the carers, visitors, anybody I could. This led to appearances in juvenile court, and more than one stay in a young offender institution. I would come off the drugs cold turkey – there wasn't a lot of rehab around, not for kids like me anyway. Then I'd come out, go back on the smack every time, and do anything I could to fund the habit. Not only stealing. Begging, of course. And having sex for money. I was on the game at sixteen.'

'At sixteen?'

Vogel didn't mean to interrupt, but he wasn't able to help himself. Delia would have been not much older than his daughter Rosamund when she became a prostitute.

'Yes. Sixteen. And I looked younger. So there were plenty of customers. Old men mostly. Well, old compared to me at that time. Paedophiles, I suppose, but that wasn't a term you often heard back then. There didn't seem to be anyone to help me. I had bucked the system, broken all the rules. And I suppose most people would have thought I only got what I deserved after mugging that poor woman. I thought that myself, for God's sake.

'I was just nineteen, only old enough by a few weeks to be treated as an adult in law. I suppose there's little doubt that I had it coming, big time. I'd been out of control for years. I was advised to plead guilty, which I'm sure was only right and proper.

'But the woman I had knocked over appeared in court to give a statement before I was sentenced. It was her choice, I understood at the time, at the request of the prosecution who wanted me put away for as long as possible. She was still on crutches, and she looked so weak and vulnerable. It seemed she had no children or immediate family and had lived alone, quite contently, looking after herself, until I'd mugged her, and she'd been left unable to fend for herself any longer. She spoke of how frightened she was, following the attack, of even trying to go out anywhere on her own. She'd had to move to a care home, and she hated it.'

Delia paused again.

'Not much of a back story for a famous romantic novelist, is it, Mr Vogel?' she asked. 'You probably think you've heard everything in your line of work. But I expect you are just a little surprised, aren't you?'

Vogel thought both questions were probably more or less rhetorical, but he answered anyway.

'It's certainly not the kind of background I would have expected you to have, Delia,' he commented mildly. 'And I assume this is why you think you've received those threatening anonymous letters. And why somebody out there, perhaps somebody connected with the woman you mugged, is attacking you. Is that right?'

'Yes, I suppose so. What else could it be? But this is the first time in all these years that I've suspected that my past might be catching up with me. I was a different person then, you see. I had a different name, of course.'

'Yes, when you told me earlier that you'd served a prison sentence, I thought you must have changed your name. Otherwise, the court records would have been bound to have come to light over the years. We checked and found nothing. Would you tell us your previous name, please, Delia?'

She took what seemed to Vogel to be a very long time to answer.

'I was Elizabeth Brown,' she answered quietly. 'And it's been many, many years since I've even said that name.'

Vogel glanced very quickly at Saslow. The two officers knew each other well. It was clear that she had read his signal at once. She immediately started discreetly tapping away at her phone, and Vogel had no doubt that she would be contacting DI Peters in the incident room and asking her to orchestrate every possible check on anyone called Elizabeth Brown with a criminal record.

'You managed to completely leave Elizabeth Brown behind, did you not, Delia?' Vogel commented.

She nodded.

'It is quite extraordinary that you were able to build a new identity so completely,' Vogel continued. 'To the extent that you have been able to lead such a high-profile life as a world-famous author without your past being revealed. Until now, maybe. Would you tell us how you did it?'

'Yes. The beginning was straightforward enough. I did not want to be Elizabeth Brown any more. It seems I did have a conscience of sorts, even then, albeit buried somewhere pretty deep. I do remember, probably for the first time in my life, feeling shame as I stood in the dock listening to that poor woman. And appearing in an adult court on such a serious charge, and seeing the effect my actions had had on her life, did serve as a massive wake-up call.

'For a start, I vowed that I would change, that I would clean myself up. I suppose the odds were stacked against me managing to do that. I was more or less off drugs by the time of the court hearing, having gone pretty much cold turkey while on remand. There were always drugs about in prison – at a price, of course, and the price wasn't always money. But I vowed not to get hooked again. I tried to turn being in prison into something positive. I don't know where my intent came from, let alone my resolution, but there were some people there trying to help the prisoners, particularly the young ones. And I think I was the youngest there. I got a job in the kitchen. I thought it might help me in future if I learned to cook. I signed up for every class I could. Including a pottery class, although I still have no idea how I thought that was going to assist me in anything. And a creative writing class. I didn't glean much out of school. I was never in one long enough really. But I had at least learned to read and write, although I'd never done a lot of either. But in prison, I discovered, completely out of the blue, that I was quite good at making up stories.

'The writing class was fortnightly, run by a young woman teacher from the local grammar school, Sue Warner. She was twenty-four, just five years older than me. And her prison class had only been going a month when I joined. One way and another, she brought out the best in me. She got me reading books and, more importantly, writing. To the surprise of us both, I didn't find it difficult. I suppose it was in me. Every fortnight, we were tasked with producing a short story. We started with eight women in the class, but one by one they mostly dropped out. I think it was rather too much like hard work. Writing is hard work, although nobody ever believes it. And Sue was quite a tough taskmistress. Eventually, there were only three of us, and the other two weren't that interested, just treated the class as a bit of a diversion.

'After about a year, Sue read a story of mine which she thought was particularly good. She told me about this competition and said I should enter it, after doing a bit more work on my story, of course. I asked how on earth I could enter a competition from prison. I didn't have any other address I could use. It would be a waste of time, I said.

'She said she didn't entirely agree – prison could work in my favour. I found that hard to believe. In any case, I didn't want to make my imprisonment any more public than it was already. And what I wanted, more than anything else in the world, was to leave my old life behind me. Do you believe that people can change, Mr Vogel?'

Vogel found himself blinking. Just a little. That was quite an awkward question for a police officer.

'I'm not sure,' he answered honestly. 'I deal with serial offenders all the time. But I do believe that people should be given a second chance, the opportunity to change. Absolutely.'

'Well, I guess that's exactly what I wanted,' said Delia. 'To reinvent myself, and to do one hell of a lot better as the new me. I told Sue I would like to enter the competition as somebody else. I didn't even know the term "pseudonym". I just didn't want to be me, Elizabeth Brown, any more. And I certainly didn't want any more people knowing what I had done, what I had become.

'Sue agreed to help me. I could use her address, she said. It was way before the days of the internet and email, of course. She asked me what name I wanted to use. I'd just been to the prison library and, having become interested in cooking, had taken out a Delia Smith cookery book. Delia seemed like a good, strong name, and it was relatively unusual. So I chose to become Delia.

'Then Sue said, "Well, this could prove to be a momentous day – perhaps the first day of a new life for you. What about Delia Day?" I jumped at it. I liked the sound of the short, sharp alliteration. Although, back then, I didn't know that was what it was called.

'We worked together polishing up my story. Sue would have made an excellent editor, but she never wanted to do anything except teach. When we thought it was as good as possible, we sent it off. A month or so later, we heard it was longlisted, then shortlisted, and eventually that I'd won. Sue had been much more confident all along than me, but I think we were both a bit shocked.

'I was asked to pose for a photograph and give an interview, which was a bit tricky. But we got over it. Sue snuck in and took a photograph of me in my cell, black and white, soft focus and moody. Actually, more like murky. I wore a long platinum-blonde wig, with hints of purple, and far too much makeup, including false eyelashes and layers of heavy lipstick, all of which became part of my trademark style. I looked so different from the usual me that even if anyone in the prison or whom I had known before ever saw that picture, we reckoned they would never recognize it as being the dowdy me of those days. Then we sent off the photograph along with a letter from me explaining that I had just come out of hospital and was recovering from a serious illness. I didn't feel well enough to pose for any new photographs or take part in face-to-face interviews.

'The magazine liked the story a lot. Almost immediately, they commissioned another story. Before long I had a monthly spot. They called it "Day-Time". I rather liked that.

'They published my monthly offerings – two thousand words, no more, no less – across a double-page spread bearing Sue's original Delia Day picture. Every so often, they made noises about arranging a photo shoot. They wanted a new picture. And they wanted to meet me, to take me out to lunch, to put together a profile piece on me. I had my excuses on tap. I had not fully recovered from my illness. I'd always been very shy. Unfortunately, I had become agoraphobic. I was a recluse.

'Meanwhile, I started to write a book. And when I'd finished, Sue began to send it out to publishers, saying she was my manager. It was easier to pretend to be whoever you wanted to be back then in the days before the internet. The third publisher she sent it to bought my book, and from then on my real story becomes pretty much the same as my public version, and—'

Vogel interrupted again then. He had to, even though Delia's story was fascinating. Not only was he heading an investigation into the attacks on Delia and the murder of James Harding, by the most unusual and extraordinarily toxic kind of poison, but he was also now a major part of the operation to ensure that the people of North Devon would no longer be at risk from that toxin.

'Delia, I'm sure you can imagine, knowing what has happened, that I need to speed things up a little. Do you mind if I fire a few questions at you?'

'Of course not.'

'Right. Are you sure there could not be someone in this area, particularly someone at the festival, who could have recognized you as Elizabeth Brown?'

'I'd be very surprised. Apart from the passage of time and so many other considerations, I was born with a huge nose – Cyrano de Bergerac, eat your heart out – and no chin. I had plastic surgery to sort both of those out, and my appearance was transformed. Plus my hairdo. Elizabeth Brown had nondescript mousey hair, brown to match her name. And hair alone changes people enormously, particularly women. Once I became Delia, I was platinum blonde with purple streaks for years, then I went silver, in deference to my age.'

'What about any legal loopholes?'

'I shouldn't think so. I just changed my name by deed poll, and Elizabeth Brown was gone.'

'But you must have gone to a solicitor?'

'Yes. Nearly forty years ago. Just a high street solicitor chosen at random. He wasn't a young man then, and I should imagine he's long dead. In any case, why would he have been interested? Delia Day wasn't famous then.'

'Presumably, that deed must still exist somewhere?'

'Maybe, but anybody who knew it existed would have to find it. And then there's data protection.'

'Did you never try to check Elizabeth Brown out?'

'When I first came out of prison, I did, but without much success. I had one of those short birth certificates which were commonplace then, mostly given to children who were adopted to protect both them and their natural parents. It led me nowhere. And don't forget, after I changed my name to Delia Day, all I wanted to do was to forget Elizabeth Brown ever existed.'

'What about Sue, your mentor? Obviously, she knew everything about your past?'

'Sue died, tragically, of an aneurism when she was in her early thirties. In any case, she would never have done anything to hurt me. We had fallen in love, you see. We didn't go public with it – you didn't in those days. But I'm sure we would have eventually, had she lived . . .'

Delia's voice tailed away. Vogel thought there might be tears in her eyes. He was never comfortable with personal revelations and displays of emotion, and he was confident that Delia's relationship with Sue would have little or no relevance to his enquiries. So he changed the subject.

'Do you think someone close to the woman you mugged might have found out who you were and come to get you?'

'After all this time? And the poor woman had nobody – that was part of the horror of it.'

'Yet you still suspect that somebody did find out that you were Elizabeth Brown and has launched these attacks against you, don't you?'

'I don't know what to believe, to tell the truth.'

'You suspected James Harding, didn't you?'

'I thought he might have sent the notes, yes, but clearly, he couldn't have attacked me. He was already dead! I mean, I told you before, he wasn't exactly blackmailing me, but he had certainly threatened me before.'

'What about?'

'Oh, it was nothing to do with my past, with Elizabeth Brown. Do you remember the Pandora Papers?'

Vogel nodded.

'Yes, an investigation into tax avoidance billed as the world's biggest ever journalistic collaboration,' Delia continued. 'A couple of years ago now. Millions of documents were leaked revealing the hidden tax dealings of some of the richest, most privileged and most important people in the world. From world leaders to high-earning celebrities.

'Well, I was involved. It transpired that I had invested a great deal of money into what turned out to be little more than a scam, a tax-avoidance scheme, exposed as such in the Pandora Papers. I'd put my money into an overseas company which didn't even exist. Unwittingly, I promise you. I didn't even know about the investment. Should have done, obviously. But I didn't. I'd left my financial affairs in the hands of an accountant who turned out to be extremely dodgy, and my then agent, who had recommended him and turned out to be even dodgier. I escaped being named at the time, though I've never known quite how. I was certainly being investigated. And when I found out what had been going on I dropped both agent and accountant like stones. The accountant managed to remain in business, slippery bastard, and James ended up going to him when he started to make big money out of my work. Ironic really. The accountant clearly held a grudge against me. He was never going to publicly admit that he'd led even more people astray than had already been revealed, but he and James went out drinking one night and he spilled the beans. According to James, who was a serious drinker by the way, he suggested that I should be in jail for what I had done. Ironic again really, considering my hidden past.'

'So, however you put it, Delia, James was blackmailing you?'

'Yes, well, he probably thought he was. However, unlike my deeply buried past as Elizabeth Brown, I was kind of expecting this one to catch up with me. I was ready to deal with it. And still am. I made a big mistake, allowing other people to control my affairs. No more than that. And I always thought James's threats were mostly hot air. After all, it was totally against his interests to damage my reputation. He just liked to make it known that he had something over me, or thought he did. Also, to be honest, I'm not sure if I would have refused to work with James under any circumstances, much as I would have liked to have done. Netflix liked him too much. So it was easier to go along with the man. Even though I loathed him. He never gave me any indication that he knew anything about my life before Delia. How would he?'

'I've no idea, but I was hoping you might,' said Vogel. 'What about the dodgy accountant? Could he have played a part in any of this?'

'I can't imagine he's pissed off enough with me to try to murder me, nor that he has a lot to do with lethally poisonous frogs,' said Delia with a smile. 'Unless he's a closet psychopath.'

Vogel smiled back. A tad wearily. There was nobody he had so far encountered in the process of this investigation who seemed likely to have anything to do with lethally poisonous frogs. That was the crux of his problem.

'All the same, would you let us have the accountant's name and contact details, please; he should be checked out.'

Delia said she would text them to Vogel and began to do so at once.

'Is there nobody else at all you might suspect of having had a hand in any of this?' Vogel asked, just as he heard his phone ping.

'Not really. The worst thing that's ever happened to me before as Delia Day is the odd vicious review or a bit of trolling on Twitter.'

She paused for a moment.

'Look, there's something else you should know. I have no childhood memories from before I was about eleven, maybe twelve. I'm not sure. Maybe that's not that unusual. I don't know. But it has always bothered me. I vaguely remember being in hospital, I remember when I was taken into care, I remember my first foster home, or I think it was my first foster home, and my foster parents saying they couldn't cope with me and returning me to the local authority children's home which I was then in and out of for years. I remember all of that clearly. But nothing before.'

'Really? Nothing at all?'

'No, except . . .'

'Except what, Delia?'

'Well, ever since I arrived here, starting on the train actually, that last bit between Exeter and Barnstaple, I've felt a
tad uneasy.'

'Uneasy?'

'Yes, nothing much more than that. But I have once or twice
had the feeling that certain things were familiar.'

'That you'd been here before?'

'Which I haven't. Not as Delia Day, certainly. And not quite
as strong as that. Just that certain places and people were very
vaguely familiar.'

She told Vogel then about Amelia Bowden.

'You thought you may have recognized her from the
past?'

'David, she's well into her eighties. Over twenty years older
than me. And when I was eleven, she would have been thirty-
something. Even if I had known her then, I probably wouldn't
recognize her now, would I? But there was also something
about the way she looked at me. Just as we were leaving, I
felt her eyes on me, and she had a look I couldn't quite
fathom. But I found it disconcerting. Mind you, as I've told
you. I've been disconcerted ever since I got here.'

'Have you met anybody else whilst you've been here who
made you feel uneasy?'

'No, not particularly.'

'Anybody else who might have a grudge against you.'

'Only that bloody Penelope Peabody-Jones.'

'Ah, yes, we're checking her out at the moment. Who else
have you been in close contact with at the festival?'

'Generally, I try to avoid close contact with people at
these events, to tell the truth, but there's Carolyne Smedley,
the festival director, of course, Janey Lucas, our ill-fated panel
moderator, the Smythes and the Tucker twins.'

'Yes, we've talked to all of those,' said Vogel. 'Anyone
else?'

'Michael my driver, whom you've just met. He's been one
of the bright sparks amid this madness, to tell the truth.'

'Anybody else you've spent time with, chatted to?'

'Well, yes, of course, but half the time it's people whose
names I don't even know. Fans, helpers at the festival, Jenny

on the front desk at the Imperial and several other staff, I suppose.'

'Did you know anybody from the area before you came here?'

'No, I don't think so. I knew that James had lived here for a while. Apparently, the dreaded Penelope lives around here somewhere now, but I didn't know that. And I'd never met Carolyne Smedley before, just talked on the phone.'

'Let's go back to Amelia Bowden. Are you sure you couldn't have met her somewhere else and can't quite remember?'

'I suppose I can't be sure, not entirely. But she is quite memorable. Very tall for a woman of her generation and quite commanding.'

'I think she would say you were memorable, too,' commented Vogel.

Delia smiled. 'Yes, she did say that actually, when I asked her if we had met before.'

'You asked her that?'

'Yes. Not unusual for me. If I think there's a chance I may have met somebody before and can't remember, I just ask them. I find they do usually remember.'

'I'm sure they do,' responded Vogel with a wry smile. 'So what exactly did Amelia Bowden reply?'

'She said no, we hadn't met before, and she was sure she would have remembered.'

'Yet you still weren't sure?'

'It was just later, when we all left, in that storm, and my hair was blowing all over the place. And well, when I caught that look in her eye, I just found myself wondering . . . Oh, I'm sure it was nothing . . .'

'Please, Delia, if there's anything at all that you know that might help us find who is responsible for all of this, please tell me. It's not just you who might still be in danger – hundreds if not thousands of people could be at risk.'

Delia stared at Vogel for several seconds.

'All right,' she said eventually. 'There is something about me that could lead people to recognize me from a very long time ago. Or make them think they might.'

'A physical characteristic?' queried Vogel.

'Yes, I suppose you could call it that. Something I was born with, I believe, that I've always tried to conceal. Just because I've always been so self-conscious about it.'

She put up her hand to her hair, which, in spite of everything, she had effectively smoothed down into its usually slick bob.

'I told you the wind was blowing my hair everywhere when I caught Amelia staring at me in a funny sort of way. It was quite disturbing. Well, this is what she would have seen.'

She pushed her hair back, revealing her right ear.

'Ah,' said Vogel, who understood then, although he couldn't see what the fuss was about. But then, he was a middle-aged heterosexual man.

Delia's ear was seriously deformed. In fact, it was barely an ear. More of a fleshy stump.

'It's always been a secret part of me. I don't think there's ever been a photograph taken of it. I always try to make sure people don't see it. But there are people who know, of course. Like my hairdresser.'

Saslow looked on with interest. So that was why Delia didn't want help drying her hair, she thought.

'As you're so self-conscious about your ear, have you never considered remedial surgery on it?' Vogel asked.

'Of course,' said Delia, 'But I've always been told it would likely do more harm than good, and probably destroy the hearing I have in that ear, which is actually quite good. So, long ago, I chose to use a hairdo to hide it. Which has always worked pretty well. Most of the time.'

Much as he wanted to hear more of Delia's story, Vogel ended the interview then. Or, rather, suspended it.

He needed to get back to the Bideford incident room in order to oversee the operation in its entirety. But first, he wanted to talk to Amelia Bowden. He didn't think Delia was a fanciful sort of person, in spite of being a writer of romantic fiction.

If she thought her meeting with Amelia Bowden had some sort of hidden and disturbing significance, then it almost certainly did.

TWENTY-FOUR

Vogel and Delia were on their way to confront Amelia when Jenny eventually arrived at Bideford Police Station, which was no longer open to the public at the best of times.

She was prevented from driving her car up the steep ramp which led to the station yard by a uniformed constable who told her in no uncertain terms that members of the public were not allowed in the station, and that she should back off and contact the investigations team by phone or email.

Having made the decision, as she felt, to put not only her freedom but her whole life on the line, Jenny was having none of it.

'I want to confess, I have to confess now,' she yelled at the top of her voice, in what was for her a rare show of considerable spirit. 'I have to see someone in charge, and I have to tell them what I did. It was me who delivered those threatening letters to Delia Day. It was me.'

By now, everybody knew about the anonymous letters Delia had received. The constable took a step backwards.

'Just wait there,' he said. 'Don't move.'

Then he turned his back on Jenny and called DI Peters, who told him to let the young woman into the station.

The constable, not without difficulty, found Jenny somewhere to park her car, then led her to Janet Peters' office.

When she had extracted all the information she could from Jenny, DI Peters called Vogel to tell him of the hotel receptionist's arrival at Bideford and her unexpected confession.

'I talked to her myself because there was nobody else available,' the DI began. 'She claims she was made to deliver the two letters to Delia by someone who was more or less blackmailing her.'

At once, Vogel asked the big question.

'Did she tell you who that was?'

'Yes, boss. And it's quite a bombshell. Her uncle made her do it. Her uncle, the mayor. Jeremy Roberts. The mayor of Bideford.'

Vogel could hardly believe his ears.

'Why?'

'She said she didn't know why, boss.'

'Did she know what these letters were, the messages they contained?'

'No to that too, boss; she claims she never opened the envelopes.'

'Blackmail, you said? By her uncle. What's all that about?'

'Jenny's mother suffers from multiple sclerosis; she's in the final stages and has recently gone blind. Her father walked out when Jenny was a baby, so it's just the two of them. Roberts, who is quite a wealthy man, it seems, has been paying both for drugs not available on the NHS to help with the MS and for private nursing so that Jenny and her mother can stay in the home they both love, and Jenny can continue to work. Roberts threatened to pull the plug on it all unless Jenny delivered those letters, which he took to her on the night of the opening ceremony.'

'What a nice chap!' commented Vogel. 'Jenny's uncle, you say? Does that mean he's her mother's brother?'

'Brother-in-law,' she said. 'Jenny's father is Roberts's wife's brother.'

'Umm, maybe he would have behaved differently if he were blood, if he were the brother. Probably not, though, I suspect. Had he ever asked Jenny to do anything like this before?'

'She said no to that. Not exactly. But she did say that he never failed to grasp an opportunity to let her know the huge favour he was doing her and her mother. And he was always getting her to run little errands for him. But never anything that gave her cause for concern. Not until this. He called her and said he was bringing the letters round to her, to her home, and she'd better do what she was told. She was off duty at the time, apparently she'd been to the opening ceremony herself earlier.'

'So when did she deliver the letters?' asked Vogel.

'Very early the next morning. She started work at the Imperial at six a.m.'

'Right,' said Vogel. 'Send me Mayor Roberts's address. Saslow and I were on our way to seek out Amelia Bowden. Delia is suspicious of her in all sorts of ways, although she can't quite explain why. But I think we'd better go see Mayor Roberts right now.'

He checked the clock on the dashboard. It was just coming up to eight p.m.

'Let's just hope he's at home. Where does he live? Can we get there with all these roadblocks?'

'He lives out towards Hartland. As long as you don't try to come through Bideford, you should be all right. Shall I send Saslow some directions avoiding the town?'

'Yes, please. And you'd better give me an update on what else is happening.'

'Most importantly, no further cases of possible contact with the toxin have been reported,' said Peters. 'We have specialist military units all over the area now, and a clean-up operation has started at the festival site. The Seagate is still closed, of course, and indeed Appledore is almost entirely cut off.'

Vogel grunted.

'And all we have to do is find the bastard who's caused all this,' he muttered. 'Who killed James Harding? Almost certainly by accident, it now seems. And who has made two attempts on Delia's life, and why? Did we get anywhere with Penelope Peabody-Jones?'

'We couldn't get her on her phone, but we tracked her down to a holiday cottage out towards Torrington where she's been staying through the festival. And, guess what, boss, it was rented by James Harding. Seems they were having an affair. She clearly loathes Delia, but it's a big step to trying to kill her. And the landlord, who lives in the cottage next door, saw her return in floods of tears early on Sunday evening and is sure she didn't leave again that night. Says the lights of her car would have woken him. So that pretty much rules her out of the two attacks on Delia, and I can't see her carrying lethal toxins in her handbag.'

Vogel chuckled.

'The affair doesn't surprise me,' he said. 'Any news of Harding's wife?'

'She was in LA, where they rent a flat, apparently. And she should soon be boarding a flight to Heathrow. Not that distraught by her husband's death, we understand.'

'Doesn't seem like anybody other than Penelope is,' replied Vogel.

'Indeed,' said Peters. 'One more thing, not long after Perkins and Saslow removed Delia from the hospital, the Tucker twins were found wandering around looking for Delia. We sent a team out, and they interviewed the twins on the spot. They said they knew that James Harding was blackmailing Delia and they wanted to tell her that he'd been shooting his mouth off. Drunk at another book fair, apparently. Boasting about having Delia in the palm of his hand. They said they'd wanted to tell you on Sunday evening, but at that time they thought you suspected Delia of killing James Harding, boss.'

'Did they tell you if he said what he was blackmailing her about?'

'Yes, allegations of bullying and cheating, which originally came from Peabody-Jones, it seems, and an allegation that she was involved in some tax-avoidance scandal . . .'

'I know about all of that,' interrupted Vogel. 'Delia told me. She was never as worried about any of it as we might think, either. Didn't regard James as very credible; same with Penelope, I should think.'

'Right. The twins also said the Smythes were present when Harding launched his drunken rant. We've checked with them, and they confirmed that. Said they'd been fretting over whether or not they should do something about it ever since.'

'What a nice man he was,' commented Vogel. 'Good work from everybody, though. We need to tie up every possible loose end.'

'Yes, boss, of course, and good luck with Roberts,' said Peters.

'He's the one who's going to need luck,' replied Vogel grimly.

Mayor Roberts answered the door to his large and luxurious home, which boasted superb views out to sea over Hartland

Point, just where the Bristol Channel meets the Atlantic Ocean.

He visibly paled when Vogel introduced himself and Saslow. But he didn't look surprised.

'You'd better come in,' he said quickly, ushering the two officers into a small but comfortable room just off the hall, which was set up as a home office. As he was shutting the door, a woman's voice called out. Presumably Roberts's wife.

'Who is it, Jeremy?'

'Somebody for me, dear,' Mayor Roberts called back. 'We won't be long.'

Vogel wasn't at all sure he would be proved right about that.

Roberts sat in the chair behind a desk that filled almost a quarter of the room. Vogel and Saslow sat on the two upright chairs on the other side of the desk.

Vogel came straight to the point.

'Mr Roberts, we have reason to believe that you were responsible for two threatening notes which Miss Delia Day received at the Imperial Hotel. We believe you, uh . . .'

Vogel hesitated, he wanted to say 'coerced', but knew that might not be the best choice of word in order to elicit the answers he was looking for.

'We believe you persuaded your niece Jenny to deliver them to Miss Day's room. Is that correct?'

Roberts looked stricken. But he did not prevaricate.

'Yes, it is true,' he said. 'I've been going out of my mind with worry. And the news is just getting worse and worse. I've been trying to pluck up the courage all day to give myself up. But . . . well . . . anyway, now you're here.'

'Can you tell us, please, why you wrote those notes to Miss Day,' asked Saslow.

'I didn't. Well, I typed the words and printed them out, and took the notes to Jenny to deliver to Delia Day, but I didn't write them – those weren't my words. They were the messages I was given over the phone. I typed them out, that's all. I just did what I was told.'

'Told by whom, Mr Roberts?'

'By that bastard James Harding. That's who.'

This case was not only developing into one of the most disturbing that Vogel had ever dealt with, but also one of the most bewildering.

'Why on earth did James Harding tell you to do that, Mr Roberts?'

'How the hell do I know?' asked the mayor. 'He enjoyed putting the fear of God into people, I know that. He'd probably got something on that Delia Day, just as he had something on me for years. And he liked you to know it. He started blackmailing me years ago when he was still living in Irsha Street. His work and his marriage went pear-shaped at the same time. He was pretty much broke, although I didn't know that then. So it was money he wanted from me in the beginning. Like a fool, I paid him what he asked, and for quite a while he tapped me up regularly, just for a couple of grand or so at a time. Not enough for me to think it was worth making a fuss. So I took the easy route. Then he hit the big time again with Netflix and everything went quiet. I realized he must have good money coming in again, and I thought I was off the hook. I saw him across the room on the opening night of the festival, and he didn't come near me. To my relief. Then, when we were driving home, he called and asked me – no, *told* me – to get those notes printed and delivered. Put under Delia's door to add to the threat. He didn't know about Jenny. He just said he was sure I'd find a way. The Imperial was on my patch. And I better had, he said, or else.'

'I see, and what exactly is the "or else", Mr Roberts? What is it that James Harding was blackmailing you about?'

Roberts sighed.

'I expect you know that I run a waste disposal business,' he began.

Vogel had not known that.

'Well, I've made a lot of money out of it. I latched on to recycling very early on, and I also used to deal with the disposal of hazardous waste.'

Hazardous waste? Vogel's ears pricked, and he bet Saslow's did, too.

'Thing is, I got a bit greedy, and the regulations weren't as tight as they are now. You could slip a few quid to the right people and dump stuff in places you wouldn't like to know about. We didn't separate the waste like we should have done, either, and we certainly didn't do what we should have done with the hazardous waste. Most of it is not all that hazardous, to tell the truth – I mean, batteries and light bulbs are classed as hazardous waste. We had no trouble for years, and I suppose I got a bit complacent about it. But we had the contract for that chemical research plant near Cirencester, and I guess some of their waste was toxic. It all came to us in sealed containers, though, and we just buried the lot. Looking back, I've never been able to believe I could have been so foolhardy. It was an accident waiting to happen.

'After a time, near where we had a couple of dump sites on Exmoor, fish started to die in the River Exe. And people started to get ill, too – mostly kids who'd been swimming in the river. Several ended up being taken to hospital, and one little boy nearly died. It was touch and go for days. You may have heard of it, Mr Vogel; it was a big scandal at the time.'

Vogel nodded. He'd still been in the Met in London, but the incident had been national news, and he had a vague memory of it. The local water board was pilloried, he seemed to remember.

'Well, the water was tested, of course, and they found traces of highly dangerous toxins, and it was clear that there had been chemical spillage. There was a real witch hunt. And how it didn't get traced back to us, I'll never know. It didn't, though. Of course, the farmer asked no questions when he accepted a significant stack of cash in return for letting us utilize a remote patch of land which had no other purpose for him – he certainly wasn't going to say anything. But despite us having that contract with the Cirencester chemical research plant, nobody contacted us. And eventually, miraculously, the river cleaned itself up and tested free of toxins. Most toxic substances do dissolve in water, Mr Vogel, given time and a big enough quantity of water.'

Even *Phyllobates terribilis*, thought Vogel, remembering what Raoul had told him at the mortuary early that morning. Was it really only that morning? He couldn't believe it.

Roberts was still talking.

'. . . so it seemed I had got away with it. Except for one thing. James Harding guessed my company had been responsible—'

'He guessed?' interrupted Vogel. 'How on earth did he do that? How well did you know each other?'

'Not that well. We met when he gave a talk to the local Rotary club. I was chairman at the time. We went out drinking afterwards, and, boy, could he drink! I wasn't in the same class. My tongue was loosened, and I think I must have started showing off. Boasting about the money I'd made out of other people's rubbish. How easy it was to get rid of anything if you spread your cash around. Who cares about the rules? Hazardous waste is where the real money is. That sort of thing. So when the River Exe scandal broke, he put two and two together and started to put the squeeze on me.'

'But he couldn't have had any evidence, could he?'

'He didn't need any. If he'd alerted the authorities and there'd been any sort of investigation into my company, they would quickly have found out what we'd been doing. For a start, I had one guy working on all the dodgy stuff with me, and he would never have breathed a word to a soul – I paid him too well – but if the police or anyone in authority had given him the third degree, I knew he would have caved in at once. I had no choice. I just paid up. And it was much the same when Harding called me on Friday night. He could still have ruined me. So I did what he asked. But I never expected what happened. Not any of it.'

For a few seconds, Vogel sat in silence, just looking at Jeremy Roberts.

'I want you to be very careful how you answer this, Mr Roberts,' he said. 'You must be extremely relieved that Jeremy Roberts is dead, are you not?'

'I was at first, yes,' Roberts admitted readily enough. 'But not when all the other things started to happen. And, look, I know where this is leading. I didn't kill Harding. I detested him, but I couldn't do that. And I wouldn't know how to handle a lethal toxin, either. Certainly not how to use it against somebody without killing myself.'

'Is there any way your company could be inadvertently

responsible for this toxin having been used as a murder weapon, and in such a way that it might still be a danger to the public?'

'No, absolutely not. The River Exe thing scared the life out of me. I pulled out of the hazardous waste business soon afterwards. And all our recycling, everything we've ever done since, has been strictly by the book. It's all logged, too.'

'I see.' Vogel thought for a moment. 'Mr Roberts, I am still not entirely convinced that your company is in the clear on this. And you are certainly involved to some extent because of the letters you caused to be delivered to Miss Day. We will continue with our enquiries, and I think it is likely that we will need to see you again very soon.'

Roberts lowered his face in his hands. When he looked up, Vogel could see that there were tears in his eyes. The DCI was not impressed.

'What is going to happen to me?' Roberts asked plaintively. 'Whatever is going to happen to me?'

'You will almost certainly be charged with committing the offence of malicious communications,' said Vogel coldly. 'I will pass on your confession concerning the previous incident of toxic contamination of a major waterway to the relevant authorities, and no doubt they will investigate further with a view to criminal prosecution. We will also continue to investigate your possible involvement in our current crisis here in North Devon. And I must ask you not to leave home until we have completed our enquiries. The actions you have so far admitted have caused near death and widespread distress, both physical and mental. And yet you have expressed no remorse, Mr Roberts, only concern for your own skin.'

'I am sorry, I am so sorry, really I am,' babbled Roberts.

'Are you really?' asked Vogel rhetorically. 'C'mon, Saslow, let's go.'

Jeremy Roberts's tears turned into full-on sobbing. The two officers did not look back.

Just as they were driving away from the Roberts home, Vogel's phone vibrated. It was Perkins. The DCI put the call on speakerphone so that Saslow could hear.

'You're not going to believe it, boss, I think the bastard might have been trying to have another go at Delia.'

'What? Is he mad?'

'Or she – afraid I still can't be sure it's a man.'

'Whatever it is, you'd think they'd realize we were watching over Delia. What happened? What did you see?'

'Well, as you know, Docherty's here with me, and one of us has been looking out of the window all the time. There's only one way in, of course. I caught a glimpse of someone – dark clothes, hoodie – just peeping out from the alleyway across the road. They were there for some time, so I told Docherty that I thought I'd better go down and have a look.

'When I got outside, I couldn't see anyone. I had a look around. Walked up and down the alleyway, which is a dead end, by the way, and I thought it was probably nothing. So I started to make my way back to the flat. But then I reckoned I'd just make sure. So I waited in the doorway, looking out on to the street, just in case. And sure enough, this same person came out of the doorway to the newsagents down the road, looked both ways, then started to walk away. In the opposite direction to me.

'I went after them, just walking fast at first so as not to draw attention, but they were looking all around and probably realized where I'd just appeared from. Anyway, they took off. At speed, I can tell you, boss. Man or woman, faster than me, I'm afraid. Although I wasn't far behind, they just disappeared on me up another back alley and then they were gone. Somebody who knows Braunton well. Somebody local, I reckon.'

'All right, Perkins, at least nobody got to our Delia. Make sure she doesn't do anything else stupid.'

Vogel ended the call and turned to Saslow.

'So, who knows where Delia is, apart from we two, DI Peters and Perkins?'

'Michael the driver,' said Saslow straight away.

'Yes, Michael the driver,' repeated Vogel. 'Anyone else?'

'Well, you can never be totally sure, can you, boss?' responded Saslow. 'Maybe Michael talked about it to the wrong person. People like to show off, don't they? Or maybe somebody followed him from the Imperial to Braunton when he delivered Delia's laptop. Also, it is possible that Perkins, Delia and I could have been followed going to Braunton, although we didn't think so. But the only person we know for certain is aware of Delia's present whereabouts other than the four police officers on our team is Michael.'

'Indeed,' said Vogel. 'We need to talk to him straight away, Saslow. I have his address.' He opened his notebook. 'Michael Souch, East-the-Water, Bideford. Let's head that way. But he's a taxi driver, so he may not be there, and we're half an hour's drive away, possibly more if the bridge is still blocked off and there's a tailback. I'll call Peters, see if we can do a quick background check on him, and find out if he's at home.'

They got lucky. Peters called back only five minutes later to say PC Lake had called Michael's home and learned from his wife that the driver had arrived there a few minutes earlier. There hadn't been time to find out much about him, except that he was ex-army and a decorated soldier.

It was just gone ten p.m. when Michael opened the door of the pretty little terraced cottage just a couple of streets back from the river. Vogel told Michael sternly that he had reason to believe that he could help with the ongoing police enquiry into the death of James Harding and the two attacks on Delia Day. Michael looked both nervous and surprised.

'I don't think there is anything I can help with. All I've done is drive Delia wherever she has needed to go,' he said. 'But, please, come in. Only, do you mind being quiet? We've just got the baby off to sleep.'

He held a finger to his lips as he led the way into the open-plan living area, where his wife, Rosie, was sitting on the edge of the sofa looking somewhat bewildered.

Michael introduced the two officers to her. She offered tea or coffee, which both officers refused. They also refused her invitation to sit. Saslow cut to the chase at once.

'First of all, we would like to know exactly where you have been this evening until now?' she asked.

Michael looked puzzled then.

'Well, you know that I went to the Imperial earlier, picked up Delia's laptop and took it to her at that flat in Braunton, like she asked me to; we met on the doorstep, Mr Vogel, and I think you were inside with Delia, weren't you, DC Saslow?' he said.

'Yes,' said Saslow curtly, still annoyed with herself for the part she may unwittingly have played in putting Delia in further danger. If only she hadn't forgotten to pick up the laptop.

'What about afterwards?' she added. 'That was nearly four hours ago.'

'I had a fare – some lads wanting to go to a gig in Combe Martin.'

'Right, well, that will be logged then. On your mobile at least.'

'Uh, no. I just, uh, picked them up.'

'You picked them up? What, off the street?'

'Uh, yes. As I was going through Barnstaple.'

'Isn't that in contravention of the terms of your licence as a private hire driver?' asked Saslow.

'Well, yes, maybe, but I knew them by sight, and, uh, times aren't easy. We have a new baby; I need every penny.'

'I'm not really interested in the way you run your business, but we do need to know your movements this evening,' Saslow reposted. 'In detail.'

'I've more or less told you. I don't have any of the lads' numbers or addresses in my phone, but I'm sure I can find them again. The round trip to Combe Martin and back home here took over an hour and a half, including a stop for petrol . . .'

'There still seems to be a missing hour or two,' commented Vogel quite gently. 'What else did you do this evening, Michael?'

'Oh, all right, I picked up another couple of dodgy fares – and no, I don't have any proof, but that's what I did,' admitted Michael, resignedly. 'Why are you asking me all this, though? Has something happened to Delia again? Is she all right?'

Michael sounded genuinely concerned. Saslow and Vogel didn't care.

'We have a report of someone behaving suspiciously outside the property where Delia is currently staying,' Vogel pronounced. 'As far as we are aware, you are the only person outside the police force who knew where Delia was this evening. So I suggest you do all you can to corroborate what you have just told us. We also need to know where you were on the two occasions when she was attacked. On Sunday afternoon and in the early hours of this morning.'

'I was on my way to Appledore to pick Delia up when she fell off the quay,' replied Michael. 'I arrived well afterwards. You saw me, Mr Vogel. And later on, well, I was here in bed with my wife when Delia was attacked the second time, in the early hours, as you put it.'

Rosie nodded her agreement.

'What about after the opening ceremony of the festival, Friday evening – where did you go then?' asked Vogel.

He was thinking about the two letters Delia had received, the first having been delivered sometime overnight on Friday. Jenny had already confessed to delivering both letters, and Mayor Roberts to writing them, but Vogel had learned that little was quite how it seemed with this case. Michael was a person of interest to the police. And Vogel wanted to know his whereabouts throughout.

'Well, uh, when I'd finished driving Delia, I came straight home,' he said. 'But . . .'

His wife completed the sentence for him.

'But you were quite late, weren't you, because you had to take her to see friends in Ilfracombe, didn't you?' she commented.

Michael nodded.

'We have talked to Delia at length about anyone she might know in North Devon, and she has at no stage mentioned friends in Ilfracombe,' said Saslow.

'Well, uh, maybe it slipped her mind.'

Saslow treated him to what her mother would have called an old-fashioned look.

'Really,' she commented. 'Well, I'd like the name and address of the Ilfracombe friends from you, please.'

'Uh, I didn't know their names. And Delia directed me to their home . . .'

'What? You didn't use sat nav? And how could she direct you? Our understanding is that she has never been to North Devon before.'

'Hasn't she? Um, I didn't realize.' Michael paused. 'Yes, come to think of it, of course I used sat nav. Just for the last bit. If you'd like to come out to the car, I'll check it back for you.'

They left Rosie still sitting on the sofa, and still looking bewildered.

Once outside, Michael shut the front door quietly and led the way to his car parked in a designated parking area just across the road. He stopped alongside the car, but instead of unlocking it, he turned to face the two officers.

'Look, I swear I had nothing to do with the attacks on Delia or James Harding, I didn't even know the man.'

'We are investigating the possibility that he may have been killed by mistake, instead of Delia,' said Vogel.

'What? I like the woman. I think she's great. I would never do anything to hurt her.'

'That's all well and good, Michael, but we still need proof of your whereabouts. So let's have a look at that sat nav, shall we?'

'All right, all right. I did go to Combe Martin tonight, and I put my sat nav on like I said. But I didn't take Delia to Ilfracombe on the opening night of the festival. That was a lie. She has no friends there, as you both suspected, I, uh . . .'

Michael looked down at the ground.

'C'mon, Michael, spit it out,' said Saslow. 'Where were you on Friday evening?'

'I was in Barnstaple, at the Marmaduke Club. I went there straight after dropping Delia at the Imperial at about half past nine.'

'Ah,' said Saslow.

The Marmaduke was a gay club. Saslow lived in Barnstaple. She knew the club. Everybody knew the Marmaduke.

'Ah, indeed,' repeated Michael. 'And yes, I am gay. I am also happily married to a woman I love.'

'Whom I presume doesn't know you are gay, or you wouldn't have concocted the Ilfracombe story,' remarked Saslow.

'I'm not sure. Sometimes I think she does know. But we've never talked about it. We both wanted a family life, and that's what we have. A wonderful family life, actually. I try never to do anything to upset that.'

'You were in the army,' Vogel interjected. 'A decorated soldier, I understand? Is that one of the reasons you've kept your sexuality quiet?'

Michael laughed wryly.

'The modern diverse army?' he queried. 'By and large, the military is inclined to be more broad-minded than a lot of folk around here, I'd say. It's just, well, Rosie and I were childhood sweethearts. We only split when I joined up, and I only joined up because I had to get away. I needed to be free to do my own thing and find out who I was. Then, when I met Rosie again many years later, at just the time when I was becoming disillusioned with the army for all manner of reasons, I realized she was still the one for me. The only one. She was the person I wanted. Thankfully, it was the same for her, too. We both wanted children badly. And we were running out of time. So I quit the army and we married, and I've never regretted it. But I guess I knew the other stuff would catch up with me sooner or later.'

'The Marmaduke is hardly the most discreet of venues, is it?'

'I only go there once in a blue moon,' said Michael. 'The Imperial is right by it. I guess I gave in to temptation.'

Saslow was gay. She lived with her girlfriend. The Marmaduke was mainly for men, but some women went there. Saslow would rather have extracted her own teeth than go to the Marmaduke. She was out to friends, family and neighbours, and had been pretty much all her adult life. But she was a very private person who saw no need to go public with her sexuality. And public included the Devon and Cornwall Police. She never talked about her personal life when she was at work. Vogel knew. He had met Sam, Saslow's girlfriend, on a few occasions – chance meetings, sharing transport and so on. But Vogel respected other people's privacy more than anybody Saslow had ever known. And the matter was never discussed. After all, if she ever brought it up, poor Vogel would start blinking like mad. For sure.

But choosing to keep your sexuality private was one thing. For a man to live with and marry a woman, have two children with her, then frequent a gay club with a pretty sleazy reputation, and describe himself as gay, not even bisexual, was another. Saslow was distinctly unimpressed.

'Your sexuality is your own business,' she said coldly. 'We still need to establish your whereabouts for all the times we have mentioned to you. If you were at the Marmaduke Club, then you had better let us have the names of the people you met there. We may well need to talk to them.'

'Of course,' said Michael weakly.

'This is a massive and far-reaching operation, Michael,' said Saslow. 'And if I were you, I'd tell your wife what you've just told us, before somebody else does.'

Michael agreed that he would, although Saslow wasn't entirely convinced. He turned and went indoors.

'What do you make of that?' asked Vogel, as he and Saslow walked back to her car, but his phone buzzed before she had a chance to answer. It was Peters with an update.

'We've just got a load of military info in on Michael,' she began. 'He was special services, SAS, and his last tour of duty was in Colombia. And not just Colombia – that district the size of New York City which we are told is the natural habitat of the golden poison dart frog – indeed, the only place in the world where the deadly little creature can be found in the wild.

'Oh, and something else – he's related to Amelia Bowden. She's his great-aunt.'

TWENTY-FIVE

This changed everything. Vogel at once asked Peters to send uniformed back-up and set aside an interview room at Bideford nick. She replied that she had already done both. Which, of course, was why Vogel loved her.

He and Saslow returned immediately to the house they had just left, and Vogel hammered loudly on the door.

Again, Michael opened it. Simultaneously, a siren heralded the arrival of a squad car. Michael remained standing in the hall, just inside, his face etched with anxiety.

'What now?' he asked. 'Why have you come back? Why have more police arrived?'

'We have new information which makes it necessary for us to question you further,' said the DCI.

'And we have to ask you to accompany us to the station for questioning,' he added.

'Why?' asked Michael shakily. 'I've told you all I know.'

Two uniformed officers, a man and a woman, had by then approached the house.

'Mr Souch, will you please step outside and come with us,' said the male officer.

Michael looked stricken. He didn't move. Rosie came to the door then and asked him what was going on.

'Ask *them*,' he said, gesturing towards the four police officers now standing on his garden path.

'Michael, you must come with us straight away,' instructed Vogel.

'I can't,' said Michael. 'Why should I? I don't know anything and I haven't done anything. I'm not coming.'

'I must warn you that if you do not cooperate fully, I shall have no choice but to arrest you on suspicion of the murder of James Harding and the attempted murder of Delia Day,' Vogel declared.

'All right, all right,' said Michael eventually, adding again, 'But I haven't done anything.'

Vogel addressed Rosie. 'Mrs Souch, in view of the nature of the offences that have been committed and the toxic substances that may still be in existence, I'm afraid I have to ask that you and your children leave the house tonight. A constable will stay with you. Properly equipped personnel will be searching the premises in due course.'

'Oh my God,' said Rosie. The female officer moved to her side.

'Do you have family you can go to, Mrs Souch?' she asked.

Rosie nodded very slightly. She seemed rooted to the spot. Vogel wasn't surprised.

Saslow and the male PC were already on their way to Saslow's car with Michael. Vogel followed them.

He began the formal interview with Michael as soon as they reached the station and were installed in an interview room.

Vogel dived straight in, informing Michael that he had been brought in for questioning because it was now known that he was ex-SAS, and had spent his last tour of duty in Colombia, and in the relatively small area where the golden poison dart frog, the *Phyllobates terribilis*, the venom of which had killed James Harding, has its natural habitat.

Michael looked bewildered.

'You're not seriously suggesting that I brought some of these damned frogs back with me, are you?' he asked. 'I'd never heard of the creatures until today. It was years ago I was in Colombia, anyway.'

'The venom the frogs secrete remains toxic indefinitely,' interjected Saslow.

'Really,' commented Michael. 'So what do you think? I packaged some up and carried it home in my hand luggage?'

'Please do not be flippant,' said Vogel. 'I suggest you take this very seriously indeed.'

'You think I'm not taking it seriously? You've arrested me, for God's sake. You're accusing me of murder.'

'You're ex-SAS, Michael,' said Vogel. 'You do know how to kill, do you not?'

'Not with the venom of toxic frogs, I don't.'

Bizarrely, Vogel wanted to laugh. And there was certainly nothing to laugh about. But Michael Souch did have a point.

'There is something else,' he began. 'I understand you are Amelia Bowden's great-nephew.'

Michael agreed that he was, although he looked somewhat taken aback by the question.

'Have you seen your great-aunt lately?'

'Uh, yes. I popped over on Saturday afternoon, in between driving Delia about.'

'Was there any specific reason for going to see her then?'

'Well, I do usually see her quite often, but . . .'

'But what?'

'She asked me to go. So I did. I'd been busy, hadn't seen a lot of her lately.'

'Did she want anything in particular?'

'Well, she said she just wanted a catch-up, only when I got there, she started to ask me lots of questions about . . . about . . .'

Michael stopped.

'I hadn't really thought this through before,' he said. 'But now, well, I'm not sure that I should say . . .'

'You certainly should say, whatever it is. You're already on the verge of being arrested on suspicion of murder. There could well be terrorism charges pending.'

Michael gasped.

'It was all about Delia. She asked me loads of questions about Delia.'

Vogel was beginning to feel that this investigation was finally getting somewhere.

'What sort of questions?' he asked.

'Oh, all sorts of stuff – what I knew about her past life mostly. Had she ever talked to me about her childhood, did I know where she came from originally or anything about her life before she became rich and famous? That sort of thing. Of course, I didn't know anything about any of that.'

'Did Amelia tell you why she was asking these questions?'

'No, she didn't. And I asked her, too. Several times. She just brushed me aside and asked me something else. She's a pretty formidable woman, you know.'

'So I hear,' said Vogel.

He suspended the interview and asked Saslow to step outside with him.

'I think we need to get Amelia Bowden in here,' he told the DS. 'Delia Day's instincts about her were probably spot on. She clearly knows something. Tell Peters to arrange a squad car to bring her in for questioning. And tell them to go in heavy. No deference to her age. Nor the fact that it'll be gone midnight by the time they get to her. If she shows any reluctance to cooperate, which I doubt she will, but if she does, they're to arrest her on suspicion of conspiracy to murder and two counts of attempted murder. Everyone keeps telling us how formidable the woman is. I want her well softened up before we even sit down to talk to her.'

TWENTY-SIX

Within less than an hour, Amelia Bowden had been collected from her home and brought to Bideford Police Station. It had not proved necessary to arrest her. She had cooperated fully, even though she had been just about to go to bed, albeit managing to maintain an air of disdainful superiority throughout, according to the two PCs who brought her in.

She sat with an extremely straight back in the chair across the table from Vogel and Saslow, and made no comment as the DCI completed the necessary introductions for the record.

Vogel began by explaining to Amelia that her great-nephew Michael had also been brought in for questioning, largely because of his military tour of duty in Colombia, the only place in the world which is home to *Phyllobates terribilis*, the golden poison dart frog.

Amelia raised a curious eyebrow.

'Just a tad tenuous, don't you think?' she asked coolly.

Vogel was inclined to agree. But he ploughed on.

'Another factor is that he's your great-nephew,' Vogel continued.

'And what on earth do you think I've got to do with any of this?' asked Amelia, even more coolly.

'I have no idea, but Delia Day, who, as I'm sure you know, has just survived two attempts on her life, thinks that you and she may have some past connection, but she doesn't know what it is.'

For the first time, Amelia's mask of composure seemed to slip a little.

'And you think I do?'

'I don't know what to think, Mrs Bowden, but in addition to one murder and two attempted murders, we are dealing here with a situation on the scale of a major act of terrorism, which could still lead to many more deaths.'

He paused. This woman would not be easily bullied. He decided to appeal to her sense of decency. To her humanity.

'Mrs Bowden, if there is anything, anything at all, that you know about Delia Day, Michael, or indeed anyone else, that may have some bearing on the quite frightening chain of events we are dealing with here in North Devon, please, please, tell me. I beg you.'

Amelia took a moment or two to reply.

'There is something, of course,' she said. 'You're quite right about that, Detective Chief Inspector. But I couldn't be sure. I've been trying to find out more. When I heard about the mix-up over the name cards at the festival, and how Delia might have been the target all along – well, then I did wonder about coming to the police. But I still can't be sure, you see, not absolutely sure. It all seems so extraordinary . . .'

'Coming to the police about what, Mrs Bowden?' asked Vogel.

She took a deep breath. Suddenly, there was nothing at all disdainful or superior about Amelia Bowden.

'Once upon a time, I had a husband, Gordon, whom I loved dearly, and a beautiful six-year-old daughter, Anna,' Amelia began, almost as if she was telling a story. 'We had a lovely home on the edge of the town, the house I still live in, with a big garden which backs mostly on to fields and trees beyond. I worked part-time as a teacher, which suited us all well. It was a good life. Then, in 1972, came the day which changed everything. I will never forget it. Anna was playing in the garden with her cousin, Gillian, who was older – she was eleven – and another little girl, our neighbour's daughter, June, who was just a year younger than Gillian. We were never keen on having Gillian around, because she had always been such a problem child, but her mother was very ill at the time, and her father, my brother, begged us to take Gillian that day. It was a Saturday. Gordon and I were in the kitchen preparing lunch when we heard this tremendous bang and we felt the whole house move. It really did. Several panes of glass cracked. Gordon and I just looked at each other. We guessed at once what it was. There was a firework factory, not much more than half a mile away from us as the crow flies. It had gone up.

'Gordon and I ran out into the garden. You could already see flames and huge palls of smoke. Then we looked around and realized the girls weren't there. They'd gone. We both had the same premonition. Gordon just took off, leapt over the fence at the bottom of the garden – he was always very athletic – and ran across the field towards the factory. I tried to follow, but I took a lot longer than Gordon to get over the fence, and I was only halfway across the field when there was a second explosion.

'I never saw my husband or daughter alive again. Gordon must have just got to what was left of the factory when the second blast happened. It seemed he was flung into the air by the power of the explosion and killed instantly. I could see his body lying on the ground, but I couldn't get close.

'It was patently obvious that anyone who had been inside that building was bound to have been killed. And the three girls had got into the factory somehow and were presumably playing there. God knows why. There was little doubt that Gillian would have been the ringleader, though. She always was.

'Afterwards, it was revealed that there were far bigger quantities of gunpowder on the premises than there should have been, and various fire enhancement compounds.

'The intensity of the heat generated was so intense that the girls' bodies were almost totally destroyed. The families were told there wasn't anything left to formally identify . . .'

She stopped, seemingly unable to go on. The tears had started to run down her cheeks. This was not the Amelia Bowden that Vogel had expected to encounter. This was a woman still wracked with grief from long ago. Grieving not only a husband and a daughter, but a life she had lost forever.

Vogel waited until she had composed herself a little.

'That's terrible, Mrs Bowden, so very terrible,' he commented gently. 'But – and please forgive me – what has it got to do with Delia Day?'

Amelia sighed.

'Well, I know it sounds crazy, but I think Delia Day might be Gillian . . .'

'What!' Vogel couldn't help exclaiming. 'Why on earth do you think that?'

'Well, there was something about Delia that was familiar. I thought that when I was first introduced to her on the opening night, and then, when we were all leaving, in a raging gale, Delia's hair blew back off her face and I saw her ear. An ear that is little more than a stump, a bit like a bud that has never opened, and it was just like the ear Gillian was born with.'

'But Gillian is dead,' Vogel responded. 'She died in the fire along with your daughter and the other little girl. You've just told us that.'

'And I accepted that, until this past Friday night when I saw Delia's ear. Even then, I told myself it probably meant nothing. There was no reason to assume Gillian's ear deformation was the only one of its kind. But, at the very least, Delia was the right age, and the seeds of doubt were sown.

'I decided to tell my brother. I decided to ask Harry if it was remotely possible that Gillian had survived the explosion and the fire. Harry is a sick man. I'm afraid to say, I showed him no mercy. I suppose you could say I bullied him into telling me the truth.

'Gillian had a fascination with fire, so the family had always believed that she had started the fire which led to the explosion, probably by lighting fireworks. Albeit not necessarily with any intention of hurting anyone. You could never be sure with Gillian, though. She was a very dangerous child. She had started fires before. At her home. In the woods. And in our garden. But she had died as well, it was believed. So the family, what was left of it, closed ranks. There was no point in stirring anything up. Even I believed that. Gordon and Anna were dead. Nothing could bring them back. And my brother was distraught. His wife was dying of cancer, for God's sake. So I kept quiet. A witness came forward, a neighbour, to say he'd seen Gillian at the factory before, and she seemed to know how to get through the fence. But nobody took much notice. Three little girls had died. Past misdemeanours didn't seem to matter.

'Then, on Friday night, Harry told me that Gillian hadn't died. She'd run home, covered in soot, her hair scorched, burnt hands, and told him that she'd done a terrible thing.

She'd lit a couple of fireworks, inside the factory, a fire had started which she couldn't put out, so she'd just run away. Our Anna and the other girl had gone further into the factory, exploring. Gillian just left them behind.

'Harry told me that he'd panicked. He said he didn't know how on earth he was going to tell me that Gillian was responsible for Anna's death, that she had in effect killed my darling daughter. He was already finding it almost impossible to deal with Gillian, whilst nursing Miriam, her dying mother. He'd heard of a place in London, a hospital, where they gave therapy to problem children. It was experimental and highly suspect, I should think. Principally, it was electric shock treatment. Designed to make patients forget, so that they could start again. This was what Harry wanted. He convinced himself it was not only better and easier for him, but better for Miriam to think that her only daughter had died rather than have to face the consequences of what the child had done. Harry just whisked Gillian away and handed her over. Under another name. Elizabeth Brown, he said.'

Vogel tried to keep his expression neutral. It looked like Amelia was quite right in her suspicions. Delia had told him her previous name had been Elizabeth Brown. But he didn't want to tell Amelia that yet.

'Then, when Elizabeth had completed her treatment, he contrived to have her put into care, citing some story about her parents having died in a car crash,' Amelia continued.

'Hang on a minute – you can't just give a child away like that,' said Vogel. 'Any local authority would require documentation.'

'And they got it. Harry was the district registrar here. He gave them all the documentation they needed and filed a short-form birth certificate for Gillian.'

'But it was all reliant on Gillian's memory being wiped out, wasn't it? That could have backfired dreadfully.'

'Yes, it could have. But it didn't.'

'This is the most bizarre story I've ever heard,' said Vogel.

'I know,' said Amelia.

'But I will tell you, Mrs Bowden, that it does match with what Delia Day has told me. She was called Elizabeth Brown until she changed her name to Delia Day. And she still has absolutely no childhood memories before she was eleven.'

'Oh my God,' said Amelia.

'Yes. It seems you correctly deduced that Delia Day was your niece, Gillian, and that, at the very least by foolhardiness, she was responsible for the death of your daughter. I have to ask you, Mrs Bowden, did you attempt to kill Delia in revenge?'

'You can't be serious,' replied Amelia, sounding rather more like herself. 'In the first place, I wasn't sure Delia was Gillian, until now. And if I had become sure, I would probably have done my best to destroy her world by revealing to her, her publishers, her readers, to everybody, what she had done. That would have been my revenge. I wouldn't have tried to kill her, because in the second place, I am not a psychopath. And in the third place, I don't have a great deal of access to the toxic venom of poisonous frogs. Oh, and at my age, physical attacks are not my forte.'

Vogel thought that was probably fair enough.

'What about your brother?'

'Oh, Mr Vogel, she's his daughter. Fifty years ago, he made a split-second decision to tell a terrible lie, to say that Gillian too had died, and set in motion a sequence of events which proved unstoppable. He's not a killer – he couldn't kill his own daughter. In any case, he's a very sick man, he can barely walk.'

Vogel said that in spite of that, Harry Souch would have to be interviewed. He asked Amelia for her brother's address and texted Peters to get her to send a team round. Then he turned his attention to Amelia again.

'Does anyone else know any of this?' he asked. 'Have you told anyone what Harry told you?'

'No, absolutely not.'

'What about your nephew Michael? You asked him to visit you. He says you questioned him at length about Delia. Did you not tell him why?'

'No. I was just trying to find out if it was possible that Delia was Gillian. He knew nothing, anyway.'

'And there's no one else.'

'No. Well, there's William, I suppose. Although I can't be sure . . .'

'Who's William?'

'My other great-nephew.'

'You talked to him about it?'

'No, of course not. It's just that he drove me to Harry's house on Friday evening. Harry and I talked in his bedroom. Once, I thought I heard a noise outside and wondered if William might be listening. But I didn't do anything about it. I was too stunned by Harry's story.'

'Did you ask William about this?'

'No. And he didn't mention anything. William is not the brightest, Mr Vogel. Even if he'd heard anything, I doubted he'd respond like other people.'

'Have you seen William since Friday?'

'Yes, he popped in earlier today. It was a strange visit, I must admit. There seemed to be something he wanted to talk to me about, but he couldn't quite spit it out. Mind you, he always has been a bit of a strange lad, and he couldn't stay long. He was working.'

'What does he do?'

'Oh, he works for Jeremy Roberts's recycling company. Has done since he left school. Jeremy seems to think a great deal of him, goodness knows why. Pays him a lot more than he could possibly be worth, I would say . . .'

Vogel glanced at Saslow. She was on the edge of her seat. He felt that tingle running up and down his spine which always came when he believed there was about to be a major development in a case.

'Mrs Bowden, did you know that Mr Roberts's company used to deal with hazardous waste?' he asked.

Amelia shook her head and said nothing. But Vogel could see the shock in her eyes and knew that she was ahead of him.

'They used to have a contract with a major chemical research plant to dispose of toxic materials,' he went on.

'Dear God,' she said. 'But you don't . . . you can't think William could have done all this? He's too stupid. I mean, he wouldn't . . . couldn't . . . I just don't believe it. Anyway, how? And why?'

'I don't know the answer to either of those questions, Mrs Bowden,' said Vogel. 'I do know we need to speak to your nephew at once. Could you give us his address, please?'

TWENTY-SEVEN

Vogel and Saslow arrived at William Souch's isolated cottage just before two in the morning. They were accompanied by a squad car and a police armed response vehicle, both with sirens blaring, a specialist military unit dressed in gear which made them look like space explorers, and a CSI team in full PPE.

Nobody needed to knock on the cottage door. The commotion of their arrival had woken William. He was standing in the porch, bleary-eyed, wearing striped pyjamas. He was holding a twelve-bore shotgun across his body.

Vogel was about to step out of the car, but the leader of the AR team stopped him at once.

'Everybody keep back,' he ordered, taking cover behind his own vehicle along with his team. Each held an MP5 carbine aimed at William Souch.

'Put down your weapon, sir, put up your hands and step forward,' ordered the senior authorized firearms officer.

Souch levelled the shotgun and pointed it at the AFO. Well, thought Vogel, Amelia Bowden had said he was stupid.

'Put down your weapon sir, or we will shoot,' said the AFO calmly.

Souch put the gun down. Not completely stupid, then. Vogel was allowed out of the car. He walked towards Souch.

'William Souch, I am arresting you on suspicion of the murder of James Harding and two counts of attempting to murder Delia Day,' Vogel began.

He then cautioned Souch and ordered that he be handcuffed and taken to Barnstaple police station – which, unlike Bideford, had police cells – processed and locked up until Vogel was ready to interview him.

William did not speak at all. Nor did he look surprised or particularly distressed. Amelia had said he was a strange one. And he most certainly was, thought Vogel. Scarily strange.

Vogel then instructed the specialist military unit to begin the search of the premises, primarily to ascertain whether or not hazardous toxic substances were present.

There was a heavily padlocked windowless shed on the far side of the yard.

The military unit, in their space explorer kit complete with breathing apparatus, split into two sections. One section, assault rifles raised, raided the house, the other, making short work of the padlocks, entered the shed. Both sections were on red alert just in case Souch had not been alone on the premises.

After just a few minutes, the leader of the team inside the shed stepped out and approached Vogel.

'I think we've got him, sir,' he began. 'The shed is set out like a laboratory inside, with a fridge, a sink and temperature-controlled storage units holding dozens of glass vials of the kind chemicals are usually stored in. Including toxic substances, of course. Obviously, we don't know what is in those vials and that's going to be a specialist job for forensics. But we can be pretty sure he's been up to no good.'

'Excellent,' said Vogel. 'My sergeant and I will go back to Barnstaple nick and give the bastard the third degree, whilst you lot carry on here. Please keep me posted.'

'Right,' responded the soldier, his voice sounding strange through the breathing apparatus he was still wearing. 'There are also some dead animals laid out on a bench, with various instruments alongside, as if for dissection. A couple of rats, and a cat. God knows what else we're going to find . . .'

Vogel interrupted at once.

'What sort of cat?' he asked.

'A black tom,' replied the soldier, a note of puzzlement in his already strange voice. He wasn't to know that the DCI had a special family interest in cats.

Vogel breathed a small sigh of relief. So did Saslow. Bless her, he thought. But he knew she too had a cat at home.

In the car on the way to Barnstaple police station, they were both quiet, experiencing the anti-climax which often follows a key arrest.

'Looks like we may have our cat-napper as well, then,' commented Saslow.

Vogel grunted.

He was about to reply that he wondered just how many cats Souch had snatched, more than likely experimented on and killed, when his phone buzzed. The caller was the leader of the military unit back at Souch's cottage.

'In the house, we found a large quantity of PPE,' he began. 'Hooded suits, headgear and even breathing apparatus not unlike ours, boxes of rubber gloves, overshoes and so on. Also stacks, literally stacks, of newspaper cuttings concerning death by poison, murderers who got away scot-free, and the slaughter of animals. We haven't let CSI in yet, but we brought Souch's laptop out to them. They've only had time for a quick look so far, but it seems to contain more of the same. And a clip from something that looks like a snuff movie.'

Vogel looked at Saslow, who was driving as usual. She glanced at him. She knew they were thinking the same thing. Was it possible that James Harding was not William Souch's first victim?

'We also entered a second shed in which we found a number of live animals, in cages. There were rats again, three of them, some mice and two cats.'

Vogel asked again what sort of cats they had found.

'Two females, one ginger, one tortoiseshell.'

Vogel felt a surge of optimism. Rosamund's female cat Storey was a tortoiseshell. He told himself off. Tortoiseshells were common. This was a long shot, under the circumstances. However, Storey was distinctively marked, with a brown and white head, a white collar and front, and two white back legs.

'What sort of condition are they in?'

'Surprisingly good,' came the reply. 'Their cages are clean and they have food and water.'

Vogel knew the members of the specialist unit all wore headcams and that everything they saw was automatically filmed and recorded. He asked if he could be sent footage, which arrived within seconds.

He showed Saslow his phone. She knew his daughter's cat. 'That's Storey,' said Saslow. 'Definitely.'
'I think so too,' said Vogel.

William Souch had been processed by custody, he'd been photographed, fingerprinted, had a DNA sample taken, his clothes removed for forensic examination. Now, wearing a station-issue paper suit, he was sitting at the table in the interview room when Vogel and Saslow entered.

He was a pleasant-looking young man, thirty-four years old apparently, with wavy sandy hair and gentle light-brown eyes. Not for the first time in his career, Vogel was reminded that monsters do not necessarily have horns. And he was beginning to suspect that the benign-looking William Souch might turn out to be a monster.

Souch spoke first, before Vogel had time to record the formal introductions and begin the interview.

'I suppose you've found my laboratory by now,' he said, with a small smile.

Vogel indicated that Souch must wait, and only responded after the formalities had been completed.

'Yes, we have indeed entered the shed which is what I assume you mean by your laboratory. And we are currently investigating the contents.'

'You'll find everything in order,' said Souch curiously. 'I've labelled every substance I could identify – of course, I've never had the facilities to be able to identify everything.'

'Mr Souch, let me ask you a simple question. Why are you storing large quantities of lethal substances at your home?'

'They're not all lethal. You'll find everything is properly catalogued. I expect you've found the animals, too.'

'Yes, we have.'

'Um, it's a shame. But I have to be sure, you see, that I cause as little pain as possible. I'm like all scientists. Experimenting on animals is a necessary evil.'

So he reckoned he was a scientist, thought Vogel.

'What do you mean by that?' he asked.

'Well, all I want to do is help people, without pain if possible.'

'How do you want to help people?' Vogel persisted.

'I put people out of their misery. I stop the suffering.'

Vogel felt the hairs stand up on the back of his neck. He could sense Saslow tensing in the chair beside him. Perhaps Amelia was right and this young man was plain stupid. He appeared to have no idea at all of the enormity of what he seemed to be saying. Vogel pressed on.

'Would you like to tell us exactly how you do that, William?' he asked.

'Yes. Of course. I have decided that I will tell you everything. I don't have any choice, do I? Not now. Not now you've been to my place. And I don't mind being honest with you, because I have only ever tried to help people. And I'm so sorry I won't be able to do that any more. I'm sure you will understand.'

Vogel could hardly believe his ears. This seemed to be developing into the most extraordinary interview of his long career. But Souch had stopped talking and was making no attempt to start again.

'Please go on,' Vogel murmured, his voice little more than a whisper. It felt as if he were being held in a spell and he so didn't want to break it.

'Yes, of course, sir,' said Souch politely. 'Well, my grand-father had a friend who ran an old people's home. He used to take me there sometimes when I was a boy, and then the friend offered me a Saturday job. I was about sixteen, I think. I'd run errands, help serve the food, that sort of thing. Well, some of them were all right, but some of the people in the home were just vegetables, and I used to think how wonderful it would be if I could end their suffering.

'Then, when I left school, I went to work for Mr Roberts. In particular, I got rid of the hazardous waste for him, because he trusted me, you see. And then when I began to realize what we were dealing with, well, I thought it could be very useful to help those poor people. And when I got my own place, I began to take the odd container home with me. And I started trapping rats and taking cats. They like me, do cats; they always come to me. I don't like killing cats, but I have to, you see. Like any scientist, I need to experiment on animals first. I would never move on to people until I was sure, I told you that, sir.'

'What exactly do you mean by moving on to people?' Vogel asked. 'I need you to explain that to me, William.'

'Well, it's when I felt confident enough to administer a substance which could end people's suffering, of course, with as little pain as possible.'

Vogel took a deep breath. He wondered if the question he intended to ask next might be going too far. He decided to risk it.

'Do you mean that you started to kill people?'

Vogel held his breath. He thought Saslow was probably holding hers, too. But Souch replied quite quickly, without any apparent concern.

'Yes. That's it. I had to be sure I could do it right before I started putting people out of their misery.'

'Again, I have to ask you to answer this properly, William. Do you mean, by killing them?'

'Yes. I began to kill people. But only when they were barely alive anyway.'

'And when did you begin to do that?'

'Oh, a couple of years before that leakage on Exmoor, when Mr Roberts stopped handling waste. I helped five people in that first couple of years. Not all in the same nursing home, of course. I began to volunteer at several. I had to go more slowly after that because I knew I couldn't get any more supplies. I couldn't help nearly as many people as I would have liked.'

'So how many people altogether have you, uh, helped, William?' asked Vogel, using Souch's own terminology with some reluctance.

'Twelve,' he answered promptly. 'Including that Mr Harding. But he didn't need helping yet. He was a mistake. So I haven't catalogued him.'

Twelve people. Poisoned by this pleasant-looking young man. Vogel had to struggle to keep his voice level.

'You did put a lethal serum into an apple juice bottle at the festival, though, didn't you, William?' he asked.

'Yes, I did. Well, I put the serum in a bottle at home actually, in my laboratory. Safely. In controlled conditions. We have the contract for waste disposal at the festival, so I could come and go as I liked. I went into the marquee by the back entrance, just after the earlier panel, when I knew the marquee would be empty. I put out the name cards and two bottles of juice, one of them my poisoned one. But I put it there for Delia Day. Behind her card. And then they sat behind the wrong cards. It wasn't my fault, was it?'

Vogel ignored the question.

'Delia Day didn't need help to die, either, did she?' he enquired, almost casually.

'No, I was trying to help Aunt Amelia.'

He then told the story Vogel and Saslow already knew, of what Delia had done as a child when she was Gillian Souch, and all that came after.

'I overheard my grandfather telling it all to Aunt Amelia,' said Souch, which, of course, was exactly what Amelia Bowden had suspected. 'Confessing that Gillian was still alive, and Amelia saying she believed Delia Day was Gillian. And how she wanted revenge, that she would like to destroy Delia.'

'So did you think that meant that Amelia wanted Delia dead?' asked Vogel, who knew perfectly well that wasn't what Amelia had meant at all.

'Of course I did. And I knew how to do it, didn't I? How to get rid of Delia Day. Aunt Amelia always underestimates me, you see. Michael's her favourite. The day after she went to Grandpa's, I popped round to see her, to ask her if I could help her. But Michael was there. I saw his car outside. I thought, I'll do it anyway. I only had a drop or two of *Phyllobates terribilis* left, but I knew there would never be a better use for it. I wanted to impress Aunt Amelia. To prove that I could do special things. Only it all went wrong. The wrong person died. I didn't even know what to say to Aunt Amelia. I tried, but I couldn't tell her that I'd made a terrible mistake. She's always saying I'm stupid. All I wanted was for her to be proud of me.'

'I see,' Vogel murmured.

Souch had even pronounced *Phyllobates terribilis* perfectly, the only person other than Raoul that Vogel had heard do so. He really was a quite terrifying young man, thought Vogel.

'So were you also responsible for the further two attempts on Delia Day's life?' asked the DCI.

'Yes, of course I was. I wanted to finish the job.'

'And did you seek her out a third time in Braunton?'

'Yes, I followed Michael. I knew he'd lead me to her sooner or later.'

'But the attacks on Delia were quite out of character for you, William, weren't they? Why did you not use poison again, as you have told us you have been in the habit of doing?'

'Oh, I would never take poison into a hospital, Mr Vogel,' replied William. 'That would be irresponsible. There are young people in hospitals, children. And when I pushed Delia off the quay, well, that was just chance. I was getting myself an ice cream when I saw her standing right by the quayside. It was fate. I just gave her a little push. That's all.'

He's mad, thought Vogel, keeping his facial expression neutral, *quite mad*.

'I need to ask you about the lethal toxin which killed James Harding,' the DCI continued. 'After you had dropped it into that juice bottle, what did you do with the used vial?'

'Oh, I disposed of it properly, of course, if that's what you're worried about, Mr Vogel,' Souch replied. 'I walked right out to the point at the far end of the estuary and threw it into the sea. When the tide was going out, of course. If any toxin dilutes enough, it becomes harmless, you know.'

Vogel did know. He had only one more question for the time being.

'The people in the nursing homes whom you helped, William, how precisely did you do that?' he asked.

'Oh I gave them chocolates, delicious chocolates that I'd doctored with lethal serums,' he said. 'Old people love chocolates, you know.'

Vogel suspended the interview, stepped outside the room and immediately called the specialist military unit team leader he had been speaking to earlier.

'Have you found any chocolates in the house?' he asked.

'Oh, yes, a couple of dozen boxes at least,' said the man. 'Is that significant?'

'I think it might be very significant,' Vogel replied quietly.

TWENTY-EIGHT

Whilst Vogel and Saslow had been interviewing William Souch, news had come through from the uniformed team sent to the home of Harry Souch, William's grandfather.

They had been unable to raise Harry, and eventually, after gaining permission from their senior officer, had broken into the house.

Harry was lying dead in his bed. The opinion of the paramedics who arrived quickly at the scene, having coincidentally just completed another call nearby, was that he had almost certainly died of a stroke. He had, after all, suffered several strokes previously, and this prognosis would almost certainly never have been questioned were it not for the fact that his deluded grandson had just confessed to multiple murders, almost all of vulnerable elderly people.

Vogel returned to the interview room and gave the news to William, who barely reacted. But then Vogel had come to the conclusion that the young man was almost totally unconnected with reality.

'I thought he might go soon,' murmured William.

Vogel asked him bluntly if he had killed his grandfather.

'Oh, no,' said William. 'Grandpa didn't need my help. Not yet anyway. He wasn't unhappy, you see.'

It was nearly five in the morning before Vogel got home. He set his alarm for three hours later. He had to have some sleep, but he also needed to see Delia as soon as possible.

He arrived at the Braunton Airbnb well before nine and told Delia the whole story. He saw no reason to hold back.

She looked stunned.

'So as well as having mugged a vulnerable old woman, I have killed two little girls; what a lovely person I am,' said Delia. 'My father has died suddenly, probably also because of me. My aunt – my closest living relative, I suppose – wants to destroy me. And I have a nephew who is a psychopathic serial killer, it seems. A truly dysfunctional family, wouldn't you say, David?'

Vogel did not comment.

'Perhaps no coincidence that I turned out to be such a disturbed child, though, eh?'

'Perhaps indeed, but you came through it.'

'Did I? I'm not so sure about that any more.'

'You really had no idea, did you?'

'About what happened when I was a child, about what I did? No. And even now, it remains a blank.'

'And yet you did have that feeling of having been here before, didn't you?'

'Yes, I did. And if I hadn't accepted the invitation to the Appledore Book Festival, if I hadn't come back here, do you realize, none of this would have happened. James would not have been killed. Harry would probably still be alive. You wouldn't have had to bring in the army to shut down half of North Devon.'

'That's true. You set this chain of events in motion, Delia – you alone. But if you hadn't done so, we would not have caught a deranged serial killer.'

'There is that, I suppose,' said Delia. 'OK, so what happens next?'

'Well, assuming William pleads guilty – and he has made a full confession – there will be no jury trial, just sentencing by a high court judge. And it is unlikely that you will be required to attend.'

'Will I be charged with anything?'

'Almost certainly not. You served your time for that Covent Garden mugging. You were only eleven when the firework factory exploded and your cousin and the second girl were killed. And there is not even any evidence that you were responsible for that fire. You're still a free woman, Delia Day.'

'Really? I certainly won't be after all of this becomes public knowledge. Aunt Amelia will get her wish. There will be an avalanche of negative publicity, and I will be destroyed.'

'Not necessarily. Don't they say there's no such thing as bad publicity?'

'Only those who have never experienced it,' said Delia.

Later that day, William Souch was charged with the murder of James Harding, and the attempted murder of Delia Day. The investigation into his confession of twelve other murders began at once, and further charges were expected to follow.

A post-mortem on his grandfather was fast-tracked. Harry Souch had indeed died of natural causes. He had suffered a massive stroke.

However, it seemed apparent to all concerned that the shock of the confrontation with his sister Amelia, coupled with the realization that the legacy of his extraordinary actions of half a century earlier had come back to haunt him, was the real cause of his death.

The specialist military unit at William Souch's cottage found no signs of toxic contamination in the shed where Souch kept his live animals. The two cats that had been discovered alive were released to a vet who was able to check the tabby's chip and confirm that she was Rosamund's beloved Storey. And Vogel was able to take her home to his daughter.

The festival was abandoned. The Smythes, the Tucker twins and all the other participants left for home. They had yet to learn the truth about Delia Day's involvement, and her life before her extraordinary reinvention.

EPILOGUE

Six months later

S ouch ultimately pleaded guilty to thirteen counts of murder and three of attempted murder, and was sentenced by a high court judge to a full-life term of imprisonment. This meant that he would never be released.

The extent of his killing spree, spread over several years, had caused a sensation. The relatives of those whose lives he had so arbitrarily ended were unlikely ever to recover.

Vogel was almost mesmerized by Souch as he stood in the dock, listening to the judge's devastating summing up and hearing the severity of his sentence. William Souch again barely seemed to react. His features were arranged in a pleasant expression throughout.

This was a true psychopath, Vogel thought.

It was not the first time he had been confronted by someone whose crimes had taken his breath away. But he would never forget the agreeable-looking William Souch, unmoved, it seemed, both by the terrible crimes he had committed and the punishment that had quite properly been meted out to him. Souch looked to be completely dissociated from the world around him.

Amelia Bowden had not attended court, and nor had Delia Day.

It had been suggested in the media and by various victim support groups that the two women might like to meet.

'I have no wish to meet the woman who killed my daughter,' said Amelia.

She had become near reclusive since William's arrest, and Vogel had been told that she was a broken woman, a shadow of her former self.

Michael, looking stricken, had turned up for the final part of his brother's hearing. As far as Vogel knew, he had never contacted Delia Day again, despite becoming aware that she was his aunt. And Vogel had no idea whether or not he had told his wife the truth about his sexuality. Nothing concerning that was a police matter anymore.

The day after William was sentenced, Vogel tried to phone Delia. There was no reply.

He tried again the following day, with the same result.

Her horrific past had been fully revealed in court by the prosecution, and again in some detail by the judge in his summing up. There had been a huge press presence outside her home for several days. But no one had caught sight of Delia.

Her whereabouts were no longer a police matter. However Vogel still had old chums in the Met. At his request, they mounted a limited investigation.

It transpired that not only had Delia been absent from her home for several weeks, but she had sold the property. She had also liquidated all her known available assets, withdrawing everything possible in cash and then closing her accounts. She had even sold her car. For cash.

The last sighting of her in London seemed to be some CCTV coverage at Euston Station. She was seen at the ticket office, towing two large wheeled suitcases. But if she had bought a ticket, she had used cash. Because of the time scale, and the rarity of cash transactions and paper tickets nowadays, it seemed that Delia had probably bought a ticket to Birmingham. There the trail ended.

Delia Day had disappeared.

Vogel was not particularly surprised. She had done it before, after all. Albeit in a different era. He thought that if anyone could do it again, then it would be Delia. He wondered, though, if she'd had help, as she'd had when she'd previously reinvented herself. It was extremely difficult to disappear in the modern world. And it was the perceived wisdom within the police force that it was pretty much impossible without some degree of outside assistance. But was there anyone whom the fiercely independent and somewhat insular Delia might have trusted enough to share her new secret with?

Vogel liked Delia. He didn't like what she'd done in the

past, either as Elizabeth Brown or Gillian Souch. But Gillian had been just a child, a disturbed child, when she had been responsible for those long-ago deaths, and Elizabeth had already paid the price for her crimes. Vogel was unsure whether or not Delia deserved to be so cruelly overwhelmed by that past, after so long, and after the transformation of herself that she had brought about.

Either way, he found that he was wishing her well.

A woman wearing no makeup, with grey hair now almost long enough to reach her shoulders, stood on a bleak hillside somewhere in the extreme north of Scotland, gazing into the distance. A narrow twisting road wound its way towards her along the valley below. There was snow on the mountain peaks beyond.

She had rented a remote cottage. Under an assumed name. With cash. Which, it seemed, still opened doors and closed mouths.

She had huge amounts of cash. The two big suitcases she had brought with her had contained very little except cash. And most of it was now buried in various containers in her newly acquired garden.

There was no Wi-Fi. She had no computer or tablet. Just a burner mobile phone. And a television. She had begun to watch a lot of television. And she was reading. Something she had never done a lot of when she was writing. She had taken the smaller of her two wheeled suitcases on the bus to the nearest town, which fortunately had a bookshop, and very nearly filled it with books. Paid for in cash.

She had no desire ever to write another word. She could not write another word. That part of her life was over. Delia Day was dead. Or as good as dead. But then the extraordinary reality was that, despite the fame and fortune, Delia Day had never really existed.

She did not know how long it would be before she was found. As she felt sure she would be one day. Or, alternatively, how long it might be before she was tempted back into the world in some form or other.

She was not afraid of solitude. In many ways, she welcomed

it. In spite of there always having been so many people around her, she had in reality been alone for most of her life, ever since Sue had died.

It was the guilt that was now her greatest burden. All her life as Delia Day, she had felt guilty about what she had done as Elizabeth Brown, and guilty about having so successfully escaped her past. Now she was also burdened with the guilt of what she had done as eleven-year-old Gillian Souch.

She'd always regarded the loss of Sue as the greatest tragedy of her life.

But now, seeking again to put her past behind her, yet still haunted by the terrible sins she had committed in her previous lives, it seemed like a kind of poetic justice.

However, Delia Day was not beaten. It was not in her nature to be beaten. She still thought she had, by and large, been wonderfully lucky in her life. Certainly through most of her adult life.

Neither was she entirely alone. She had known from the moment she had begun to plan her disappearance that she could not do it alone. Not entirely alone. Vogel had been quite right about that.

She had placed her trust in two people she felt sure, or as sure as it was ever possible to be, would never betray her. They had dealt with everything she could not without revealing her identity. They had proved themselves surprisingly inventive and resourceful. They had picked her up from Birmingham station in the brand-new motor car she had bought them, having first checked out a CCTV-free parking spot just a few minutes' walk from the concourse, and driven her on the last leg of her journey to the Scottish Highlands.

It was two days before Christmas. Her collaborators were on their way to share the festive season with her. She had instructed them to bring with them a turkey, a Fortnum and Mason hamper and a case of good wine. She narrowed her eyes and stared across the valley. Yes, in the distance she could just make out the speck of an approaching vehicle. And as it drew nearer, she could see that it was indeed the customized pink Mini Cooper she had been watching out for. The car could perhaps be considered a little too distinctive under the circumstances. But Delia didn't care. Her entire life had been a gamble. She had never been dull. Never been ordinary. Never ever been boring.

And neither were the Tucker twins . . .

Tina and Tilly Tucker sincerely believed that they must have died and gone to heaven. When Delia had called them to ask for their help in what she described as her 'new venture', they had been overwhelmed. There was nothing, absolutely nothing, they wouldn't do for Delia Day. And they had told her so straight away.

They loved their pink Mini, too. It was their dream car. Not least because it took them to their beloved Delia.

The twins couldn't believe what had happened. Delia needed them. It was even possible that she couldn't survive without them. She had already told them that. More or less.

It really was like a dream to Tilly and Tina. They were completely untroubled by the revelations about Delia's early life. And they didn't even care that she would probably never write another book or appear in public again.

They had her all to themselves. She was theirs. They didn't have to share her with anyone.

As they began the steep climb up to Delia's cottage, they spotted a figure on the brow of the hill. It was Delia. Their heroine. Their idol. She was wearing a big dirty-green country coat and Wellington boots. Around her neck was a long purple scarf, perhaps a nod to her past life, which blew crazily in the wind. She was waving enthusiastically. It was clear that she was as pleased to see them as they were her.

'There she is,' said Tilly.

'Isn't she wonderful?' said Tina.

'Oh, yes, she's just soooooo wonderful.'

The twins were ecstatically happy. Happier than they had ever been. They would always look after Delia. It was their destiny.

Tina was driving. She removed her left hand from the steering wheel and held it towards Tilly, fingers outstretched. Tilly did the same. They high-fived. And each twin gave an involuntary whoop of joy.

Milton Keynes UK
Ingram Content Group UK Ltd.
UKHW050844250324
439991UK00006B/713